CW00557275

PATRICIA W
BLINDFOLD

PATRICIA WENTWORTH was born Dora Amy Elles in India in 1877 (not 1878 as has sometimes been stated). She was first educated privately in India, and later at Blackheath School for Girls. Her first husband was George Dillon, with whom she had her only child, a daughter. She also had two stepsons from her first marriage, one of whom died in the Somme during World War I.

Her first novel was published in 1910, but it wasn't until the 1920's that she embarked on her long career as a writer of mysteries. Her most famous creation was Miss Maud Silver, who appeared in 32 novels, though there were a further 33 full-length mysteries not featuring Miss Silver—the entire run of these is now reissued by Dean Street Press.

Patricia Wentworth died in 1961. She is recognized today as one of the pre-eminent exponents of the classic British golden age mystery novel.

By Patricia Wentworth

The Benbow Smith Mysteries
Fool Errant
Danger Calling
Walk with Care
Down Under

The Frank Garrett Mysteries
Dead or Alive
Rolling Stone

The Ernest Lamb Mysteries
The Blind Side
Who Pays the Piper?
Pursuit of a Parcel

Standalones
The Astonishing Adventure of Jane Smith
The Red Lacquer Case
The Annam Jewel
The Black Cabinet
The Dower House Mystery
The Amazing Chance
Hue and Cry
Anne Belinda
Will-o'-the-Wisp
Beggar's Choice
The Coldstone
Kingdom Lost
Nothing Venture
Red Shadow
Outrageous Fortune
Touch and Go
Fear by Night
Red Stefan
Blindfold
Hole and Corner
Mr. Zero
Run!
Weekend with Death
Silence in Court

PATRICIA WENTWORTH

BLINDFOLD

With an introduction by
Curtis Evans

DEAN STREET PRESS

Introduction

BRITISH AUTHOR Patricia Wentworth published her first novel, a gripping tale of desperate love during the French Revolution entitled *A Marriage under the Terror*, a little over a century ago, in 1910. The book won first prize in the Melrose Novel Competition and was a popular success in both the United States and the United Kingdom. Over the next five years Wentworth published five additional novels, the majority of them historical fiction, the best-known of which today is *The Devil's Wind* (1912), another sweeping period romance, this one set during the Sepoy Mutiny (1857-58) in India, a region with which the author, as we shall see, had extensive familiarity. Like *A Marriage under the Terror*, *The Devil's Wind* received much praise from reviewers for its sheer storytelling élan. One notice, for example, pronounced the novel "an achievement of some magnitude" on account of "the extraordinary vividness...the reality of the atmosphere...the scenes that shift and move with the swiftness of a moving picture...." (*The Bookman*, August 1912) With her knack for spinning a yarn, it perhaps should come as no surprise that Patricia Wentworth during the early years of the Golden Age of mystery fiction (roughly from 1920 into the 1940s) launched upon her own mystery-writing career, a course charted most successfully for nearly four decades by the prolific author, right up to the year of her death in 1961.

Considering that Patricia Wentworth belongs to the select company of Golden Age mystery writers with books which have remained in print in every decade for nearly a century now (the centenary of Agatha Christie's first mystery, *The Mysterious Affair at Styles*, is in 2020; the centenary of Wentworth's first mystery, *The Astonishing Adventure of Jane Smith*, follows merely three years later, in 2023), relatively little is known about the author herself. It appears, for example, that even the widely given year of Wentworth's birth, 1878, is incorrect. Yet it is sufficiently clear that Wentworth lived a varied and intriguing life that provided her ample inspiration for a writing career devoted to imaginative fiction.

It is usually stated that Patricia Wentworth was born Dora Amy Elles on 10 November 1878 in Mussoorie, India, during the heyday of the British Raj; however, her Indian birth and baptismal record states that she in fact was born on 15 October 1877 and was baptized on 26 November of that same year in Gwalior. Whatever doubts surround her actual birth year, however, unquestionably the future author came from a prominent Anglo-Indian military family. Her father, Edmond Roche Elles, a son of Malcolm Jamieson Elles, a Porto, Portugal wine merchant originally from Ardrossan, Scotland, entered the British Royal Artillery in 1867, a decade before Wentworth's birth, and first saw service in India during the Lushai Expedition of 1871-72. The next year Elles in India wed Clara Gertrude Rothney, daughter of Brigadier-General Octavius Edward Rothney, commander of the Gwalior District, and Maria (Dempster) Rothney, daughter of a surgeon in the Bengal Medical Service. Four children were born of the union of Edmond and Clara Elles, Wentworth being the only daughter.

Before his retirement from the army in 1908, Edmond Elles rose to the rank of lieutenant-general and was awarded the KCB (Knight Commander of the Order of Bath), as was the case with his elder brother, Wentworth's uncle, Lieutenant-General Sir William Kidston Elles, of the Bengal Command. Edmond Elles also served as Military Member to the Council of the Governor-General of India from 1901 to 1905. Two of Wentworth's brothers, Malcolm Rothney Elles and Edmond Claude Elles, served in the Indian Army as well, though both of them died young (Malcolm in 1906 drowned in the Ganges Canal while attempting to rescue his orderly, who had fallen into the water), while her youngest brother, Hugh Jamieson Elles, achieved great distinction in the British Army. During the First World War he catapulted, at the relatively youthful age of 37, to the rank of brigadier-general and the command of the British Tank Corps, at the Battle of Cambrai personally leading the advance of more than 350 tanks against the German line. Years later Hugh Elles also played a major role in British civil defense during the Second World War. In the event of a German invasion of Great Britain, something which seemed all too possible in 1940, he was tasked with leading the defense of southwestern England. Like Sir Edmond and Sir William, Hugh Elles attained the rank of lieutenant-general and was awarded the KCB.

Although she was born in India, Patricia Wentworth spent much of her childhood in England. In 1881 she with her mother and two

younger brothers was at Tunbridge Wells, Kent, on what appears to
have been a rather extended visit in her ancestral country; while a
decade later the same family group resided at Blackheath, London
at Lennox House, domicile of Wentworth's widowed maternal
grandmother, Maria Rothney. (Her eldest brother, Malcolm, was in
Bristol attending Clifton College.) During her years at Lennox House,
Wentworth attended Blackheath High School for Girls, then only
recently founded as "one of the first schools in the country to give
girls a proper education" (*The London Encyclopaedia*, 3rd ed., p. 74).
Lennox House was an ample Victorian villa with a great glassed-in
conservatory running all along the back and a substantial garden--
most happily, one presumes, for Wentworth, who resided there not
only with her grandmother, mother and two brothers, but also five
aunts (Maria Rothney's unmarried daughters, aged 26 to 42), one
adult first cousin once removed and nine first cousins, adolescents
like Wentworth herself, from no less than three different families
(one Barrow, three Masons and five Dempsters); their parents,
like Wentworth's father, presumably were living many miles away
in various far-flung British dominions. Three servants--a cook,
parlourmaid and housemaid--were tasked with serving this full score
of individuals.

Sometime after graduating from Blackheath High School in the
mid-1890s, Wentworth returned to India, where in a local British
newspaper she is said to have published her first fiction. In 1901 the
23-year-old Wentworth married widower George Fredrick Horace
Dillon, a 41-year-old lieutenant-colonel in the Indian Army with three
sons from his prior marriage. Two years later Wentworth gave birth to
her only child, a daughter named Clare Roche Dillon. (In some sources
it is erroneously stated that Clare was the offspring of Wentworth's
second marriage.) However in 1906, after just five years of marriage,
George Dillon died suddenly on a sea voyage, leaving Wentworth with
sole responsibly for her three teenaged stepsons and baby daughter. A
very short span of years, 1904 to 1907, saw the deaths of Wentworth's
husband, mother, grandmother and brothers Malcolm and Edmond,
removing much of her support network. In 1908, however, her father,
who was now sixty years old, retired from the army and returned to
England, settling at Guildford, Surrey with an older unmarried sister

named Dora (for whom his daughter presumably had been named). Wentworth joined this household as well, along with her daughter and her youngest stepson. Here in Surrey Wentworth, presumably with the goal of making herself financially independent for the first time in her life (she was now in her early thirties), wrote the novel that changed the course of her life, *A Marriage under the Terror*, for the first time we know of utilizing her famous *nom de plume*.

The burst of creative energy that resulted in Wentworth's publication of six novels in six years suddenly halted after the appearance of *Queen Anne Is Dead* in 1915. It seems not unlikely that the Great War impinged in various ways on her writing. One tragic episode was the death on the western front of one of her stepsons, George Charles Tracey Dillon. Mining in Colorado when war was declared, young Dillon worked his passage from Galveston, Texas to Bristol, England as a shipboard muleteer (mule-tender) and joined the Gloucestershire Regiment. In 1916 he died at the Somme at the age of 29 (about the age of Wentworth's two brothers when they had passed away in India).

A couple of years after the conflict's cessation in 1918, a happy event occurred in Wentworth's life when at Frimley, Surrey she wed George Oliver Turnbull, up to this time a lifelong bachelor who like the author's first husband was a lieutenant-colonel in the Indian Army. Like his bride now forty-two years old, George Turnbull as a younger man had distinguished himself for his athletic prowess, playing forward for eight years for the Scottish rugby team and while a student at the Royal Military Academy winning the medal awarded the best athlete of his term. It seems not unlikely that Turnbull played a role in his wife's turn toward writing mystery fiction, for he is said to have strongly supported Wentworth's career, even assisting her in preparing manuscripts for publication. In 1936 the couple in Camberley, Surrey built Heatherglade House, a large two-story structure on substantial grounds, where they resided until Wentworth's death a quarter of a century later. (George Turnbull survived his wife by nearly a decade, passing away in 1970 at the age of 92.) This highly successful middle-aged companionate marriage contrasts sharply with the more youthful yet rocky union of Agatha and Archie Christie, which was three years away from sundering when Wentworth published *The Astonishing Adventure of Jane Smith* (1923), the first of her sixty-five mystery novels.

Although Patricia Wentworth became best-known for her cozy tales of the criminal investigations of consulting detective Miss Maud Silver, one of the mystery genre's most prominent spinster sleuths, in truth the Miss Silver tales account for just under half of Wentworth's 65 mystery novels. Miss Silver did not make her debut until 1928 and she did not come to predominate in Wentworth's fictional criminous output until the 1940s. Between 1923 and 1945 Wentworth published 33 mystery novels without Miss Silver, a handsome and substantial legacy in and of itself to vintage crime fiction fans. Many of these books are standalone tales of mystery, but nine of them have series characters. Debuting in the novel *Fool Errant* in 1929, a year after Miss Silver first appeared in print, was the enigmatic, nautically-named *eminence grise* Benbow Collingwood Horatio Smith, owner of a most expressively opinionated parrot named Ananias (and quite a colorful character in his own right). Benbow Smith went on to appear in three additional Wentworth mysteries: *Danger Calling* (1931), *Walk with Care* (1933) and *Down Under* (1937). Working in tandem with Smith in the investigation of sinister affairs threatening the security of Great Britain in *Danger Calling* and *Walk with Care* is Frank Garrett, Head of Intelligence for the Foreign Office, who also appears solo in *Dead or Alive* (1936) and *Rolling Stone* (1940) and collaborates with additional series characters, Scotland Yard's Inspector Ernest Lamb and Sergeant Frank Abbott, in *Pursuit of a Parcel* (1942). Inspector Lamb and Sergeant Abbott headlined a further pair of mysteries, *The Blind Side* (1939) and *Who Pays the Piper?* (1940), before they became absorbed, beginning with *Miss Silver Deals with Death* (1943), into the burgeoning Miss Silver canon. Lamb would make his farewell appearance in 1955 in *The Listening Eye*, while Abbott would take his final bow in mystery fiction with Wentworth's last published novel, *The Girl in the Cellar* (1961), which went into print the year of the author's death at the age of 83.

The remaining two dozen Wentworth mysteries, from the fantastical *The Astonishing Adventure of Jane Smith* in 1923 to the intense legal drama *Silence in Court* in 1945, are, like the author's series novels, highly imaginative and entertaining tales of mystery and adventure, told by a writer gifted with a consummate flair for storytelling. As one confirmed Patricia Wentworth mystery fiction addict, American Golden Age mystery writer Todd Downing, admiringly declared in the 1930s, "There's something about Miss Wentworth's yarns that is contagious." This attractive new series of Patricia Wentworth reissues by Dean Street Press provides modern fans of vintage mystery a splendid opportunity to catch the Wentworth fever.

Curtis Evans

Chapter One

"HALF PAST TEN," said Mrs. Green—"and time you took 'er Benger's up. Half past ten to a tick she 'as it, so you'd better look sharp."

Flossie Palmer stifled a yawn.

"And what about my beauty sleep? How am I to keep my complexion if I got to sit up till half past ten?" She finished on a giggle, and then added, "Pertickler, is she?"

Mrs. Green turned round from the gas stove with the saucepan of Benger in her hand.

"Everything to the tick," she said. "If you're late, you get the sack, so I keeps me clock a bit on the fast side to be safe. 'Ere, give me that cup! And now up you go. And you knock on 'er door, but you don't go in, not for nothing. You waits on the mat till Nurse opens the door and takes the tray, and then you come along down. Same way with the tea in the morning—half past eight, and you knocks, but you don't go in. And mind you clear the corner with your tray—the stair's that awkward."

Flossie Palmer took the tray and went out of the kitchen. The stair which led from the basement was steep and narrow. She wouldn't have taken the job if she had known that there was a basement. "Carrying trays up these stairs all day and half the night, I *don't* think!" Well, she'd obliged Ivy, and Ivy'd obliged her, but she needn't stay more than her month. That'd give her time to look round. Aunt's tongue had got to be beyond a joke, so basement or no basement, she'd have to stay her month. She giggled a little as she pushed open the door at the top of the stair. It was Ivy's month really, come to think of it. "And you just remember your name's Ivy Hodge this journey, Flossie my girl," she said as she went up the stair from the hall to the first landing.

The drawing-room took up the whole of this floor. To reach Miss Rowland's room she had to go up one flight more. Funny kind of start to have a mistress you didn't see. It must be awful to be an invalid and lie in bed all day. Seemed she did come down to the drawing-room on her good days, so perhaps she'd see her to-morrow.

She knocked on the bedroom door and waited with her tray. It was the nurse who opened it—starched cap, starched apron, starched cuffs, starched belt. "Coo! I wouldn't like to have her looking after *me*!" She proffered the tray, and it was taken.

"You're the new maid?"

"Yes, Nurse."

"Ivy Hodge?"

"Yes, Nurse," said Flossie Palmer.

"You're nearly a minute late, Ivy. Don't let it happen again. Miss Rowland expects punctuality."

The door was shut. Flossie tossed her head as she went down to the next landing—"Thinks she's a duchess, I suppose!" She stopped to recapture the nurse's chilly tone: " 'Miss Rowland expects punctuality.' And if I was half a minute late, it was as much as it could have been!" She tossed her head again. Her hair was fair and fluffy under the neat cap. Nurses who gave themselves the airs of duchesses were worse than the backbreakingest basement stair that ever was. She paused on the top step of the next flight and looked back over her shoulder. And then next moment she didn't know why she had done it. Come to think of it, there was something funny about that.

She stood there, little and trim, in her black dress with its white turn-down collar and thin pleated apron, her fair hair bound with a black velvet ribbon to which was attached a little white frill like a coronet. Her blue eyes searched the landing. There were two doors, both leading into the L-shaped drawing-room. The one nearest the stairs was shut, but the other stood a handsbreadth ajar. She tiptoed up to this door, pushed it half way open, and looked in. The light from the landing showed an old-fashioned carpet with bunches of flowers on a ground of faded drab.

Flossie put up her hand to the switch and hesitated. She hadn't seen the drawing-room yet. "S'pose I'll see plenty of it before I'm through." And as the words came into her mind, her fingers moved on the switch and with a little click the light went on in two bracket-lamps on the other side of the room. They were one on either side of the mantelpiece, just where the gas-brackets of an earlier day had been. They preserved the illusion of that day. The whole room preserved it.

Flossie stepped inside and looked about her. There was the big couch where, she supposed, Miss Rowland would lie when she came down. It was upholstered in dark green tapestry, and so were the chairs. The curtains were of dark maroon velvet with deep fringed pelmets. In the middle of the white marble mantelpiece was a gilt clock supported by massive golden cherubs. It startled Flossie with a silvery chime of three strokes. "Quarter to eleven. Coo! I must hurry!" And then, "The blinking thing must be fast." Just one look round into the L. She came a few steps farther. There was a piano round the corner— the upright sort, with flutings of faded green silk, and tarnished brass candle-holders. It stood flat against the wall just beyond the second door and was reflected in the very large gilt-framed mirror which hung on the opposite wall. She wondered how you cleaned all that gilt stuff. She'd never had it to do. There was a bit of work in this room; she could see that.

She looked down the L to the window at the end of it. Another pair of those velvet curtains. Handsome stuff, but a bit too heavy for her taste. Someone had drawn them crooked—"That there nurse, I shouldn't wonder." Funny how it worried you to see things crooked like that.

She went down to the end of the L and pulled at the soft, rich folds. There was a noise that frightened her. She had never heard a curtain make a noise like that before. Suppose someone came. "Well, I'm not doing nothing wrong, am I?" She turned round with that little toss of her head and stood, her eyes widening to a horrified stare. The noise hadn't come from the curtain at all. It had come from the wall of the L. She was looking at the wall. She was looking at the place where the six-foot mirror had hung in its broad gilt frame. It had reflected the piano, but it didn't reflect it any more. It didn't reflect anything, because the glass was gone. Instead there was a blackness, a dark hole full of shadows.

Flossie's mouth opened in a stiff O. She screamed in her mind, but it made no sound in the room. There was a sound there, but it was another sort of sound altogether. It came from the black hole with its wide gilt frame. There was a shuffling and a sighing, and a deep and dreadful groan. And then something moved and, moving, came into view.

It was a man's head. It seemed to rise out of the darkness at the bottom of the frame. At first she only saw the head. It had dusty hair and glazed, straining eyes. There was blood running down over the forehead. It rose a little, waveringly, and she saw the shoulders and arms. The man was crawling with a slow, painful motion. One of the hands rose like a dirty claw. It came groping over the edge of the gilded frame. Flossie stared at it in a terror beyond anything she could have imagined. It was worse than the worst nightmare she had ever had. She wanted to scream, and she couldn't scream. She wanted to fly, and she couldn't move.

And then all at once another hand came out over the frame, high up, and someone was looking at her. A long, pale face—with eyes—it was the eyes which shocked her alive again. They were pale too—pale, cruel eyes—and at the sight of them Flossie screamed and ran. She didn't remember opening the door in the L, but she must have got it open, because the next thing she knew she was tumbling through the doorway and down the stairs into the hall three steps at a time and four at the last, and then helter-skelter through the baize door and down the basement stair. They'd come after her those eyes would. "*Oh, Gawd— don't let them!*" breathed Flossie.

The kitchen door stood open and the kitchen was dark. Mrs. Green had gone to bed in one of the two dingy basement bedrooms. The other waited for Flossie Palmer. *And it might wait.*

Her coat hung on a peg in the passage. She snatched it and, without waiting to put it on, stooped to the heavy bolt which fastened the area door. It came creaking back, and the key creaked too as she turned it. Mrs. Green's voice came to her on the threshold—Mrs. Green's voice, and—was someone opening the door at the top of the stairs? She didn't wait to see, but slammed the door and ran up the area steps and down the foggy street. Thick fog, so that no one could see her. Thick, blinding fog, so that she couldn't see where she was going. Thick, deadening fog—

She ran on wildly, clutching her coat, not daring to stop and put it on, or to listen for the footsteps that might be following her.

Chapter Two

MILES CLAYTON had not felt the hand in his pocket. It had come and gone, and he had felt nothing at all. His own hand, following it after some lapse of time which he could not measure, found only emptiness, a most disconcerting emptiness. There should have been a bulging pocket-book, but it wasn't there. His hand came away, and then went back again. There are things you simply can't believe. This was one of them. The pocket-book was there, because he had put it there. It bulged with the Treasury notes into which he had, only an hour or two ago, changed his French money at Dover. It contained, besides, his passport, his letter of credit, and his luggage check. It was impossible that it should be gone.

His fingers explored the neatly fitting lining of his right-hand inside pocket. There was nothing in it except the lining. He withdrew his hand, rummaged his other pockets, and, having drawn a blank, made such remarks as seemed suitable to the occasion. There was twenty pounds in the pocket-book, but the letter of credit was the worst of it. The passport didn't matter so much. He wouldn't be going back yet awhile. Personally he considered the whole thing a wild goose chase, but if old Macintyre didn't mind footing the bill, that didn't matter to him.

He left that. The immediate question was, what next? He supposed the police, and groaned in spirit. He foresaw an endless vista of the most devastatingly bromidic interviews in which he supplied earnest and well-meaning officials with his entire history from the cradle to what interviews call present day, while in return they assured him that they would do their best to trace his money—and his letter of credit— his passport—his luggage check.

He found himself presently in the middle of such an interview.

"My name is Miles Clayton. I am a British subject. I have just landed at Dover and come up by the boat train."

The man whom he was addressing said, "Wait a minute, sir," and melted away. He was a fat man with rather a sympathetic face.

After about five minutes he was replaced by a little ginger-headed man with a swivel eye. Miles began all over again.

"My name is Miles Clayton. I am a British subject. I have just landed at Dover and come up by the boat train."

The little man stabbed an official pen into an official inkpot, cast a large blob of ink upon the table at which he had seated himself, and called back over his shoulder.

"George, did you fill up those forms?"

There was a thick fog outside, and a good deal of it hung about the corners of this office. From one of its dingier recesses the voice of George made answer. It said,

"No."

"Then get on with it!" said the ginger-headed man. He turned back to Miles, stabbed with his pen again, and said,

"Now, sir, what about it?"

Miles said his piece all over again. He thought this was the sixth time, if you counted the two porters and the ticket-inspector.

"My name is Miles Clayton..."

This time he got it all off his chest, and was edified by the sight of the official pen taking official notes.

"You see, it's damned awkward about my luggage," said Miles.

The official pen travelled squeakily over the official paper.

After a short interval Miles repeated his remark.

The pen continued to squeak.

Miles went on talking.

"You see, it really is damned awkward, because I've got no hand-luggage. My suit-case gave up the ghost in Paris, so I chucked it away and booked everything through. Hotels don't smile on you if you arrive without any luggage."

The ginger-headed man dipped his pen fiercely in the ink and went on writing.

Miles continued to talk. He had a friendly disposition, and he had been looking forward with immense pleasure to being in England again. He had had three very pleasant years in New York, but London was London, and old Macintyre's wild goose chase was a bit of all right as far as he was concerned. Just at the moment joyous reunion with his native land was not going quite as well as he had hoped. On the other hand if, as seemed probable, the ginger-headed man had a human heart somewhere under that official uniform, it might possibly be softened to the extent of permitting him to remove at least one of his trunks to an hotel.

It was a hope which perished in the cradle. The ginger-headed man broke suddenly into his conversation with a request for a signature.

"Name *and* address, sir, if you please."

"But I haven't got an address. You know, you haven't really been listening—I thought you hadn't. Now look here—I arrived in Paris from New York a week ago. And I arrived in Dover from Paris this evening. You don't want my New York address. You don't want my Paris hotel. And if you'll tell me how I'm to scrape up an address in London when I haven't got any money and I haven't got any luggage, I'll be most uncommonly obliged to you."

It wasn't any good, not as far as to-night was concerned anyhow. He could come back in the morning and they would see what could be done.

Miles went along to a telephone-box and rang up Archie Welling— that is to say he rang up the Wellings' house—only to be informed after considerable delay by an agitated and breathless female voice that Mr. Archie was out of town.

Miles considered. He had never met Mr. and Mrs. Welling, but they must know he was coming over. He asked if he could speak to Mr. Welling. The female voice, very flustered, said that Mr. Welling was away, and saved him the trouble of asking for Mrs. Welling by adding, "They're all away, sir." Whereupon a second female voice said in a hissing whisper, "'Ush! You shouldn't ha' said that," and the line went dead.

He stood in the box and tried to think of anyone else whom he could ring... Mrs. Bryan?... Her name wasn't in the directory... The Maberlys were in Egypt, and Tubby was in Scotland... Gilmore—there wasn't an earthly chance of connecting with Gilmore till he reached office to-morrow... He couldn't think of anyone else.

He ran through his pockets and discovered that a single penny represented his cash in hand. You can't get a bed for a penny. What an ass he had been to run himself out of change. If he hadn't—well, what was the good of saying that now? He had, and there was an end of it.

He looked at his wrist-watch. Just on eleven, and a beast of a foggy night. If it hadn't been for the fog, they'd have been in hours ago.

Eleven... By ten o'clock next morning he could start looking up Gilmore at his office and all would be well. Meanwhile he had eleven hours to put in, and a penny in hand.

He walked out of the station into the fog.

Chapter Three

A CHURCH CLOCK somewhere in the fog struck three. The strokes sounded dead and far away. Miles Clayton wondered whether it wouldn't have been better to have kept on moving. If it hadn't been for the fog, he would rather have enjoyed seeing what London looked like at night. But where were you to go when you couldn't see a yard before your face? He had found himself on the Embankment, felt his way to a bench, and stayed there until a policeman came and moved the whole benchful on. He was now in some sort of niche or embrasure behind a group of statuary. He knew this because he had barked his shin on the stone plinth and, groping, had encountered a horrid mass of monumental drapery. He was cold and stiff, and most unutterably bored.

A small whispering voice said in the dark beside him,

"They might leave you be."

The voice didn't seem to be addressing anyone; it just complained out loud because it had been moved on, and the night was long, and the fog was cold, and the stone of the seat was so hard. It was rather a pretty little voice, a girl's voice. It sounded young. Miles found himself speaking to it.

"It's not so long to morning now."

"They keep moving you on so," said the voice. "A shame, I call it!"

"Well, it stretches one's legs."

Someone on the other side of him, a man, gave a ghastly hollow groan.

The girl's voice said, "Ooh!" and came a little nearer. Miles could feel its owner pressing up against him with a shiver. After a moment she said, "D'you know why they move them on? Bound to do it they are, every two hours regular. I've got a friend that's got a cousin in the p'lice, and he says it's in case anyone goes and dies afore morning—that's what he says. He says he'd get into awful trouble if anyone was found dead on his beat and they'd been dead more than two hours, so they just keep moving them along. But I call it a shame all the same." She gave another shiver. "I've never been out all night before. Have you?"

"No, I haven't."

Flossie Palmer hesitated. His voice sounded nice—quite like a gentleman's voice. Oh well, there were all sorts out of work nowadays. Aunt 'ud have a fit—but then Aunt would have a fit anyway if she knew that her own sister's daughter was spending the night on the Embankment along with a lot of tramps. She gave her head its little characteristic toss and said with a sort of whispering eagerness,

"My name's Flossie. What's yours?"

"Miles."

"That's funny. D'you mean that's your Christian name?"

"Yes. It means a soldier."

"Are you a soldier?" Aunt had always warned her specially about soldiers.

"No, I'm a secretary," said Miles Clayton.

"Out of a job, I s'pose?"

He laughed a little.

"No—I've got quite a good job. It sounds awfully silly, but I've just come over from America, and someone pinched my pocket-book, so I haven't any money, and they won't let me take my luggage away, and I can't get hold of anyone I know until to-morrow."

"Ooh!" said Flossie on a soft breath of sympathy. "What's it like in America?"

He laughed with real amusement.

"Oh, I like it."

"Then why've you come back here?"

"To look for a needle in a bundle of hay."

"What's that?"

"Well, that's what I call it. I've got to look for a girl no one's heard about since she was ten days old. I don't know her name and I don't know where to look for her. Don't you call that hunting for a needle in a bundle of hay?"

"Sounds a bit like it," said Flossie. A quick shiver ran over her and she edged a little nearer.

"Are you awfully cold?" said Miles.

"No—I got my coat." She shivered again, because when she said that, it all came over her. The coat snatched down from its peg. The bolt on the area door—it had pinched her finger, but she hadn't felt it till afterwards. And then the panic-stricken flight up the steps and down the foggy street. She'd got to have someone to talk to, or she'd be seeing that black hole in the wall again, and the man's head with the blood running down. She drew in her breath with a shuddering sound and heard Miles say in a voice of concern,

"I say, what's the matter? Are you ill?"

She said, "No—I got my coat."

He could hear that her teeth were chattering. Then, between those chattering teeth, she said,

"I got a fright."

The man who had groaned had made no sound since then. Miles was vaguely aware of him, slumped down in a heap. He and the girl might have been quite alone. They *were* alone. The fog shut them in. He could feel her shivering and trembling against him. She sounded very young. He said,

"What frightened you?"

"Ooh!" said Flossie. "It was awful, Mr. Miles—it was, *reelly*!"

She didn't care what Aunt or anyone would say. If she didn't tell someone, she'd go potty, and even Aunt couldn't say that he wasn't behaving like a perfect gentleman. Come to that, she could have done with a bit of an arm round her—it 'ud have been company in the dark and no harm done. She slipped her hand inside the arm she was leaning against and her teeth stopped chattering.

"It was awful, Mr. Miles—it was, *reelly*! I just run out of the house like I was, in my cap an' apron, only I took off the cap and put it in my pocket, and if I hadn't grabbed my coat as I came through the passage, I wouldn't have nothing round me and I'd have got my death as like as not."

"What frightened you?"

She really had a pretty voice. The London accent struck pleasantly on his ear. It went with that breathless whispering way she talked.

"What frightened you?"

Flossie settled down to enjoy herself. Holding on to his arm like that made her feel quite safe. Coo! Wouldn't Ernie be wild if he could see her now? The thought of Ernie's probable state of mind imparted a pleasant glow. Ernie was all right, but he'd better not start any of that sheikh stuff with her.

"Well, it's like this," she said. "I got a girl friend, Ivy Hodge her name is, and she was all fixed up to go to a place—house-parlour with an old invalid lady who doesn't hardly ever come out of her room. Leastways I s'pose she's old, but Ivy never seen her, and no more did I."

Miles felt a very languid interest in the affairs of Ivy Hodge, but he liked the little whispering Cockney voice at his shoulder. Hard lines on a kid like that to be out all night in this fog.

He put in an encouraging "Well?"

"Well, it was a bit funny, don't you think? No one seeing her, I mean. They just rang up the registry in an awful hurry, and they took up her reference on the 'phone, and would she come in to-morrow? And my girl friend said she would. You see, she'd had the worst row ever with her fiongcey. The banns was up and all, but she said to me, 'I don't care, dear—if I was half way through the marriage service and he demeaned himself to speak to me the way he spoke to me yesterday, I'd say no and I'd mean no, same as I've said it now. And if he thinks he can come smarming and making it up, he'll find out where he's made a mistake, because I've just been to the registry and there's a place all ready for me to step into, and a pound more than I've had yet.' Kind of proud and independent Ivy is, and she was all worked up. See?"

Miles said he saw.

Flossie was feeling better every moment. She went on eagerly.

"That was yesterday, and this afternoon she come round and told me they'd made it up. You could have knocked me down with a feather—you could reely. Seems he went down on his knees and said he'd drown himself—and of course she didn't want him to do that. So then she put it to me, what about me taking the place instead of her? And I said, 'Well, I might, but I haven't got a reference only as a general, and I've been out best part of a year because of Aunt being ill and wanting me to help at home.' And she says, 'Well, dear, why not go as me? It's no odds to anyone what you call yourself that I can see.' And so that's how we fixed it up." A slightly dubious tone came into Flossie's voice. "It wasn't hurting anyone, you see."

"You might have got into rather a mess," said Miles.

Flossie shivered.

"I s'pose I didn't ought to have done it—but I'd had a row too—with Aunt. Threw it up at me she did that I hadn't been earning. And how she'd the face, when it was her that made me leave because she'd fell downstairs and broke her leg! Well, I didn't feel like staying after that, so I told Ivy I'd take her place for her, and I put my brush and comb and my night-things in a parcel and my coat over my uniform, and I went round to 16 Varley Street and said I was Ivy Hodge. Just about nine o'clock in the evening it was, because Ivy'd let me have her black dress and I'd had to take it in."

"Nine o'clock to-night?" said Miles.

Flossie nodded. He could feel the movement against his arm.

"Just about," she said.

"You didn't stay long," he said in a bantering voice.

She shivered again.

"Ooh—it was awful, Mr. Miles!"

"What happened? Don't shiver like that—you're all right."

"I can't help it, Mr. Miles. I'm frightened to tell you."

"Then don't tell me. But there's nothing to be frightened of."

"That's all you know. But I got to tell someone."

"All right then, tell me."

"I'm going to—I *got* to."

"Go ahead then."

Flossie pinched his arm hard.

"There was a cook there—a fat woman—name of Green. She said I'd got to take up the old lady's Benger's, and not to go into the room on no account and the nurse would take it at the door. There's a nurse, and the cook, and the house-parlour-maid. So I took it up, and when I was coming down, the drawing-room door was open and I went in, just to have a look round as you might say. Ooh! *Mr. Miles!*"

"What happened?"

"I dunno—*reelly*. There was a curtain looped crooked in the back part of the room and I went to pull it straight, and there was a great big mirror on the wall, taller than me and a handsome gold frame all round it. I noticed it pertickler. And when I'd put the curtain straight, I turned round, and—*ooh!*"

"Good gracious, Flossie—*what?*"

Flossie dug her fingers into his arm.

"*Ooh!*" she said again. "There wasn't any glass in the mirror any more. There was the frame, but there wasn't any glass—there was only a most awful black hole. Ooh—it *was* awful! And there was a man's head all over blood!" She caught at him with both hands and dissolved into hysterical sobs upon his shoulder.

"Oh, I say!" said Miles. "I do wish you wouldn't do that! Look here, someone will think I'm murdering you."

Flossie choked, gulped, and said in a trembling whisper,

"I never see such eyes."

"What—in the head? Flossie, what on earth did you have for supper?"

She stiffened indignantly.

"I never! And it wasn't that there poor unfortunate head that had the eyes I was talking about—it was the other one. Come and looked at me out of the hole in the wall he did. And how I got down the stairs I dunno, but thank Gawd I did, and grabbed my coat and up the area steps and never stopped running till my breath gave out. And I dursn't go home to Aunt, not in the middle of the night, which it would have been by the time I got there in this fog, supposing I could find my way and didn't get run over. Aunt's that *pertickler*. Ooh—I wish I hadn't told you about it!" She gulped down a sob. "I thought it'd make me feel better, but it hasn't. It's all come over me worse than ever. I didn't ought to have talked about it." Her breath came in gasps between the words.

Miles took her by the arm and shook her a little.

"Do you know what I think?"

"N-no."

"I think you dreamt it."

She pulled away and sat up.

"I never!"

"Well, it sounds like it."

"Come to that," said Flossie in a little trembling voice of rage—"come to that, what about you? Coo!" She laughed. "You must have thought I was green to swallow your tale about being a secretary come all the way over from America to look for someone you don't know nothing about! But I got some manners, thank Gawd! I didn't laugh at you, did I—*nor* tell you you were dreaming, *nor* yet telling lies?"

Miles couldn't help laughing. He'd much rather she was angry than have her crying on his shoulder.

"Well, as it happens, I wasn't telling lies. But you needn't believe me if you don't want to."

"Very kind, I'm *sure!*"

"I'll tell you all about it if you like."

She tried for a haughty, languid tone.

"Well—*reelly*—" Native curiosity came bubbling through. "You don't mean you're reelly looking for a girl and you don't know her *name?*"

"I do. Wouldn't you like to hear about it? If I tell every girl I meet, perhaps I'll strike the right one. Perhaps it's you. It might be—you never can tell."

"Ooh!" said Flossie. She edged nearer again. "Go on, Mr. Miles!"

Miles went on.

"Well, I'm secretary to a man called Macintyre. He's an American, and he's got such a lot of money that he doesn't know what to do with it. There are just a few of 'em left still. He comes out somewhere near the top."

"I'd like to have a lot of money," said Flossie in a dreamy voice.

"It's not all jam. For one thing, he doesn't know who he's going to leave it to. That worries him a lot."

"Hasn't he got any relations?"

Miles laughed.

"Dozens, but he hates them all like poison. *But* he once had a brother whom he didn't hate—they built up the business together. And the brother had a wife, but she quarrelled with him and ran away—just on her own, you know, not with anyone. And after she'd run away she had a baby over here in England, a girl, and she wrote to tell her husband. She'd spent all her money by then and she was pretty ill, and she wanted to come back."

"Ooh!" said Flossie. "What happened?"

"He never opened the letter. He died last year, and old Macintyre found it unopened in his desk. There were three or four letters. None of them had been opened. They were tied up together neatly, and right on top there was one that *had* been opened. It wasn't from the wife. It said:

DEAR SIR,

Your wife died this morning. Please send money for funeral expenses and my account enclosed and oblige,

Yours truly,

AGNES SMITH.

"Nothing about the baby?"

"Not a word."

"Did he send the money?"

"We don't know. We don't know what he did. Nobody knows. And I've come over here to find the baby. She'd be nineteen and a half by now."

"Ooh!" said Flossie, still in that dreamy voice. "I'm nineteen and a half."

"But you're not Miss Macintyre, are you?"

Flossie pounced.

"I thought you said you didn't know her name?"

"Oh, her surname's Macintyre of course. I don't know what she was christened. That's one of the things I've got to find out. There—that's my story. What do you think of it?"

Flossie sniffed.

"I think you must of dreamt it," she said.

Chapter Four

MR. GILMORE might be addicted to late hours, but he did not permit them to impair his efficiency. He was something in the Foreign Office—a very efficient and confidential something. Miles Clayton, entering upon him in an extremely hungry, cold, dirty, and disgruntled condition at somewhere about ten-fifteen, was immediately sucked into a vortex of energy which resulted in the almost instantaneous recovery of his luggage and the production of his lost note-case, minus the notes it had contained, but with his passport and letter of credit intact.

"Ordinary station thief. Little man—not up to handling a letter of credit. Note-case chucked away—too dangerous to keep. What about the numbers of the notes? Have you got them?"

Miles shook his head.

Mr. Gilmore frowned.

"Always take the numbers of notes," he said. "I do. Train yourself to memorize them... Not in the least—perfectly easy. Let your brain behave like a blancmange, and it will. Now better go and have a wash and a shave, and some sleep. Dine with me at the Luxe at eight."

Miles was very glad to agree. He found a more modest hotel than the Luxe to stay at, wallowed in hot water, ate largely, and plunged into a deep and dreamful sleep. He didn't dream very much as a rule—only when he was excited or tired out. He didn't know when he had dreamed like this. Looking back afterwards, he couldn't remember where one dream stopped and another began. He couldn't really remember much about them, and the bits he remembered gave him the feeling that there was a great deal more that was hiding in the corners of his mind. In one of the dreams he was crawling through a long dark passage after a head which kept on rolling away. *Not* a nice dream. And then, after some indeterminate lapse of time, there were eyes glaring at him from the darkness and he was trying to catch them in a butterfly net. Why? What an ass one was in a dream... And then someone said "*Miss Macintyre*" in a loud booming voice that went rolling about like lumps of thunder. And in the middle of it all there was a baby in his arms, and it looked up at him with incredibly solemn eyes and said, "You don't know my name." And after that he was running the gauntlet between two rows of girls who stretched from the Marble Arch to Waterloo Bridge. One of them was Miss Macintyre, but he didn't know which. They shouted their names at him as he ran: "Joan—Alice—Una—Marion—Flossie." *Flossie.* She said in a shuddering whisper, "There was a great black hole in the wall," and he fell over the edge of the world into another dream.

It is a long way down over the edge of the world, but it is very quiet when you get there. There was a sound of water, and a sound of trees—soft running water, and slow waving trees... Little Kay was there. It was years since he had thought about Kay... He stayed in this dream for a long time very pleasantly.

Then he woke up and dressed, and went to dine with Mr. Gilmore at the Luxe.

It was a very good dinner, and he was still hungry. Somewhere between the fish and the *entrée* he found himself telling Gilmore about his wild goose chase.

"How many girls do you suppose there are in England at this minute between the ages of nineteen and twenty, Gil?"

"Ask the editor of *Tit Bits*," said Gilmore. "His line, not mine. How many halfpennies does it take to reach the moon? If you stood all the policemen in the world one on top of the other, what would be the colour of the top one's hair? Why is a mouse when it spins?"

"Do you suppose there are a million?"

"I hope not."

"Well, half a million?"

"Why this morbid preoccupation with flappers?"

Miles shook his head.

"They've stopped flapping at nineteen and a half."

"Anyhow, why?"

"Miss Macintyre," said Miles. "I've been telling you all about her and you haven't been listening. Mother vanished into the blue twenty years ago—had a baby in Hampstead and died."

"I heard all that. Your boss wants to find the girl and leave her his money. How do you propose setting about it? Where are the clues?"

"Well there are three letters from Mrs. Macintyre, all written the same month, two before the baby was born and one afterwards. Knox Macintyre hadn't opened any of them. The boss read them and handed them on to me. They were rather—heart-rending. I don't know what they quarrelled about, but she wanted to make it up. That was the first letter, and she asked him to cable an answer. The next was a fortnight later. She was awfully worried because he hadn't cabled. She was ill, and she was running out of money. She didn't want to sell the jewels he had given her. She begged him to cable and come to her. The last was ten days later, just a scrawl in pencil. 'Very ill. Do *please* come. Baby is a girl. So pretty.' Well, that was all, except a letter which he *had* opened, from the landlady: 'Dear sir, your wife died this morning. Please send money for funeral expenses and my account enclosed and oblige yours truly, Agnes Smith.' Pretty grim, isn't it? Knox must have been a hard nut."

Gilmore nodded.

"Any address on the letters?"

"Oh yes—72 Laburnum Vale, Hampstead. *But* when I wrote to Mrs. Agnes Smith, the letter came back with *Not known* scrawled across it in blue pencil. So then the boss told me to come over and worry round."

"Jewels—" said Gilmore meditatively. "She didn't want to have to sell her jewels... Any idea what they were? Likely to be noticeable if and when sold?"

"Very much so, I should think. I hunted up a couple of her women friends. Their eyes fairly popped when they were describing them. Item—a rope of black pearls. Item—a wreath of diamond laurel leaves, said to have belonged to the Empress Maria Theresa. Item—a pair of pink pearl earrings set with brilliants. Etcetera, etcetera."

"The complete jewellers' catalogue!" said Gilmore sardonically. "Well, you hike to Hampstead, you pursue pawnbrokers, you look for Mrs. Smith, who is probably dead. Net result a cable to New York: 'Nothing doing.' "

"You're a damping blighter, Gil."

Gilmore shrugged his shoulders. His dark, lean face expressed an amused contempt.

"Twenty years—what optimism!"

Miles laughed a little. He was the same age as Gilmore, but there might easily have been seven or eight years between them—the important years between the late twenties and the middle thirties. When Gilmore smiled, the apparent gap increased. The smile brought out the lines which marked his face. Miles Clayton's laugh made an undergraduate of him again. He had a boy's fair hair and fresh complexion. It came as a surprise when his jaw set and his grey eyes looked out from under frowning brows. The boy was gone then, and his twenty-eight years could be credited. Just now he laughed.

"Optimism? Well, you'd say so if you knew when those letters were written."

Gilmore's eyebrows went up.

"July, 1914," said Miles. "There was just going to be a tidy-sized war, Gil, in case you've forgotten. That mixes it a bit—doesn't it?"

They had arrived at the sweet.

As Miles helped himself, Flossie Palmer was looking into the cracked mirror on her chest of drawers. The crack was high up in one corner, so it didn't really matter. She had on a very bright pink dress which killed her delicate porcelain tints, but she considered it a complete success. She had painted her lips a brilliant cerise and darkened her eyebrows with a burnt match. She and Ernie were going to the *palais de danse*, and the immediate problem was to get out of the house without being seen by Aunt. Aunt would make her wash her face, to a cert she would. She already thought the dress too bright to be quite respectable. Aunt was so pertickler.

Flossie tilted the glass for a last good look. She wanted something round her neck, and she'd got nothing but her old beads. She took them out of the drawer and hung them round her neck—three times round and something to spare. A bit dull in colour. Old-fashioned too, going three times round like that. The grey looked rather nice hanging down over the bright pink of the dress. She put on her coat, listened at the top of the stairs, and ran down them quick and light to join Ernie in the street.

And at the same moment in the kitchen at 16 Varley Street Mrs. Green looked up at the kitchen clock.

"Getting on for nine o'clock. I thought it'd ha' been later."

She was addressing the new house-parlourmaid, who was still in her out-door clothes. They were very neat out-door clothes, but not very warm for the time of year—a dark blue coat and skirt, a grey scarf, and a little round grey cap. The hair under the cap was dark, very dark indeed. It waved away from an extremely pretty forehead. Mrs. Green, looking at her, thought the girl a deal too pretty for service—"Why, with her hair as black as that, her skin did ought to be dark. And look at it— white as privet! Show me a girl as pretty as that, and I'll show you one that'll get her head turned before you can say Jack Robinson."

At the moment there did not seem to be any sign of head-turning or of what Mrs. Green called "ideas." The dark blue eyes looked at her in an anxious, friendly manner.

"Do I have to do anything to-night?"

The girl's voice increased Mrs. Green's apprehension. Niminy-piminy she called it—for all the world like the young ladies in her last place, and all very well for young ladies. Actually, the voice was a pretty one.

"What did you say?" said Mrs. Green. "And I've forgot your name, what with that girl running out of the house like a mad thing last night, and only come in a matter of two hours before. And two others this month, and I don't know what girls are coming to, I'm sure. And what did you say your name was?"

"Kay," said the girl.

"Rubbidge!" said Mrs. Green. "There's no such name!"

The very little beginning of a laugh changed the charming line of the lips into something more charming still. A dimple showed and was gone. She said sedately,

"It's all I've got. Please, do I have to do anything to-night?"

"Half past ten," said Mrs. Green, "you takes 'er Benger's up. Half past ten to a tick she 'as it. And you don't go in, not for nothing. You waits on the mat till Nurse opens the door and takes the tray."

"I'll just go and take off my things," said Kay.

Chapter Five

THE NEXT DAY being Saturday, Miles Clayton went to Hampstead and walked up Laburnum Vale. He was looking for No. 72, but he was not destined to find it. The row of little villas, whose small front gardens had once maintained a green wall which broke for one enchanted month into gold, were now reduced to a mere twenty shabby houses. Shops had crept in upon them at the one end, and at the other, where Nos. 50 to 100 had once stood, great modern blocks of flats reared themselves imposingly. The surviving laburnums were few, straggly, and grey in the cold light of the January afternoon.

Miles wandered to the end of the flats and turned back again. Miss Macintyre had receded in the most depressing manner. She was pre-war. Laburnum Vale was defunct. There wasn't any Agnes Smith.

He dropped into a tobacconist's and asked questions. A pleasant worried-looking little man said he didn't know, he was sure. There was a Mrs. Smith just round the corner. She was quite young—newly married couple in a hair-dressing business. It wouldn't be them? He'd only been here a matter of five years himself, but Mr. Haynes at the iron-monger's stores, he was a very old resident.

Miles sought out Mr. Haynes and found him elderly, whiskery, and bland. He rubbed his hands and bowed until Miles could see how neatly his oiled grey hair encircled the shining bald patch on the top of his head.

"A lot of changes here—oh yes, sir, a lot of changes. Improvements they call them, but I'm not so sure. Laburnum Vale, and a Mrs. Smith that used to live at 72? Before the war? Oh dear, oh dear, sir, that's a long time ago. I'd my two boys with me in the business then. We can't put the clock back—can we? Excuse me, sir."

He rubbed his hands and went away into the back of the shop. Miles heard him calling, "Mother!" and presently he came back with a brisk, plump wife.

"Mrs. Smith? Why, Father, of course you remember her! Now what's the good of saying you don't? No. 72 you said? Yes, that's her right enough—used to let apartments. Why, Father, don't you remember Bert taking a fancy to a girl she had—a forward piece of goods that I wouldn't have inside my door? Real put out he was because he wanted to bring her into tea and I said no, *and* meant it too." She turned back to Miles with a sparkle in her eyes. Bert was dead somewhere in Flanders, Mrs. Smith's Ada, that forward piece, had been gone nearly twenty years from Laburnum Vale, but the old anger came up in Mrs. Haynes as she thought of "the likes of her setting her cap at our Bert."

"Well, sir," she said, "that's Mrs. Smith right enough, but she's been gone from here, oh, getting along for eighteen, nineteen years, I should say."

Curiously enough, she had only the vaguest recollection of what must surely have provided the neighbourhood with a good deal of food for gossip—the death of Mrs. Smith's lonely lodger a week after the birth of her child. She couldn't remember the name, or what had happened to the baby. What month would it be? Oh, July 1914? Well, that accounted for it, because she was away right on into August with her sister in Devonshire, and only came home then because Bert had enlisted—"And if I'd been there, I'd have kept him home and he'd have been here yet."

"Now, now, Mother—" said Mr. Haynes.

They sent him on to two other people who remembered Mrs. Smith, but neither of them knew where she had gone. One of the two, a little faded dressmaker, remembered Mrs. Macintyre—"Very nice-looking but very sad, poor thing, and used to cry more than was good for her, I'm afraid. She died when the baby was born."

"Yes," said Miles. "Now, Miss Collins, I want you to tell me anything you can remember. Mrs. Macintyre died on 30th July 1914. Do you know what happened to the baby?"

Miss Collins' small beady eyes became moist and eager. Life was rather a dull affair for her. She served a dwindling clientele of ladies with a preference for pre-war fashions. The constant adaptation of late Edwardian styles to figures afflicted with an elderly spread was not an exhilarating occupation. There *was* a time when she had made baby clothes. The recollection warmed her, and she hastened to tell Mr. Clayton all about it.

"I used to go in and out, being a friend of Mrs. Smith's, as you might say, and the poor thing—well, Mr. Clayton, if I was to tell you she couldn't so much as hold a needle, I really shouldn't be exaggerating—no, indeed I don't think I should. Anything so helpless I never saw. She used just to sit and mope, and it would have done her good to have made some of the dear little baby's things herself—now wouldn't it, Mr. Clayton? Of course I couldn't complain, because it was money in my pocket, as you may say—or should have been." She patted her curled front with modest pride. She kept it under a net, and it had once been auburn. "I made all the baby clothes—six of everything. And then, poor thing, she died, and there wasn't anyone to settle my account. I'd quite a tiff with Mrs. Smith about that, Mr. Clayton, and I'm not saying anything behind her back that I didn't say to her face, but wouldn't you think she might have put in a word for me and my account when she was getting her own settled?"

"Did Mrs. Smith get her account settled?" said Miles quickly.

Miss Collins bridled.

"Indeed she did! And I said to her, 'If I'd a friend that had an account and it only needed a word from me—' "

"Miss Collins, who settled it?"

Miss Collins tossed her head.

"Well, it's never been settled, Mr. Clayton, not to this day."

"Mrs. Smith's account," said Miles. "Who settled that? You said it was settled."

"Oh, the poor thing's sister that came down and settled everything—*most* open-handed and generous, as you may say. Why, that worthless girl of Mrs. Smith's that used to run after young Bert Haynes, she got a present of a pound. And then to think that Mrs. Smith wouldn't so much as have mentioned my name!"

Miles was staring at her.

"A sister?" he said.

"Why, Mrs. Macintyre's sister—the poor thing that died."

"Miss Collins, are you sure?"

He had reason to be astonished, for Marion Macintyre had been an only child. There was no sister who could have settled Mrs. Smith's account. There was no relative, of any degree, who could have done so. His information was that the runaway Mrs. Macintyre had neither friend nor relative in England. She had left her husband and had buried herself amongst strangers. She had lived lonely and died alone. But when she was dead, a sister had come down and settled Mrs. Smith's account...

"Of course I'm sure," said Miss Collins with a touch of offence.

"Did she ever come to see Mrs. Macintyre?"

"I don't think so. No, I'm sure she didn't, Mr. Clayton, for Mrs. Smith used to say to me what a shame it was that no one ever came near her. And she didn't get any letters either. People talked about it, Mr. Clayton."

Miles was thinking. This *sister*—who was she? He said,

"Did she pay for the funeral?"

"She paid for everything, and I'm sure—"

"Did she come to the funeral?"

"Yes, Mr. Clayton, she did—and stayed the night and paid up all the bills, so you can't say there wouldn't have been time to mention my account."

Miles perceived that he must bear with Miss Collins' account.

"Very hard lines," he said. "Well, she stayed the night. And then?"

Miss Collins fluttered a little. Her twenty years' grievance shook her.

"And then she went away and didn't leave any address. And Mrs. Smith wrote to the husband out in America and didn't get any answer. And I sent my account to the address she gave me, and I never had any answer either—no, not from that day to this, Mr. Clayton!"

"Very hard lines," said Miles. "What did you say the sister's name was?"

Miss Collins tapped her forehead where the caged fringe left off.

"Let me see... No, I don't know that I... Wilkins?... No, that was someone else. It's a long time now, and I'm not very good at names, as you may say... Palmer now—Palmer—I'm sure there was someone called Palmer... No, no, of course—how could it have been? That was Mrs. Smith's own sister. Flo, she called her—Flo Palmer. No, Mr. Clayton, I'm sorry, but I don't seem to get hold of the name. Very likely I never heard it, not to take it in, for when I went round there the day after the funeral, and found she'd gone, and all the accounts settled except mine, well, I had words with Mrs. Smith, and we didn't speak for weeks. In fact it wasn't ever the same again, and I wasn't really sorry when she moved away."

"And Mrs. Macintyre's sister took the baby?"

"Took everything. And as I said to Mrs. Smith—"

"Was the baby christened?" said Miles.

Miss Collins shook her head.

"Oh no, Mr. Clayton—not down here."

Miles took a hasty look at the half sheet of paper on which he had made some notes.

"What was the baby like?"

"Oh, a very pretty little thing—a dear little girl."

"Fair, or dark?"

Miss Collins pursed up her lips.

"Well, I couldn't really say. Nothing much one way or the other."

"Mrs. Macintyre was dark, wasn't she?"

"Dark hair and blue eyes, and the loveliest pale skin. But all babies have blue eyes, Mr. Clayton, and most of them have fair hair when they're born, if they have any at all."

Miles took another look at his paper.

"Was there any name talked of for the baby? Can you remember?"

Miss Collins shook her head.

"There wasn't anything settled, and I'll tell you how I know. Mrs. Smith was talking about it only the day before the poor thing died, and she'd asked her just that very day what she was going to call the baby. Her name was Marion, you know, and Mrs. Smith said something about little Marion, meaning the baby, and poor Mrs. Macintyre burst out crying—'Oh, no, no, no!' she said. 'Don't call her after me! I'd like her to have a happy name. You mustn't call her after me!' " Miss Collins got out a handkerchief and dabbed her eyes. "It's a very sad story, Mr. Clayton."

Beyond the fact that the baby's name was not Marion, he had achieved nothing. He wondered how many thousand names that left. He went back to his notes.

"Do you know what doctor Mrs. Macintyre had?"

"Doctor Murgatroyd," said Miss Collins. "Such a nice man. He was killed in the war."

Miles crossed out the doctor.

"And the nurse? What about the nurse?"

"Oh, that was Miss Hobson. She died about ten years ago—and *very* much missed. Such a good nurse."

Miles crossed off the nurse.

"You don't know where Mrs. Smith is now?" he said.

"No, Mr. Clayton, I don't," said Miss Collins. She put her forefinger to her mouth and nibbled at the nail. Miles had the impression that there were words on the tip of her tongue.

He said "Yes?" in an encouraging voice.

"Well, it isn't anything to go by," said Miss Collins, "for I always thought she was a very untruthful girl."

"Who was?"

Miss Collins sniffed a virtuous sniff.

"That Ada of Mrs. Smith's. A very flaunting sort of girl. And the way she ran after that poor Bert Haynes—quite a disgrace, as you may say!"

Laburnum Vale seemed to make the most of its scandals. Bert had been dead nearly twenty years, but Ada's flaunting was unforgotten there.

"What about her?" said Miles.

"I don't suppose it's anything," said Miss Collins.

Miles groaned inwardly. It would have been a relief to swear, or it would have been a relief to burst out laughing. If he did either, she would dry up. He achieved a weary smile, which Miss Collins fortunately admired a good deal.

"Well, suppose you tell me," he said.

"She must have been well over forty," said Miss Collins.

"What—Ada?" (Were you still a girl at forty in Laburnum Vale?)

"Oh no, Mr. Clayton—*Mrs. Smith*. She was a lot older than Flo—Mrs. Palmer. Fifteen years or so, I should say. But Ada said—"

"Yes, Miss Collins?"

Miss Collins bridled.

"Well, it was nothing, Mr. Clayton, but I just happened to meet her in the street—"

"Mrs. Smith?" said Miles hopefully.

Miss Collins sniffed again. It was the same definitely virtuous sniff.

"Oh no, Mr. Clayton, not Mrs. Smith—that girl Ada I was telling you about. I just happened to meet her in the street—just after the Armistice it was. And she wasn't the kind of girl I'd stop to speak to, but she came up to me as bold as you please and asked me if I'd heard that Mrs. Smith had married again. And I said I hadn't, and I walked right on. And I don't think there's anything else I can tell you, Mr. Clayton, so if you don't mind—I've got a lady coming for a fitting."

Miles thanked her very much. There was a slow and heavy foot upon the stair. He spoke quickly and without great hope.

"I suppose you can't give me Ada's address?"

Miss Collins shook her head with a decided air of offence.

"Oh no, Mr. Clayton, I couldn't. I only saw her that once after she left. She wasn't a girl I'd have had in any house of mine. Of course Mrs. Smith pleased herself... Oh no, no trouble at all. Good afternoon, Mr. Clayton."

Chapter Six

MISS ROWLAND LAY on the sofa in her drawing-room at 16 Varley Street. The blinds were down and the curtains were drawn—those wine-coloured velvet curtains with the fringed pelmets which Flossie Palmer had thought handsome but too sober for her taste. Both the electric wall-brackets were lighted, but they were so heavily shaded that the room seemed to be full of a greenish twilight. Miss Rowland's sofa was drawn up at right angles to the fire. About the head of it a tall, light screen which displayed golden storks upon a black ground was so arranged as to shade her still further from the light.

Kay came timidly up to the sofa and set the tea-tray down upon the small walnut table which stood ready for it. This was the first time she had seen her new mistress, and she did not quite know whether to look at her or not. She put down the tray, and then she did look up, because Miss Rowland was speaking. She had a very low, weak voice.

"You are the new maid?"

"Yes, madam."

"Your name?"

"Kay, madam."

"That's a very unusual name. I suppose you have a surname?"

A deep carnation colour rose in Kay's cheeks.

"I should have said Kay Moore, madam."

All this time she had not looked directly at Miss Rowland. She had seen the pillows heaped in the shadow behind her, the crimson silk eiderdown which hid all the lower part of her body and was drawn up above her waist, the fringed edges of the shawl about her shoulders. She had seen these coverings and adjuncts, but Miss Rowland herself she had not seen. Now she looked at her. The shadow of the screen was reinforced by the shadow of an old-fashioned cap. It was made of lace and muslin and tied under the chin with a large bow of lilac ribbon. It hid all the hair and half the forehead and cheeks. There remained in the twilight a long pale nose, two half closed eyes, and a pale drawn-in mouth.

Just as Kay looked, the eyelids lifted and the eyes met hers. They were pale too, but Kay didn't think of this at the time, because when Miss Rowland looked at her she was shaken by a sudden vivid sense of recognition. It came and went in a flash and left her with shaking knees.

Miss Rowland did not speak again, and she went out of the room wondering what had startled her so. She hadn't ever seen Miss Rowland before. But she had recognized her—or been recognized. She didn't know which. Something had happened in her mind when she looked at Miss Rowland and Miss Rowland looked at her, but it had happened so quickly that she hadn't been able to get hold of it. That is the case sometimes with a word or a name that you have known and then forgotten. It hovers on the very edge of consciousness, and sometimes flashes across the conscious field, and you snatch at it, but it is gone before you can hold it. It was like that.

Kay went down into the kitchen and found Mrs. Green stirring the teapot.

"Well, did you see her?" she asked.

Kay said, "Yes."

"Nurse there?"

Kay said, "No."

"Nice and chatty you are, I don't think!" said Mrs. Green. "I suppose you got a tongue, 'aven't you? What did you think of her?"

"Is she very ill?" said Kay in a shrinking voice.

Mrs. Green began to pour out the tea.

"Five years I been here, and she's never been out. Doctor comes every week reg'lar—and not an ordinary doctor neither, but one of those high up specialists. But there—she's got plenty of money and nothing to spend it on, pore thing. Once in a way she'll be down like she is to-day, but mostly she's in 'er room and 'as to be kep' that quiet—not a sound in the 'ouse. And that's a thing you'll 'ave to remember, my girl—you don't go up on Miss Rowland's landing, not for nothing you don't, except when you're rung for and when you takes 'er Benger's up at night like I told you. I don't mind it myself, but it makes a dull 'ouse for a girl. Now how many girls d'you suppose we've 'ad 'ere since I come? Eight or nine a year, I reckon, and you can do the sum yourself. Most of them goes at the month, and if they don't go of themselves they get the sack. Two month's the limit. So now you know. Why'd you leave your last place?"

"I didn't like it."

"You're not a London girl?"

"No."

Mrs. Green pushed the jam across.

"Oh, find your tongue—*come*! The last girl we 'ad wasn't 'ere only a couple of hours and she'd told me all about 'er boy friend before she run away. And it's no use your asking me why she run, for I don't know, nor no one else. But anyhow open your mouth a bit and let's 'ave the story of your life, as they say."

Kay's lips parted. The dimple showed. Some pretty white teeth showed.

"I haven't got a story—yet," she said.

Mrs. Green put a fourth lump of sugar in her tea. She was a fat woman with a pale, moist skin and a great many rolling curves.

Her cheeks rolled into her chin, and her chin by way of two or three subsidiary chins rolled into her neck, and so to a vast bosom, a waist which still attempted to be a waist, and monumental hips. She stirred her sweet, strong tea with a vigorous spoon.

"Well, I suppose you were born like the rest of us, and I suppose you were brought up somehow by someone or other? You're not going to tell me you were found under a gooseberry bush, are you?"

The bright carnation colour came again.

"No," said Kay—"it wasn't a gooseberry bush." Then, quickly, "I don't really know anything about my father and mother. I don't remember them."

Mrs. Green finished her first cup of tea and poured herself out another, horribly black. This time she put in five lumps.

"Then 'ow were you brought up? Relations? You don't look like a norphanage girl."

"An aunt brought me up. I haven't any other relations."

"Oh, come on!" said Mrs. Green. "This isn't a police court, for me to be asking you questions and you to be saying just as little as you can for fear of what might come out. *Unless such was the case*," she added darkly and stirred her tea again.

Kay looked down at her piece of bread and jam and began to cut it into strips.

"There isn't anything to tell," she said. "My aunt wasn't well off. We moved about a good deal. She taught me, and I helped in the house. I didn't go to school. She died two years ago, and there wasn't any money, so I went as mother's help to the Vicar's wife—we were in a village then."

"Mother's 'elp!" said Mrs. Green, in a tone of scorn. "'Eaven 'elp them is what I say! All 'elp and no wages—work from six in the morning till eleven at night in return for a kind 'ome! That's about the size of it as a rule!"

"Oh no!" said Kay warmly. "They were most awfully kind to me, and they paid me ten pounds a year. They had six children and *very* little money, so they couldn't pay me any more. I only left because they couldn't afford to go on having me."

Mrs. Green scooped up the remains of her sugar lumps and ate them out of her spoon.

"Did you go for another 'elp?"

"Yes. I only stayed a few months. They were rather like you said."

Mrs. Green nodded.

"They mostly is."

"So then I thought I'd try being a house-parlourmaid. I thought I could do the work, and I should get a proper day out and much more money. But I didn't like the place I got, and now I've come here."

"And 'ow did you come 'ere?" said Mrs. Green. "That's what I want to know, my girl. That there Ivy Hodge, she come day before yesterday, and so far as anyone knew we were all fixed up. Well, she takes and runs away—banged the area door and off like a mad thing. And lunch-time yesterday Nurse comes in in 'er outdoor things and she says as cool as a cucumber, 'There's a new 'ouse-parlourmaid coming in, Green, and I 'ope you'll find 'er satisfactory.' Now that's what I call a quick bit of work."

Kay hesitated. Her colour rose. Then she said,

"I wanted a place, and you wanted a house-parlourmaid. That's how it happened, Mrs. Green."

Chapter Seven

WHILST MRS. GREEN was sugaring her strong tea, Flossie Palmer was entertaining Mr. Ernest Bowden. It was the first time he had been officially received in the family circle—Aunt being so pertickler. Flossie's return after a mere twelve hours absence had not been at all well received. In sheer self-defence she had secured another situation, and the tea-party had been conceded by Mrs. Palmer as a send-off. Not to anyone except that chance-met stranger in the fog had Flossie spoken of her headlong flight from No. 16 Varley Street. Her ordinarily voluble tongue became dry and silent under Aunt's questioning. She hadn't liked the place and she had come away, and that was all. For one thing, if Aunt knew she had been out all night, the fat *would* be in the fire. She bought herself another brush and comb, and said nothing about the hat, the night-dress, and the change of underclothes which she had left behind in the basement bedroom. Not for anything in the world would she go back and fetch them away. She came over all goose flesh at the mere idea, and by exhibiting an unusual amount of energy and securing a place as housemaid at Mrs. Freddy Gilmore's she stopped Aunt's mouth, and was graciously permitted to ask Ernie to tea.

Ernie was finding the occasion rather formidable. He was wearing a high stiff collar which hurt his neck, and his best suit, which had not kept pace with his vigorous development. He was a large young man—a motor-mechanic by trade. He had advanced political opinions and a good deal of bony wrist and thick dark hair. Flossie's aunt made him come over hot about the ears and moist about the hands. She kept a steely eye upon him, as if she expected at any moment to find him out in something he shouldn't be doing, and she called him Mr. Bowden at least once in every sentence. It was quite horribly daunting. During tea she talked about all the promising girls she had known who had married drunkards and declined prematurely into their graves. Even Flossie was subdued.

It was a little better after tea when the table had been cleared. He and Flossie were allowed to sit up to it side by side whilst she showed him the photographs in the family album, an immensely thick and heavy book with an embossed leather binding, gilt edges, and a portentous clasp. It was possible to hold Flossie's hand when she was not turning a leaf. Mrs. Palmer, knitting by the hearth, could only see the table-cloth and the heavy album tilted on an aged copy of *Stepping Heavenward*. She had stopped talking, and he gathered, to his immense relief, that it was now Flossie's business to entertain him.

They lingered over the faded pictures of whiskered young men and chignoned young women, hairy old gentlemen with beards flowing down over their waistcoats, and old ladies all shawl and cap and skirt.

"That's Aunt's grandfather," said Flossie. "A builder in a very good way of business he was—wasn't he, Aunt?"

Mrs. Palmer's needles clicked.

"*And* a life-long teetotaller," she said.

Flossie trod on Ernie's foot.

"Had a lovely house up in Hampstead—hadn't he, Aunt?" she said.

"Took the pledge at five years old and never broke it," said Mrs. Palmer. She drew out a needle and stabbed it into the sock she was knitting. "And a pity there are not more like him, Mr. Bowden."

Flossie tossed her head.

"You needn't think Ernie drinks, Aunt, because he doesn't!"

"So he *says*," said Mrs. Palmer. She sat bolt upright in a chair with a leather seat and a curly walnut back, her firm, high-busted figure tightly cased in a black stuff dress with a high-collared front of cream net over white silk. A gold locket with raised initials hung down upon the front, and an agate brooch which was exactly like a bulls-eye fastened the collar. Her thick wiry grey hair was brushed tightly back from her forehead and temples and fastened in a plaited coil about half way up the back of her head. She had a high, fixed colour, sharp grey eyes, and practically no lashes. A formidable person.

Flossie passed quickly to the next page.

"That's my mother," she said. "D'you think I'm like her? I'm called after her, you know. I don't remember her hardly at all. I'm Florence after her, but they called her Flo, and me Flossie. I like Flossie best—don't you?"

The enamoured Ernie turned a deep puce in reply to this challenge. He squeezed the hand which he found conveniently near his own and said nothing. Neither of them noticed that Mrs. Palmer had stopped knitting. Her lips were pressed together. She was frowning as if she had dropped a stitch. Presently the needles clicked again.

"My dad was killed in the war, you know," pursued Flossie. "No, of course I don't remember him! Coo, Ernie—however old d'you think I am? That's my mother's photograph we've been looking at, not me! See that brooch she's got on? Ever so pretty it was—two hearts twined together, a white one and a blue one, pearl and turquoise. I had it stolen in my first place. Wasn't it a shame? So now I've only got these old beads that I've wore and wore till I'm sick of them."

"I like them," said the infatuated Ernie.

Flossie tossed her head and fingered the beads. Her bright pink dress was upstairs in a drawer. She wouldn't have dared to wear it under Aunt's eye. She had on a dark blue jumper suit in which she looked very pretty indeed. It threw up her fair, bright tints and the whiteness of her skin. She looked down at the beads with discontent.

"They'd be all right if they were white," she said. "I'd like a nice white pearl string—it'd suit me. I'd have thrown these old grey things away long ago if they hadn't been my mother's. Dingy, I call them. Look here, this photo's slipped. I'll have to pull it out or it won't go in straight."

The photo showed a buxom middle-aged woman in an outdoor coat and an excruciatingly unbecoming hat. The hat dominated the picture. It was trimmed with about a dozen yards of ribbon and a whole pheasant. Its forward tilt obscured the sitter's features and gave the impression that it had just fallen upon her head.

"Coo!" said Flossie, giggling. "Who's this, Aunt?" She held the photo out, saw as she turned it that there was something written on the back, and read aloud: "'Yours truly, Agnes Smith'. Who's that, Aunt?"

"Why, your Aunt Ag of course. You ought to know that, Flossie, I must say. Flo's own half-sister Ag."

"Well, it says Agnes Smith. Ooh!" Flossie's fingers tightened on the old *carte-de-visite*. She turned it over and stared at the high-sleeved coat, the plump featureless face, and the hat with its load of millinery. She had a funny giddy feeling as if she were in two places at once, because whilst she looked at the photograph here in Aunt's warm parlour, she had the cold taste of fog in her mouth and she could hear Mr. Miles saying " 'Please send money for funeral expenses and my account and oblige yours truly Agnes Smith'." It was really a very horrid sort of feeling.

"What's the matter?" said Ernie in what he intended for a whisper.

Flossie caught her breath.

"Nothing. Aunt Ag's name isn't Smith, Aunt? It's never been Smith since I heard tell of her." She dragged her eyes away from the photograph and fixed them upon Aunt's unresponsive profile.

Without looking up from her knitting, Mrs. Palmer said,

"Well then, you don't know everything, though I've no doubt you think you do."

"Was her name Smith, Aunt?"

"For about twenty years it was—and a bad bargain she had. Had to leave him in the end and keep herself letting apartments. Then he died and she married again, and how she'd the courage, I don't know. You'd think one man would be enough for any woman, let alone one like Jacob Smith. But there—she'd not been a widow a twelve-month before she married again. Put the photograph back tidy, Flossie, and don't bend the corners." Mrs. Palmer's needles clicked vigorously. "Why any woman born wants a man tracking dirt into her house, coming in all hours with muddy feet, and as like as not smelling of drink and tobacco, passes me."

Flossie turned the page. She didn't want to talk about yours truly Agnes Smith. She wanted to get away from her. She nudged Ernie with her elbow and said daringly,

"Ooh! What about Syd?"

Mrs. Palmer's face relaxed. She did not actually smile, but she came within measurable distance of it. The locket which reposed upon her cream lace front contained two photographs of Syd, one taken at the age of four, and the other on his twenty-first birthday a couple of months ago. In the former he had long curling fair hair and a white muslin frock. In the latter he had rather the air of a girl dressed up in her brother's clothes. Mrs. Palmer had brought him up as much like a girl as possible. He had studious tastes, which he was able to gratify, as he worked in a bookshop. She certainly never thought of him as a man. He was her Syd, and the core of her heart.

"Syd's different," she said, and with that the door opened and Syd came in.

He was not much taller than Flossie, and his complexion was almost as pink and white as hers. He came in now more quickly than usual and shut the door.

Mrs. Palmer put down her knitting and looked anxiously at him.

"What's the matter, Syd?"

"Haven't you heard—about Ivy Hodge? Haven't you heard anything?"

"Coo!" said Flossie. "She hasn't broke it off with Billy again, has she? Anyhow, Syd, if she has, she won't take you, so you don't need to get all worked up about it."

Mrs. Palmer frowned and opened her mouth to speak, but Syd got in first.

"Haven't you *heard*?" he said again in his rather high voice.

Flossie pushed back her chair and got up.

"Ooh, Syd—what's happened?" she said. "Don't say anything dreadful's happened—not to Ivy!"

Syd nodded. He was still standing by the door, his face working and his colour coming and going.

"They found her in the river," he whispered.

Flossie caught hold of Ernie, not because he was Ernie, but because he was there. She hadn't ever fainted, but she felt as if she was going to faint. She heard Aunt say, "She isn't dead!" And then Syd had tumbled into a chair and was sitting with his elbows on the table and his head in his hands and saying,

"They don't know whether she'll get over it. Mrs. Hodge doesn't think she will." He began to cry in a gentle girlish way. "She's got a knock on the head and she was nearly drowned. And the police have been asking where Billy was. Isn't it dreadful? Poor Ivy I always liked her. Mrs. Hodge says she won't ever get over it."

Mrs. Palmer bent over him, patting a heaving shoulder.

"Now, Syd, don't you take on so. And don't you talk to me about Mrs. Hodge. Makes up her mind to the worst before anything's happened— that's Mrs. Hodge. I haven't patience! Where's Ivy? In hospital? Then you'll see she'll be all right. Flossie, don't you stand there holding on to Mr. Bowden like that! It's what I call right down forward. Now, Syd, Mother will make you a nice cup of tea and you'll be quite all right."

She went out to fill the kettle.

Syd pushed back his long fair hair and looked tearfully at Flossie.

"Isn't it dreadful, Floss?" he said with a catch in his voice.

"*Suppose it had been me,*" said Flossie in a sort of horrified whisper.

Chapter Eight

MILES CLAYTON put two advertisements in the papers, and sat down to wait for possible answers.

Mrs. Agnes Smith, formerly of Laburnum Vale, Hampstead, believed to have married again, and Ada —, formerly in service with the above, were requested to communicate with M. C. Box 150.

The advertisements came out on Tuesday. On Wednesday Gilmore took him to dine with his brother Freddy and his brother Freddy's pretty new wife. Miles and the two Gilmores had been at school together. He found Mrs. Freddy an engaging child of nature with a rolling blue eye and an amazing collection of other people's confidences. She retailed them with extreme candour and a wealth of sympathy. Miles liked her, but couldn't help wondering how long it would be before she landed Freddy head over ears in a libel action.

They had a pleasant little dinner, perfectly cooked, and deftly served by two very decorative maids in scarlet. The table and chairs were of glass, semi-opaque and icy looking, with a concession to the climate in the shape of scarlet velvet cushions to the backless chairs. Floor, ceiling, and walls were a dull, lustreless black against which Mrs. Freddy's lacquered gold hair and alabaster skin, her scarlet mouth and finger-nails, were all most flatteringly relieved. She looked like a poet's dream of a poster, and talked like the gossip page of a Society paper. It was quite entertaining.

The prettier of the scarlet maids was filling his glass, when Mrs. Freddy, with both elbows on the table and a cigarette lightly diffusing smoke over an already sufficiently flavoured omelette, addressed him in a low pulsing voice as "Darling Miles."

Flossie Palmer so nearly said "Coo!" that she turned hot and cold and her knees shook under her. With great self-control she kept her hand steady and filled the glass without spilling a drop.

"*Darling Miles*," said Mrs. Freddy—"you've been too utterly exiled, but I thought *everyone* must have heard about Moldavia and the Grand Duke. He's one of my very *greatest* friends, and he told me he had practically ruined himself buying her the Echnovinsky pearls. Fancy being able to feel you were going about with a man's *whole* fortune round your neck! Too *marvellous*! Freddy, my sweet, *won't* you ruin yourself—just to give me the thrill of feeling you *cared* enough to do it?"

Freddy, a cheerful thick-set young man with steady good-natured eyes, kissed his hand to her across the table.

"Nothing doing, darling."

The blue eyes rolled mournfully.

"He hasn't got any soul," she said. She puffed at her cigarette and the ash fell into her plate. "If anyone *does* want to ruin themselves for me, let it be *black* pearls—that's all I ask. Too marvellous on my skin, wouldn't they be? A long rope, you know, hanging down over something very filmy—not quite white—something like what I've got on."

"Miles is looking for a string of black pearls," said the elder Gilmore with a sardonic gleam in his eye. "If he gets them, you can vamp him for them, or steal them and put up Freddy to take the blame. I daresay he'd go to prison for you at a pinch, Lila."

The blue eyes rolled again.

"Would you, my sweet?"

"No, I wouldn't," said Freddy. "So you'd better not try it on, darling."

Lila Gilmore turned her attention to Miles.

"You know, when Narina Littlecote sold her sister-in-law's rubies, there was a most terrible fuss. Narina told me *all* about it afterwards. She said no one had any idea *how* unkind Victoria had been. She said if it had been her, she'd have been only too glad to think the wretched things were being some use instead of just lying in a safe. Because you know, my dear, *really* they were *too* archaic—an absolutely pre-Edwardian necklace, with great vulgar lumps of stones plastered on with diamonds. And to think of Victoria ever wearing it *positively* made one blush. Well, as Narina said, it really was doing her a kindness—and Victoria was downright disagreeable about it. Why are you looking for a string of black pearls? What are you going to do with them when you've found them? You know, if you haven't got the right skin for pearls, they make you look too, *too* repellent."

"I wasn't thinking of wearing them myself," said Miles, laughing.

"Darling Miles, you'd look *sweet*! Perhaps just a shade too bronzed, but I expect you had a quite too marvellous complexion when you were a baby. Tell me all about the pearls. Ian and Freddy can talk to each other. Is it a real string? Has it been stolen? Are you being Miles Clayton, the marvellous sleuth? Pearls are the hardest things to trace of all. Do you know how many there are in the string?"

As it happened, Miles did know. Both Marion Macintyre's women friends had been able to tell him the number of pearls in that envied rope. He ignored the other questions and said,

"Three hundred."

Lila drew an ecstatic breath.

"Casilda only has two hundred in hers! Three hundred would go at least twice round and hang right down! Wouldn't I look *marvellous* in them? Darling Miles, if I were to be frightfully nice to you, would you *give* them to me?"

"I haven't found them yet," said Miles. "And as they were stolen twenty years ago, I don't suppose I ever shall—and if I do, they won't be mine."

Lila sighed.

"And most likely some frightful old hag with a yellow neck is wearing them, and looking *too* foul for words." She took another little puff at her cigarette and some more ash fell.

Freddy burst out laughing.

"Did you ever see anyone smoke like Lila?" he said. "You know, darling, I don't know why you do it. You hate the taste, you make silly little puffs, and you cover everything with ash."

Lila nodded mournfully.

"But Fitz gave me such a pet of a holder for Christmas—I've just got to use it, my sweet. Fitz would be most *awfully* hurt if I didn't."

They played bridge after dinner. Flossie Palmer, looking across at Miles as she helped the parlourmaid to set out drinks, thought him "ever so nice." She was now quite certain that he was the Mr. Miles whom she had snuggled up to in the fog on the Embankment. It gave her a most romantic secret thrill to think she had leaned her head upon his shoulder. She'd pinched his arm too, good and hard. A shiver went over her. She let two glasses touch one another with a sharp ringing sound. The parlourmaid nudged her, and her colour rose.

Miles, suddenly aware of her gaze, thought what a pretty girl she was. She looked quickly away, her heart thumping. He was the only person in the whole world who knew just what had happened to her at No. 16 Varley Street. He was the only person she could talk to about it. And she must talk to him—oh, she *must*. Ever since she had heard about Ivy she had had the most awful sick feeling of fear. She didn't believe that Billy had pushed Ivy into the river, and she didn't believe that Ivy had thrown herself in. Ivy wasn't the sort of girl to throw herself into a river, not if it was ever so. And she'd no reason either, because she and Billy had made it up, and the day fixed and all. No, Ivy had been pushed. And Billy couldn't have pushed her, because he was over with his brother in Bermondsey, and lucky for him there were plenty to swear to it.

She shivered again. If she could talk to Mr. Miles, she might get it out of her head that Ivy had been pushed because she, Flossie, had gone to 16 Varley Street as Ivy Hodge and seen what she hadn't been meant to see. Another glass clinked. She was glad to get out of the room.

"My! You *were* clumsy with those glasses!" said the parlourmaid. "What are you shivering for? Hot as hot, I call it. I don't know how she stands it. But there—she doesn't wear anything under those evening dresses of hers—not a stitch of any sort or kind, if you'll believe me. It's not what I call nice myself."

The bridge was rather inconsequent, because Lila talked all the time. She had an artless way of looking over Freddy's hand and commenting on what she saw there, and she was also very generous in imparting information about her own.

"Oh, my poor sweet—what a perfectly foul hand! Only two court cards! I *do* wish I could give you some of mine—I'm simply stiff with them! Now, if you had my ace and king of hearts—Ian *darling*, talking of hearts, *have* you heard the latest about Posh Winterbotham? He really has broken off with that Margarita woman at last, and she's bringing an action for breach of promise against him. She must have the most positively iron nerve!"

It was during the fourth rubber that Fitz cropped up again, a drop in the incessant spray of Lila's conversation.

"Fitz says—"

And then all of a sudden Ian Gilmore was asking rather abruptly, "What's all this, Lila?"

Miles was dealing. He and Freddy had been talking, and then Freddy had cut to him and he had started to deal. He looked up from the cards when Ian spoke, and the thought went through his mind, "What's up with Gil?"

Lila looked a little hurt.

"Darling Ian! *Everybody's* talking about it! Fitz says it's what he calls a hang-over from the Vulture affair!—Miles darling, you simply *must* listen, because if you're aiming at being a sleuth, it's all in your line and really too intriguing—Fitz says the Vulture was *the* most marvellous super-crook with irons in the fire all over the place, and when he was killed it was the most *shattering* blow, but the organization's been pulling itself together again, and they *think* they've got a new head, and the American government and the French government—"

Ian Gilmore hacked his brother Freddy sharply on the left shinbone, whilst at the same moment he interrupted Lila.

"When you say the French government, which of them do you actually mean? They've had seven in the last two years."

Freddy took his kick like a man. Without any change in his agreeable expression, he said,

"I say, are we playing bridge, or aren't we? I don't mind, but I should just like to know. I say, darling, I suppose you know that your nose is all shiny at the corners?"

Lila gave a low heart-felt cry of "Oh, Freddy—you *beast!*" tore open a gold vanity-case, gazed earnestly into a little round mirror, and began to apply first aid to the maligned feature.

Freddy proceeded to drive the insult home.

"I can't see how you can expect not to go shiny when the room's as hot as this—and you know you made me swear to tell you."

Lila blew him a kiss with her lipstick. Having restored her nose, she was now reinforcing the scarlet of her mouth.

"Darling sweet, you haven't any tact. Miles darling, when you do get married, you just remember this—all any girl wants is to be told she's looking perfectly marvellous at least a dozen times a day. Freddy's no good at it at all, and if I didn't love him to *distraction*, I'd divorce him to-morrow. You know, that's why the Poker Pocklington menage broke up. Sally said if she went on much longer with Poker looking at her as if she was his grandmother's chest of drawers or any other old bit of Victorian furniture, and never noticing whether she'd got her hair on or off, or whether it was red, or black, or platinum—well, she might as well *be* a bit of furniture. So she took up flying—"

"*Are* we playing bridge?" said Freddy.

They finished the rubber, and the party broke up.

Ian Gilmore came down the stairs with Miles, but just short of the hall he said abruptly,

"There's something I want to see Freddy about. I'll say good-night." After which he let Miles out and went upstairs again.

Chapter Nine

MILES CAME OUT upon a dark, damp street. It had been raining, and it was probably going to rain again, but at the moment no actual rain was falling. The air was still, and it was much warmer than it had been some hours ago.

The Gilmores' house was about half way between two lamp-posts. Miles turned to the left and walked towards the pool of yellow light which surrounded the next lamp. He had reached and crossed it, when he heard the sound of footsteps behind him. They were light, hurrying footsteps. They came up behind him, and as they drew level, a voice called his name—a breathless voice which matched the hurrying steps.

"Mr. Miles—"

Miles stopped dead. It was a girl's voice—and, by gum, it was *the* girl's voice! The girl in the fog. The girl who had sobbed on his shoulder and pitched him a tale about a head, and a hole in the wall. He said "Well, well"—and turned round to have a look at her. He hadn't seen her at all in the fog, and he couldn't see much more of her now— just a dark blur, and something that looked like a raincoat. She stopped about a yard away, and he said,

"Hullo, Flossie!"

"Oh, Mr. *Miles!*" said Flossie in a breathless voice.

"We do seem to meet—don't we?" said Miles cheerfully.

"Oh, Mr. Miles—I just had to come after you! Did you reckernize me?"

"I knew your voice. I'm very good at knowing voices. But I don't see how you knew me."

Flossie giggled.

"It was when she said 'Miles darling.' " She giggled again.

Miles clasped his brow.

"I say, do you mind telling me what you're talking about?"

"Coo!" said Flossie. "Then you didn't reckernize me. I thought you didn't. Of course you was talking and I wasn't, so I had a better chance, as you may say."

"You know, you're right up over my head. You've got to make it easier. I'm no earthly good at cross-words."

Flossie gave another giggle.

"Coo, Mr. Miles! And I saw you looking at me too!"

"Where? Hand out the clues."

"At Mrs. Gilmore's where you've just come from. I got a place there—housemaid, and help in the dining-room when there's company."

Light flowed in on Miles.

"Were you the pretty one?"

"Ooh—Mr. Miles! You'd better not let Gladys hear that! She's not a bad sort, but she does fancy herself, and of course it isn't everybody likes fair hair best."

She *was* the pretty one. He said aloud,

"All right, I've got you placed. And now what can I do for you?"

"Well—" Flossie hesitated. "Mr. Miles, I don't want you to think bad of me. I'm not the sort of girl that runs after young men, and I've got my boy friend I told you about, Ernie Bowden, and next door to being engaged, so I don't want you to think—" There was a ring of honest distress in her voice.

Miles felt a good deal relieved and just a little disappointed.

"I'm not thinking anything, Flossie—honest I'm not."

She came a little nearer.

"Mr. Miles, I'm frightened."

An odd sort of thrill went through him at the words. It was as if they roused an echo in him. It was a quite momentary but very odd feeling. He said,

"What are you frightened of?"

"I didn't tell Aunt or anyone," said Flossie in a low hurrying voice. "You know—what I told you down on the Embankment. I don't know why I told you, but I just had to tell someone, and I never thought I'd come acrost you again. And then when I got home, it took me the other way. It didn't seem as if I could tell Aunt, or Ernie, or anyone. For one thing, Aunt'd never have let me hear the last of my being out all night, and for another, she'd have gone round straight to 16 Varley Street and wanted to know all about it, so I *dursn't*."

He got the thrill of her fear again. There was no manner of doubt about it, she *was* frightened.

"Well, if you feel like that—I mean if you think there's something really wrong about the house—why don't you go to the police and tell them just what you told me?"

Flossie caught at his wrist with both hands.

"Mr. Miles, for Gawd's sake don't you go bringing the police into it! You got to give me your word of honour you won't—*reelly*!"

"All right, all right, there's no need to get in such a flap over it. I'm not going to do anything. All the same—look here, why are you so afraid of going to the police?"

There was a cool, detached moment in which he considered the possibility that she was afraid of going to the police because she had been romancing and he had called her bluff. It was such an unbelievable tale.

Flossie had very strong little hands. They closed on his wrist and shook it.

"You're not to do it! You're not to go to the police, and you're not to try and make me go neither!"

"All right, easy on—I said I wouldn't. I'm only asking why."

Flossie stopped shaking him, but she still held his wrist. She held it very tight indeed, and her hands were very cold. She said in a different voice, low and shivery,

"Because I don't want to go in the river like Ivy."

The shiver ran down his back.

"Flossie, what on earth do you mean?"

She said still lower, "Ivy went in the river. Ooh, Mr. Miles—she did!"

"Now look here, Flossie—what's all this about? Who is Ivy? How did she get into the river? And what in heaven's name has it got to do with your going to the police?"

She pressed close to him in the dark.

"Course it's got to do with it! Put your thinking cap on! I told you about Ivy when we were talking in the fog—my girl friend, Ivy Hodge, that had a row with her fiongcey and went and took that place at 16 Varley Street to spite him—and then they made it up and fixed the day so she didn't want to go, so I said I'd go instead of her, and I went as Ivy Hodge because of not having a parlour reference—and I s'pose I shouldn't have done it, but it was more for a lark than anything else and to oblige Ivy, and they'd fixed it all up without seeing her, so it was quite easy and no odds to anyone, only of course I didn't tell Aunt—she's that pertickler."

All this came pouring out at an extraordinary rate. When she stopped with an effect of being obliged at last to take breath, Miles patted her shoulder with his free hand.

"All right, I've got it now. I'd forgotten—you went to Varley Street as Ivy Hodge. Now what about the river and the police? I'm not there yet."

"Ivy went in the river." He could only just hear the words.

"Do you mean she's drowned?"

"She's in hospital. She's awful bad. They say she must have hit her head jumping in—but, Mr. Miles, she *never*!"

Her earnestness shook them both.

"You don't think she did jump in?"

"Course I don't! What'd she got to jump in the river for? Billy's a very nice boy and he's got a good job, and they'd made it up and the wedding all fixed for to-morrow. Girls don't throw themselves in the river when they haven't got nothing to throw themselves in for. Besides Ivy *wouldn't*. I tell you she was pushed. And when Syd—that's Aunt's boy—came in and told us, it come over me that she'd been pushed in mistake for me. It wasn't poor Ivy that was meant to be pushed—it was the girl that'd been in that drawing-room in 16 Varley Street and seen what nobody wasn't meant to see. Ooh, Mr. Miles—I'm certain of it—I am *reelly*! I went there as Ivy Hodge, and none of them hadn't seen her, so when I ran out of the house they'd go and ask for poor Ivy at the registry. And of course *they*'d have her address, and all they'd got to do was to follow her in the dark next evening and push her in. Right close down by the river she lives, so it'd be easy enough, and with the fog there's been."

"But if you think that, you ought to go to the police, Flossie. Don't you see?"

"Ooh!" said Flossie. "You're the one that doesn't see, Mr. Miles. Go to the police? No, I *don't* think! I mightn't be so lucky as Ivy. They did get her out, with a bang on the head and nearly drowned, but p'raps next time there wouldn't be no one about and they'd make *sure*. You've got to hold *your* tongue, or it might be you that'd go barging and banging down the river with the tide till someone picked you up with your neck broke or the side of your head bashed in. And I've got to hold *mine*, or it might be me. See here, Mr. Miles—you've give me your promise and you got to keep it. I don't want to get knocked on the head and pushed in the river along of something I wasn't meant to see. I want to save a little money, and when Ernie asks me to name the day I'm going to marry him. He's got a good job and he's steady, and a girl expects to get married and have a nice home. I'm not going to get mixed up with a police case neither, for Aunt wouldn't like it at all, nor Ernie wouldn't. So you've got to promise me solemn you won't go to the police."

"All right, Flossie, I won't."

"You've got to say you promise," said Flossie breathlessly.

Miles laughed a little impatiently.

"All right, my dear, I promise."

"Word of honour?"

"Word of honour."

"Cross your heart?"

"Cross my heart, Flossie."

She let go of his wrist and stood away from him. The urgency had gone out of her. She said in rather a flat little voice.

"Gladys'll be waiting to let me in. Good-night, Mr. Miles." And with that she turned and ran back along the wet pavement.

He watched her pass the lamp-post and saw her fair hair under the yellow light. She had run out bare-headed with a coat thrown over her gay uniform. A gleam of scarlet showed at the hem. Then the darkness took her and she was gone.

Chapter Ten

Ian Gilmore sat talking with Freddy and Lila until Freddy sent Lila to bed. When they were alone, he got up, poured himself out a drink, and turning with the tumbler in his hand, went over to the hearth and stood looking down into the fire.

This room was all gold—the pale, dim gold of an old picture-frame. It made a very fitting frame for Lila's beauty. When she was in it, it seemed just that, but when she was away, it lacked life. There was too much of that one flat tone.

Ian drank from his glass and set it down upon the narrow golden ledge which crossed the chimney breast. As he did so, his brother Freddy said in his equable voice,

"Better get it off your chest, hadn't you?"

There was a moment's silence. Ian Gilmore did not turn round. He frowned at the fire, where the ash had sunk to a red pit, and said,

"Can you stop Lila talking, Freddy?"

"In general, no—but in particular, probably. Why do you want her stopped?"

Ian turned round with a jerk.

"Do you remember what she was saying when I kicked you?"

Freddy nodded.

"Something about the Vulture affair—a hang-over from the Vulture affair—and his organization having a new head. And then something about the American government and the French government, at which point you did your best to break my leg."

"Sorry," said Ian. There was no smile on his face.

Red Indian out for scalp, was Freddy's diagnosis. He hoped the scalp was not Lila's. A smile just touched his eyes and went away again. He loved Lila very much.

"Well?" he said. "What's it all about?"

Ian looked past him down the room. He was seething with things which it would have relieved him a good deal to say about wasters who couldn't hold their tongues, but as he couldn't damn Fitz and Fitz's set into heaps without at the same time damning Freddy's wife, he restrained himself. After a moment he said,

"The Vulture affair was four years ago. He ran the most extraordinary international blackmail business. The branch in the States also concerned itself with kidnapping."

"I remember," said Freddy. "A man called Lindsay Trevor ran him down. Very nice chap. I met him once."

"It was an extraordinary fine bit of work. The Vulture committed suicide and the organization appeared to collapse. Then last year there was the Gilbert Denny affair. I can't give you the details, but there was a woman mixed up with that who was one of the Vulture's lot. There were indications of a recrudescence of the organization then. The woman got away. All this year odds and ends of information have been trickling in.

The Americans are determined to put a stop to their kidnapping cases. I can't go into details, as I said before, but two separate lines have led to London, and it's true that a man was sent over from Washington and another from Paris." He frowned and took another drink from his glass.

"And you don't want Lila to talk about it?" said Freddy.

Ian laughed harshly.

"If you can stop her!"

"Well, if Fitz and his crowd have got hold of it, what Lila says or doesn't say will only be a drop in the ocean, you know."

Ian banged down his glass again.

"I wish somebody would tell me how things get out!" he said. "But look here, Freddy, this is how it stands. I'm in this business. I've been told things. I know things I can't even tell you. It's all frightfully hush-hush at the moment. Well then, if young Fitz and his crowd talk it's one thing, but if your wife talks it's another. Everyone'll think I told you and you told her. See?"

Freddy saw.

"All right," he said—"I'll pick up the bits."

Ian frowned.

"How many people do you suppose Lila's talked to already?"

"Well," said Freddy, "as a matter of fact I think you've got in in time, because Fitz has been away. Lila hasn't seen him for at least ten days till this evening, when she ran into him and the whole pack at a sherry party. She probably picked this story up there, but she hasn't had time to pass it on. Do you want me to find out just what she has heard—or doesn't that matter?"

Ian laughed. His face had relaxed a little.

"It's probably well mixed—*Rumour*, by *Conjecture* out of *Gossip*. What a life! Well, I'll be getting along."

Freddy got up. While Ian finished his drink, he stood looking at him. Then he said,

"I think I can fix it." And then, after a short pause, "Lila's got a damn silly mother, Ian."

Ian nodded.

Lady Latimer was most undoubtedly a Family Affliction. At forty-five, and a widow for the second time, she was still girlish, still gushing, still the creature of every wayward whim. Freddy endured, sometimes with philosophy and sometimes not.

He let Ian out and went to Lila's room. He had, as always, the half amused, half irritated feeling that he ought to take off his shoes and leave them outside—that he ought, in fact, to get into something very exotic in the way of a dressing-gown in order not to strike too jarring a note. For Lila had insisted on a white bedroom. The walls, the ceiling, and the floor were white. The deep piled carpet was white. There was a white bearskin in front of the fire, and a couch covered with white brocade drawn up at right angles to it. The same brocade curtained the windows and made a canopy and covering for the low bed with its golden foot-rail.

Lila was sitting curled up on the couch gazing into the fire. She had washed the make-up from her face, and in her thin filmy night-gown with a white velvet wrap thrown round her she looked much younger than she had done at dinner. She might have been even less than her nineteen and a half years.

Freddy came over and sat down on the couch.

"Well, darling?" he said.

She leaned towards him and put up her lips to be kissed.

"What did Ian want, Freddy?"

"How do you know he wanted anything?"

She slipped her hand into his and swung it to and fro.

"You think I'm stupid, but I'm not. What did he want?"

"He didn't want you to talk about the Vulture."

The blue eyes opened to their fullest extent.

"But, my sweet, everybody's talking about him. And besides, it *wasn't* the Vulture we were talking about. Ian and his old Foreign Office can't simply muzzle everyone—can they? And Fitz says—Freddy, you're not angry?"

"No, darling—not a bit. You just go ahead. What did Fitz say?"

"Well, I don't *know* that it was Fitz. I just said Fitz because—well, of course he was there. Does it matter?"

"Not if you can't remember. What did he say?"

Lila gazed pensively at a pretty bare foot. She curled and uncurled the toes. The foot was very white, and the toe-nails tinted a deep shell pink.

"Freddy, should you like me in sandals?"

"No, darling."

"Oh, my sweet—*gold* ones—and my feet bare of course—and perhaps a ring on one of the toes!"

"*No*, darling," said Freddy firmly. "I should hate it. Like poison. Lila, what did Fitz say?"

"But, my sweet, I'm not sure that it *was* Fitz—I told you so."

Freddy was fortunately so constituted that the workings of Lila's mind entertained instead of irritating him. He laughed and said,

"Well, whoever did say it."

"I can't really remember. It might have been Dinks."

"Let's say it was what's-his-name. Now, darling, what did what's-his-name say?"

Lila continued to gaze at her foot. She said in a murmuring voice,

"I think sandals would be *marvellous*."

Freddy took her by the shoulders and turned her round to face him.

"Darling, you're not attending. It doesn't matter whether Fitz said it, or Dinks, or anyone else. The point is—*what did they say?*"

"Well, my sweet, I was beginning to tell you about it at bridge, only Ian interrupted. It's never the same the second time—is it? But of course if you want me to—well, I told you the bit about the Vulture, and his gang or whatever it is getting together again, and the French and American governments."

"Yes," said Freddy—"that's where you'd got to. What about the French and American governments?"

"Well, that's the exciting part," said Lila. "Darling, you have got such nice strong hands. I *do* like it when you hold me like this—as if you could break me quite *easily*."

Freddy shook her a little.

"I shall if you don't get a move on, darling. What about the French and American governments?"

"I'm telling you, my sweet. Have the French *really* had seven governments in two years?"

"I expect so—I haven't counted."

"Why?"

"I expect they know—I don't. Now, darling, get on with it."

"Well, they each sent a man over. Sleuths, you know—at least not ordinary sleuths, but more sort of Secret Service people—a French one and an American one. But Fitz says, or perhaps it was Dinks, I *really* don't remember which—"

"It doesn't matter," said Freddy firmly. "Go on!"

"Well, they came over because they thought they'd got a clue. And they both dined with one of *our* Secret Service sleuths, and they kept it up till fairly late, and then they all went home. But they didn't get there—at least the Frenchman and the American didn't. The Englishman said good-night to them, and they said 'See you to-morrow' and all that sort of thing, and they went off. But he *didn't* see them to-morrow—no one did. They weren't in their hotel—they weren't anywhere. They say one of them's been found in the river, but Fitz didn't really know whether that was true. He *thought* it was the Frenchman. And our people are most dreadfully fussed about it, and they're keeping it most *fearfully* quiet. And Fitz says—or perhaps it really *was* Dinks, I'm not sure—anyhow he says no one's supposed to know anything about it, so of course everyone *does*."

"I see," said Freddy. "That all?"

She nodded.

"And as everyone *does* know, why mustn't I talk about it?"

Freddy explained.

"It might get Ian into trouble. You see, his chief might think he'd been talking."

"But Ian never talks."

Freddy laughed.

"Copy him, darling!"

He let his hands fall from her shoulders, but she did not move. She looked down into her lap, and then suddenly lifted her eyes to his face.

"Freddy—*do* I talk too much?"

Freddy nodded.

"About people," he said.

"But, my *sweet*, what else is there to talk about?"

He picked up one of her hands and held it lightly.

"Horses," he said—"cars—books—theatres—rabbits—gardens—shoes, and ships, and sealing-wax, and cabbages, and kings—"

Lila's eyes opened very wide.

"Freddy, I couldn't!"

"You could try, darling."

Something showed in her eyes. It was as if the colour deepened, as if there was a stirring of the blue waters.

"Would it please you if I tried, Freddy?"

"Very much, darling."

Her lips quivered a little like a child's.

"I'll try. I do like to please you, Freddy."

He lifted her hand and held it against his cheek.

Chapter Eleven

Flossie Palmer was still awake. She and Gladys shared a room, and Gladys had gone to sleep as soon as she got into bed. But Flossie couldn't go to sleep. She kept thinking about Ivy, and Mr. Miles, and 16 Varley Street. It wasn't the least use counting sheep jumping over a stile, because she couldn't keep her mind on them. She could begin, but before she knew where she was, there was the wall in the Varley Street drawing-room with a gilt frame which hadn't any glass in it, but only a black hole. And then she'd see the man's head with the blood running down, and the hand that clawed at the frame. And then she'd see the man with the cruel eyes looking at her out of the darkness. And then she would feel as if she must scream as she had screamed then, and run as she had run out into the fog.

Well, that wouldn't do.

She began to think about the dinner. She had never really waited at a dinner-party before, but she hadn't made any mistakes. There had only been four people, but everything had been done just as if it was a real dinner-party. Flossie admired Lila Gilmore very much. "Coo! She doesn't half dress!" she said to herself. "Wonder what I'd look like in some of her things." She began to go over the talk at the dinner-table. What was it Mrs. Gilmore had said about a rope of black pearls?... Pearls ought to be white... She couldn't think what black pearls would look like. She pictured them rather like bits of coal. Funny Mrs. Gilmore should want to have black pearls... And Mr. Miles was looking for some. He was looking for a girl and a string of black pearls... Three hundred pearls in the string... Coo! That seems an awful lot! She wondered how long a string three hundred pearls would make. Well, she could tell that easy enough by counting her old grey beads. Better to count beads than sheep.

She got out of bed, rummaged in her drawer, and got back again with the beads in her hand. She began to count from the clasp, slipping her fingers from one smooth bead to another in the dark. Twenty, twenty-one, twenty-two... fifty, fifty-one, fifty-two... a hundred... two hundred and fifty... two hundred and ninety-five, ninety-six, ninety-seven, ninety-eight—it was much better than counting sheep—ninety-nine... two hundred and ninety-nine... three hundred...

There were three hundred beads in her string... three hundred beads... three hundred pearls... Flossie was asleep, with the string of three hundred beads clasped tightly under the bed-clothes.

Kay Moore woke in the darkness of her basement bedroom at 16 Varley Street. She woke with a start, and she was afraid, but she didn't know why she was afraid or what had waked her. She thought it was a sound, but she didn't know what sort of sound.

She lit her candle and looked round the room with relief. It was a very ugly room, and in the daytime very dark, but it contained nothing more frightening than a large window which looked upon the area, and the battered washstand, chest of drawers, bedstead and chair which furnished it. The bedstead was of chipped enamelled iron, and the rest of the furniture had once been painted a hideous shade of mustard yellow, but it was now so dirty and so old that the colour was gone away into a general ochreish drab. The pattern of the linoleum on the floor had long since been worn out by the feet of all the girls who, according to Mrs. Green, had come to No. 16 and left at their month. Kay looked round this dreadful little room and was reassured. There was nothing that could have startled her.

She slipped out of bed, opened the door a little way, and looked out into the passage. There were the stairs going up, the kitchen door opposite, Mrs. Green's door on the same side as her own, and the door leading into the area at the end of the passage on her right. From Mrs. Green's room there came the sound of Mrs. Green's deep and steady snoring. But it wasn't Mrs. Green who had waked her; she felt quite sure of that. It was some sharp little sound, and she had heard it half in and half out of her sleep, but she couldn't quite remember what it was.

She took her candle, opened the kitchen door, and looked in. Warmth and a smell of cooking came to meet her. The fire was low in the range, but not dead. The air was sleepy-still. A mouse turned bright inquisitive eyes upon her from the white-washed hearth. The sound had not come from here.

She shut the door and looked doubtfully at the stairs. Suddenly she saw that the candle flame was shaking. Her hand was shaking. And the reason it shook was because she really did think that the sound had come from the stairs—from the top of the stairs. It was the thought that she must go up the stairs and open the door at the top which made Kay's hand shake. Yet she knew that she couldn't go back to bed without going up those stairs and opening that door.

She began very slowly to go up one step at a time with the candle in her left hand and her right hand following the wall. When she got to the top, she stopped. There was the door right in front of her—an ordinary painted door with an old-fashioned wooden knob. Kay looked at the knob. The candle-light shook.

At last she put out her right hand, took hold of the wooden handle, and turned it back as far as it would go, pushing outwards so as to open the door.

But the door didn't open.

Kay's heart began to beat with a sudden violence. The door didn't open because it was locked on the other side. It was open when they went to bed, but since then someone had come down and locked it. Someone? Nurse Long. There wasn't anyone else. That was the sound she had heard—the little sharp, clicking sound of the key being turned in the lock. She and Mrs. Green were locked in on the basement floor. Why should anyone want to lock them in?

Kay hadn't any answer to that. She went back to bed, blew out her candle, and lay down in the dark. She was shivering a little. She didn't like the feel of 16 Varley Street, and she didn't like that locked door at the top of the stairs. She had said her prayers before she went to sleep, but she said them again now. At the end she said, "I don't like this place very much, but You can keep me safe—can't You? Please do, because I haven't anywhere else to go. Amen."

It wasn't Mrs. Moore who had taught her to say her prayers. It was Eleanor Clayton. There was one halcyon period in Kay's life when for six months she was under Eleanor Clayton's care. Mrs. Moore, taken suddenly ill, had had to go into hospital, and much against her will had accepted her next-door neighbour's offer to take care of Kay. It was to be for a month only, but the month stretched to six, and for that time Kay had a family and a home. She was twelve years old, and she had never had a home before or been allowed to play with other children. Aunt Rhoda demanded all her time, her attention, her very thoughts.

The six months passed like a flash, but they influenced her profoundly. She gave her whole heart to the Clayton family. Kitty was only a year older than herself, gay and pretty; George a cadet at Sandhurst, a jolly, teasing boy; and Miles just down from Oxford. As for Eleanor the mother, loving idealistic and romantic, she opened to Kay all the worlds from which her strange upbringing had debarred her.

At the end of six months Mrs. Moore returned, more gaunt of frame, more hard of feature, and more fiercely possessive than before. She had no gratitude for the care which Kay had received, and when the child clung silently to Eleanor in a farewell which tore them both, her jealousy broke out in a frantic scene. Kay's last recollection was of Eleanor Clayton, white-lipped but still gently courteous in the face of Aunt Rhoda's crazy reproaches. Then the Eden gates were shut and they went back to the wandering wilderness life again. But Eleanor Clayton remained as a standard, an inspiration, a gracious presence which was never quite removed. When, years afterwards, she heard that Eleanor was dead, Kay had very little sense of loss.

Now, lying in the dark, her prayer said, her thoughts quieted, she went back over those six lovely months again. She and Kitty reading aloud by turns. Eleanor singing in the twilight. George putting a key down her back to make her jump. And Miles swinging her up and up in the swing which was fastened to an apple-tree. It was very good of Miles, because he was so much older. The sunshine, and the apple-blossom, and a bit of blue sky began to blot out the darkness of the basement room. The swing went to and fro, to and fro... It was very kind of Miles... Sunshine... apple-blossom... blue... Kay swung off into a dream.

Lila Gilmore woke for the space between one happy dream and the next. It was only a drowsy waking as she turned a little in bed. Nice dream... nice sleep... nice, happy sleep... lovely sleep... Freddy wasn't angry... please don't let him ever be angry... my Freddy... lovely to know that if she put out her hand, it would touch him... Freddy... quite near—always... Freddy... Lila slipped deep into her dream again.

Chapter Twelve

NEITHER THE Wednesday nor the Thursday post brought any answer to the advertisements in which Miles Clayton had appealed for information about Mrs. Agnes Smith and her former maid, Ada. Miles sent the advertisements in again, and wrote a long letter to James Macintyre in New York giving him the result of his preliminary inquiries. He didn't say anything about Flossie Palmer or the house in Varley Street. Perhaps it was on this account that he thought about them the more. Flossie's story was such a very, very odd one, and perhaps the oddest thing about it was that it seemed to him that it rang true. That is to say, it did seem to him that Flossie thought she was speaking the truth. He thought her intelligent, and he thought her honest, and he was absolutely dead sure that she was frightened. Whether she had any real cause to be frightened was another matter. She might have had a nightmare, or she might be subject to delusions, or somebody might have played her a trick. He discarded the possibility that she might be playing a trick on him, because he did feel so absolutely sure that she was frightened. He did not think that any merely acted fear would have touched his own thought and given him that momentary feeling of dread. It had gone over him like a shiver and passed, but the chill which had caused it was the authentic cold of fear. He thought he would go and have a look at Varley Street after lunch.

He came into the bottom end of it as the clock of St. Barnabas' struck three. It was a quiet street of dingy houses whose brickwork, now almost black, had been red and fresh in a bygone Georgian day. It had a very decided air of having come down in the world. None of the brass was very bright, and most of the paint was shabby. The windows kept their secrets behind close-hung curtains of muslin, lace, or net.

He walked slowly up the street, noticing as he did so that the numbers began at 70 on his own side and 71 on the other. It certainly was a very quiet street. No traffic seemed to pass, and so far the only living creature he had seen was the tortoiseshell cat which dozed with folded paws upon the step of No. 69.

When he had gone a little way he crossed over so as to be able to observe No. 16 from the opposite side. There was really nothing at all to mark it out. The paint was perhaps a shade fresher and the brass certainly cleaner than the paint and the brass on either side, and it had old-fashioned lace curtains on the ground floor and the floor above it, as against cream net curtains at No. 14, and blue net curtains at No. 18.

He walked to the end of the street and came slowly back. The windows on the first floor would be the drawing-room windows—two tall windows looking down upon the street. According to Flossie, the room ran right through to the back in the L shape common to London houses, and just inside the L, facing a door which gave upon the passage, was the mirror in its broad gilt frame—the mirror which had become a gaping hole in the moment when she turned her back upon it to adjust the curtain of the window which looked out to the back. A gaping hole—and a man's head—and a clawing hand. And another man, with cruel staring eyes. An incredibly fantastic tale.

The gaping hole in the left-hand wall of the L as you faced its windows—well, that would mean a gap in the wall between No. 16 and No. 14. He thought it would be interesting to know who lived at No. 14.

He had reached No. 7 on his side of the street, when a girl ran up the area steps of No. 16 and came out upon the pavement. She wore a dark blue coat and skirt and a little grey cap and scarf. She was, in fact, Kay Moore, and her heart was dancing joyfully because this was her afternoon out and the sun was shining in a pale winter-blue sky.

Kay hadn't really got accustomed to having an afternoon out. When you are a mother's help you take the children for a walk, but you don't have an afternoon to yourself—at least Kay had never had one. But a house-parlourmaid has a whole afternoon and evening, and every other Sunday. Kay's heart danced whenever she thought about it.

She stood on the pavement and looked up and down the street, partly because she wasn't quite sure which way she wanted to go, and partly because it was so nice to be out. Sometimes the basement smelt of mould, and sometimes it smelt of mice, and sometimes it smelt of food, but it always smelt of something. It was lovely to stand on the pavement and snuff up some perfectly smell-less air. It was the first time she had been out since she came. If she turned to the right, it would, according to Mrs. Green, take her up into the Square. If she turned to the left, it would take her down to the shops. Kay decided to turn to the left, because where there are shops there are buses, and she meant to begin her afternoon out by going for a ride on the top of a bus. She would go as far as the bus went, and then she could come back and go to a cinema. She turned her back on the Square and began to walk, not hurrying, because she had all the afternoon and evening before her and she didn't want to hurry over a single moment of it.

She had just passed No. 18, when a man came up beside her and lifted his hat. He said, "How do you do, Miss Moore?" and Kay looked at him with a puzzled frown. She could not remember that she had ever seen him before, and she had an instant and very strong conviction that she didn't want to see him again. Yet he would have passed for an agreeable man—well dressed, well mannered, and well enough to look at. Kay couldn't have said why she didn't like him, but she hadn't the least doubt about it. He had rather light eyes but you don't really like or dislike people because of the colour of their eyes. Or do you? Kay wasn't sure. But she was quite sure that she wanted to get rid of the man and begin her afternoon out. She looked at him with a sort of gentle severity and said,

"You seem to know my name, but I don't know you."

The man fell into step with her as she walked.

"That is because it is such a long time since we met. I used to know you when you were a little girl. I knew your aunt, Mrs. Moore."

Something inside Kay said, "That's true—he knew Aunt Rhoda," but it didn't make her any better pleased with his company. She stood still and said,

"I'm afraid I don't remember you at all."

On the other side of the street Miles had reached No. 17. He saw the man come up with Kay and speak to her, and he saw Kay flush and walk on. He thought she was very pretty, and that she didn't look as if she were accustomed to knocking about London by herself.

And then all of a sudden he thought he would cross the road. He wasn't quite sure, but it looked as if the girl was trying to get rid of the man and not finding it any too easy. He didn't want to interfere, but if the fellow was being a bit above himself, it might have a sobering effect to discover that he hadn't got the street to himself. He came up therefore on the outside of the pavement and set a pace which kept him a couple of yards behind them. Almost at once he heard Kay say "No, thank you," and a thrill of surprise ran through him, not at the words, but at the voice of this girl who had come running up the area steps of No. 16. He had liked Flossie's little Cockney voice because it told him that he was in London again, but this was another matter. A pretty voice. But lots of voices are pretty. This one had quality and breeding. The three words had a young dignity, and the turn of her head matched them.

The man slipped a hand under her elbow and spoke low in her ear. Miles could not hear what he said, but he saw the distressed colour rise high in the girl's cheek. If he hadn't been a fool, he wouldn't have crossed the street. He was now going to get involved in an affair which had nothing whatever to do with him. Thus the voice of reason. Kay's voice drowned it. She pulled away her arm, swung round to face the man, and said,

"I don't know you, and I won't go out with you. Will you please go away—or must I go back home again?"

"Oh, come, come!" said the man. He put his hand on her arm again, and Miles thought it was time to interfere. He came up on Kay's other side and said,

"I beg your pardon, but can you direct me to Bassett Street?"

The man's hand dropped. Miles caught a gleam of pale fury in his eyes. The gentleman's annoyance was extremely gratifying. He wondered if there *was* a Bassett Street in London.

Kay said a little breathlessly, "I'm afraid I don't know."

Her voice was prettier than ever with that flutter in it.

"Bassett Street," said Miles with an air of hopeful simplicity.

"There's no such street round here," said the man.

Miles produced a genial smile.

"Do you think they can possibly have changed the name?" he inquired.

"There is no such street," said the man curtly. He touched Kay on the arm. "Shall we be coming, Kay?"

A shutter went up with a snap in Miles' mind. It was little Kay Moore, grown up. *Kay*—yes, of course it was. And not changed anything to speak of either. She had been an awfully pretty kid, and she was an awfully pretty girl. He had been very fond of Kay. And here she was, colouring up to the roots of her hair and looking at him with appealing eyes.

"Oh, come along, Kay!" said the man.

Kay burnt her boats. She looked steadily at Miles Clayton and said, "Please will you tell this person to go away? I don't know him."

It was all over in a moment. Miles took a step forward, and the man with the light eyes dropped her arm and took a step back. A look passed between the two men, and that was all. The man with the light eyes lifted his hat. He said, "Another time, Kay," and turned and walked away.

Chapter Thirteen

KAY LEANED against the railings of No. 28. The paving-stones were tilting under her feet. She wondered why she was so frightened. People had spoken to her before; it wasn't that. She thought it was his eyes. Then a voice said, "Are you all right?" and she said "Yes," because the voice was a very reassuring one and the pavement stopped tilting.

She looked up at Miles and said, "Thank you so much," and he wondered why he hadn't recognized her at once, because no one but Kay ever had such dark blue eyes.

He said, "That's nothing. Are you sure you're all right? May I walk a little way with you? I don't know where you were going."

Kay said "Thank you" again.

They began to walk up the street. Kay was the first to speak.

"I didn't know him at all," she said.

"You don't know me," said Miles.

Kay took another look at him. She didn't really need to do this, but it was pleasant.

"You're different," she said.

Miles felt unreasonably pleased. But of course she oughtn't to go about with people she didn't know. It wasn't safe, and she was so awfully pretty. It wasn't as if she knew who he was. It would look a bit odd if he started warning her against himself. All the same—

"How do you know I'm different?"

Kay took another look. He thought the dark blue eyes said "Don't be silly." And of course it was silly, because he and Kay—he and Kay... He had a curiously touched recollection of Kay kissing him good-bye. She had kissed them all with soft, cold childish lips, but when she came to his mother there had been a desperate clinging. And then that horrible scene with the aunt. An impossible woman if there ever was one—crazy with jealousy because the poor kid was fond of them all. He wondered how she had fared. It was eight years ago. She must be nearly twenty now... He turned to her and said,

"I'm Miles Clayton, Kay. Do you remember me?"

The colour came into her face like a wind-blown flame. Her eyes shone like stars above the lovely tint. She stopped. Her hands went out and met his own, and her voice broke on his name.

"Miles!" And then, with a sort of bubbling joyfulness, "Oh, it is—it is—and I didn't know you! Did you know me? At once—just like that? It was very clever of you, because I've grown ever so much. But I ought to have known you, because you haven't changed a bit."

"Nor have you, really," said Miles.

At this point he became aware that a milkman emerging from the area of No. 30 was regarding them with an expression of gloom. He was a perfectly worthy young man of the name of Edward Jones, and the housemaid of No. 30 had just informed him that she wasn't coming out with him any more because she liked Bob Stevens a lot better than him, so there. In these circumstances the sight of Miles and Kay holding hands and gazing at one another in the middle of the pavement was more than flesh and blood could bear. His expression became so homicidal that Miles reluctantly let go and, taking Kay by the arm, began to walk her along.

"Where are you going? And can I come with you, or will you turn me down like you did the other chap and ask that ferocious milkman to protect you?"

"I'd rather have you than the milkman. I was going on a bus."

"What bus?"

"Just any bus—just for the ride. It's a lovely day."

"All right, we'll go on a bus together."

Kay's heart beat joyfully. Miles—as well as a bus ride, and a fine day, and her afternoon out. It was almost too much. She felt as if there were wings under her feet.

She said "Lovely!" and then, "Miles, tell me all about all of you. I haven't heard anything, not for years."

"My mother's gone," said Miles.

She said, "I know. When Aunt Rhoda died I wrote, and someone wrote back and said she had gone—two years before."

"She was very, very fond of you, Kay."

Kay was silent for a little. Then she turned a curious beaming look on him and said,

"I love her—always."

Miles felt an extraordinary rush of emotion. It was four years since anyone had used that present tense in speaking of Eleanor Clayton. It seemed to bring her very near. He was so suddenly and deeply moved that he found it quite impossible to speak. His hand tightened on Kay's arm and they walked on in silence.

When they came to the corner, he began to tell her that George was in India with his regiment, Kitty married and in India too. "And I've been over in New York for three years." And then the story of how he had come over here to try and find out what had happened to a baby who had disappeared nearly twenty years ago.

They chose their bus, climbed on the top, got a seat right in front, and went on talking. Such a lot can happen in eight years, and it was nearly eight years since Kay had gone sadly away from the only home she had known.

"And what did you do then, Kay? Where did you go? You never wrote."

Kay looked away over the top of the bus rail to the houses crowding up into the misty blue sky. It hadn't been misty a moment before, but clear. The mist was in her eyes—the mist of an old weeping for things which she had loved and lost. She said at last,

"I couldn't write—not until Aunt Rhoda died, and then it was too late."

"Where did you go, Kay?"

Kay said, "Everywhere. We kept moving—three months—four months—six months. We just kept moving on until she died."

"When was that?"

"Getting on for three years ago."

She told him about being mother's help to the Vicar's wife, and how she had had to leave because they couldn't afford to keep her.

"The next place I went to I didn't like at all. There was a perfectly revolting boy of twenty. His mother spoilt him, and he would come into the nursery, so I simply couldn't stay. And so I thought I would be a house-parlourmaid, because you get better wages and proper times off, but I got into a horrid place. Oh, Miles, it really was."

Miles frowned. She had come up the steps of No. 16 Varley Street. He said quickly,

"What sort of horrid? You mustn't stay there, Kay."

"Oh, but I didn't. I was only there two months. I didn't like the people or their friends—rather horrid men. I left as soon as I could."

"And came to 16 Varley Street?"

She nodded.

"Perhaps it was ungrateful to say that about their friends being horrid, because it was really one of their friends who helped me to get another place—at least not exactly a friend—" She broke off. "Miles, she told me not to tell anyone, so perhaps I oughtn't—"

"You're to tell me at once!"

"But she said—you see, it might make it awkward for her with her friends. You do see that?"

"Well, I'm not any of her friends. You're going to tell me at once!"

When he looked like that, she could believe that it was nearly eight years since he had last ordered her about. She had been very ready to be ordered about, but it *was* nearly eight years ago. She smiled a little fleeting smile, because the eight years which had changed them both so much hadn't really changed anything at all. She would still do what he told her, but she would do it with a little secret amusement.

"Well, it was like this," she said. "Nurse Long used to come to the house sometimes—not to the parties, you know, but just quietly in the afternoon to see Mrs. Marston. I think they'd been at school together, so she wasn't like the other people who came. And one day she spoke to me going down the stairs. It was rather curious, Miles, because she said, 'Is your name Kay Moore?' and when I said it was, she asked me if I had an aunt called Rhoda. She said she used to know her long ago. Then she asked me if I liked the place, and of course it was rather difficult to say I didn't, but when we got down to the door she gave me her address and said if I wanted to make a change she might be able to help me."

"What was the address?" said Miles quickly.

"16 Varley Street," said Kay.

"How long have you been there?"

Kay looked at him. There was something in his voice which she didn't understand. It seemed to ring an echo in her own mind. She couldn't understand what it said. It was just an echo. She answered his question.

"Only since Saturday. I came in on Saturday evening." She went on talking, because she rather wanted to drown that echo. "Miles, it was rather funny. I gave notice at the Marstons about a week ago, so I really had almost another month to put in there. Then on Saturday afternoon Mrs. Marston sent for me and said she would like me to go at once, because she was suited, but her friend Nurse Long was wanting someone and would I speak to her on the telephone. So I did, and she told me the girl there had left in a hurry and she would like to engage me. So of course I was very glad, because I really hadn't anywhere to go, and I haven't been able to save anything yet because of having to get uniform and all that sort of thing. Mrs. Marston got the things and stopped it out of my wages. That was why I couldn't leave before."

"Tell me about 16 Varley Street, Kay."

Kay's heart gave a little flutter of happiness. Lovely to have someone to tell. It was when you had to bottle things up that they were sort of frightening. There wasn't anything to be frightened of, and there wasn't anything to tell, but it was lovely to have someone to tell it to. She was in the outside seat, and she sat right round with her back against the rail so that she could face Miles. There was hardly anyone else on the top of the bus, only two giggling children about half way down on the other side, and a workman with a large bag of tools on the back seat. To all intents and purposes they were alone. That was a lovely feeling too. They could talk secrets if they wanted to. And then Kay laughed, because of course they hadn't any secrets. She thought it would be rather nice to have a secret with Miles. She looked at him with the laugh in her eyes and began to tell him about No. 16 Varley Street.

"It isn't Nurse Long's house, you know. She's looking after an old invalid lady who hardly ever comes out of her room. She's a Miss Rowland, and I've only seen her twice. There's a lot to do, because there's only the cook and me, and Mrs. Green never comes upstairs at all. She ought to do the dining-room and the hall of course, but she says she's too fat to get up the stairs, and I really think she is. She's very good-natured, and she's been there for years and years."

"Is there anyone else in the house?" said Miles.

"No—just Miss Rowland, and Nurse Long, and Mrs. Green, and me. And they don't seem to have any visitors. It's a good thing, or I'd never get through. Nurse Long does the old lady's room, but I've got everything else, and all the trays to take up and fetch. It's a basement house, and that always makes work."

Miles asked a funny question. Afterwards she thought it was a very funny question indeed. He said,

"What's the drawing-room like?" and she laughed and said,

"Oh, my dear, it's exactly like the pictures in the old *Punches* your mother had—bunches of flowers on the carpet, and a table with photograph albums, and a gold clock with cherubs, and things like that."

"What sort of shape is it?"

"Wide across the front of the house and narrow at the back, like an L. Two doors—one in the wide part and the other behind."

"Is there a mirror in the narrow part?" said Miles.

Kay nodded.

"A great big one with a wide gilt border. How *did* you know?"

Miles laughed.

"That sort of room ought to have a mirror in it," he said.

But he hadn't laughed because he felt like laughing. He was thinking that Flossie Palmer hadn't invented the mirror. And Flossie Palmer said that she had seen a gaping hole within the wide gilt frame—a gaping hole with a frame round it—and something else so frightening that she had then and there run out of the house into the fog... The thought of Kay in the house from which Flossie had fled filled him with disquiet. It also filled him with an unreasonable resentment against the very pleasant and agreeable Captain Grey who had married his sister Kitty and taken her out to India. If Kitty had been available, he could have insisted on Kay leaving 16 Varley Street immediately. Kitty being some thousands of miles away and no longer of the least use, he racked his brains in vain for a substitute. He had two aunts and a sprinkling of cousins, but as far as Kay was concerned they were a wash-out. The aunts were his father's sisters, and they had always deplored what they called "dear Eleanor's vagaries." He blenched at the thought of explaining Kay to them. The cousins he remembered as pretty, conventional girls entirely taken up with their own affairs. His thought glanced at Lila Gilmore, only to provoke him to rueful laughter at his own expense. Besides, Kay and Flossie under the same roof—He thought not.

He found Kay looking at him as if she would like to know what he was thinking about. He would have liked to tell her too, but he restrained himself. Instead he asked her,

"Who was the fellow you wouldn't go out with?"

Kay flushed.

"I don't know."

"But he called you Kay."

"I know he did—but I don't know him all the same."

"Do you mean you've never seen him before, or just that you don't want to know him?"

"I've never seen him before—at least—I don't think so—" Her voice faltered a little on the last words.

"Well?" said Miles. "What about it?"

He saw a distressed look come into her eyes. She said,

"Miles—he said he knew Aunt Rhoda. You know, she did have some horrid friends. I *might* have seen him—long ago—because just in the middle of saying I didn't know him a horrid sort of feeling came over me as if I was just going to remember something. I think it was his eyes—he had such horrid eyes."

Miles was thinking that Aunt Rhoda's friends seemed to be rather too much in evidence. Here was Kay newly come to London, and Nurse Long, who had known Aunt Rhoda, came visiting at the house of Kay's employers and offered to find her a place. And after taking that place another of Aunt Rhoda's friends turns up on her first afternoon out and makes a nuisance of himself. Strange ubiquity of Aunt Rhoda's friends.

Why on earth couldn't Kitty have stayed in England? He frowned, and asked,

"What was the fellow's name? Did he say?"

"He said it was Harris," said Kay doubtfully. Then she laughed. "Oh, Miles, do you know what that reminds me of? Kitty and me reading *Martin Chuzzlewit* out loud, and your mother telling us what to skip, and Mrs. Gamp always talking about Mrs. Harris."

Miles laughed too.

" 'I don't believe there's no such person,' " he quoted.

Kay nodded earnestly.

"That's just what I think about *him*," she said.

Chapter Fourteen

WHEN MR. HARRIS walked away he went on walking until he reached the Square. Varley Street runs into it at the right-hand corner. Mr. Harris turned to the right, which took him out of the Square into Little Banham Street. Almost at once he turned to the right again, and entered Barnabas Row, which runs parallel with Varley Street.

Barnabas Row is one of those odd streets which are to be found here and there in London. They contain a little of everything, like a village street, and are in fact survivals from an earlier day when a great deal of what is now London clustered about the city as village or hamlet.

Barnabas Row begins with a modern house or two, dwindles into a line of old mews, part of which has been turned into a garage, and continues by way of some small shops, a rickety warehouse, and a row of very archaic cottages to its lower end, where it breaks into shops again. The garage is on the right, backing upon Varley Street. Mr. Harris entered it.

A little later he was in conversation with Nurse Long in that L-shaped drawing-room with the wine-coloured velvet curtains, the Victorian furniture, and the handsomely framed mirror so faithfully described by Flossie Palmer. Mr. Harris was leaning against the mantelpiece, and Nurse Long was sitting in a very unprofessional attitude on the arm of one of the rather uncomfortable easy chairs. Her cap was pushed back to show a line of reddish hair. Her pale and indeterminate features wore a decidedly unamiable expression. She was smoking a cigarette in a series of short angry puffs, and between each puff and the next she had something to say.

"You would do it... I told you it wouldn't come off... She's not that sort of girl... I told you she wasn't."

Mr. Harris spoke in a cold, displeased voice.

"That'll be enough about that! You make me tired!"

Nurse Long laughed.

"And what about me? I told you were going to muff it. I didn't want her here, but you would have it. It's dangerous—I've said so all along. If anyone's looking for her, you don't want them coming here, do you?"

"They won't come here," said Mr. Harris.

"Says you!" said Nurse Long.

"Why should they?" said Mr. Harris. "That trail's lost—years ago."

She finished her cigarette and lit another.

"Lost trails can be found again," she said. "Besides, how do you know that it's lost? If we could keep track of her, so could other people. I never did trust Rhoda Moore."

Mr. Harris looked as if this amused him.

"Do you know, I seem to have heard that before."

A little colour came into her pale face.

"And you'll hear it again if I feel like it. Rhoda'd got her own game, and she'd only play yours as long as it suited her. I've always said so, and I've never come across anything to make me change my mind. What did she go dodging about all over the map for if it wasn't to cover her tracks? You told me yourself there were years when she'd given you the slip and you didn't know where she was."

Mr. Harris laughed. It was not an attractive laugh.

"You needn't get excited. I knew all I wanted to know. If I'd wanted Rhoda or the girl, I could have found them—but I didn't happen to want them—then."

"Well, whether you wanted her or not, for all you know, Rhoda was double-crossing you. That's my point—she didn't go hiding like that for nothing."

"She wanted to keep the girl. She was crazy about her. Queer how it gets people. Of course she's a taking little thing—always was. But that's neither here nor there. She's a good business proposition, and that's what interests me."

Her voice was sharp with sudden anger.

"What's the good of talking to me like that? If you think it takes me in, it doesn't—so there! The beginning and end of it is that you've taken one of your fancies, and I'm telling you straight out that you're asking for trouble. Go after any girl in London you like, but leave this one alone! Don't try and mix business and pleasure, or you'll come a most almighty smash. I don't care who you take up with, but we don't want any more girls running out of the house in a fright."

"Chuck it!" said Mr. Harris. "We've had all this out before! I'm not doing anything in the house, am I? No, my next move will be to write her a charming little note. Apologies for having startled her, reminiscences of dear Rhoda—and what do you think of a reference to her mother?—a hint perhaps of an old romance. That always goes down with a good girl—and you say she's a good girl."

Nurse Long nodded.

"Then she ought to be easy," said Mr. Harris. "As a matter of fact, Addie, you're wrong about my fancy. She's all right, and I'd sooner she was pretty than plain, but I've not gone off the deep end about her." He laughed a little. "Is it likely? No, this is business—big business, Addie. In certain circumstances, my dear, my intentions will be strictly honourable. Meanwhile, I'm not committing myself. But I want her here, and I'm going to get friendly."

Nurse Long laughed, a short disagreeable laugh. Then quite suddenly she shivered, knocked the ash off her cigarette, and jumped up.

"I wish you wouldn't look at me like that!" she said.

Mr. Harris did not remove his pale stare.

"You know, Addie," he said, "some day you'll vex me. I shouldn't wonder if it wasn't some day soon." He shrugged his shoulders very slightly. "I shouldn't if I were you. No, I shouldn't."

Chapter Fifteen

MILES CLAYTON found a batch of letters waiting for him when he got back to his hotel. They were mostly from people who wanted him to dine with them or lunch with them. There was one from each of his aunts. There was one from the girl who had refused him three years before because, as she said, you really can't live on six hundred a year. She was now married to something a good deal nearer six thousand. Her name was Angela, and she doesn't come into this story.

Miles laughed and frowned a little. He would certainly dine with Angela. For the last two years and nine months approximately he had thought of her with relief and gratitude. She might have accepted him.

He took up the next letter, which was pale blue and of a heady fragrance. He was about ten years too old to be getting a letter like that, he reflected. He wondered who on earth. As he tore open the envelope, a golden forget-me-not winked at him from the top right-hand corner of the sheet inside. He unfolded it and read: "Dear Mr. Miles." It was Flossie.

"DEAR MR. MILES

When we were talking I quite forgot there was something I was going to tell you. It is about yours sincerely Agnes Smith, and I would have told you only for being all upset about Ivy which put it out of my head. No more now and hoping you are well."

From

"FLOSSIE PALMER."

P.S.—I've got my evening out to-day Thursday and if you get this in time Ernie will be bringing me back p.m. half past nine and if I explain he won't mind waiting by the pillar-box down at the church end of the street."

"FLOSSIE."

This was Thursday. Miles looked at his watch. He and Kay had had tea and done a cinema together. She had refused to dine with him and he had just taken her back to Varley Street. It was half past eight. He could do it all right.

Then he burst out laughing. Life was becoming one giddy whirl of assignations with house-parlourmaids. But behold the rigid propriety of Flossie. A chaperone was to be provided. Ernie the boy friend would be there.

He went off to get something to eat, humming under his breath:

"Then, just when I least expected it,

  I met you."

The church end of Merriton Street was easily found, because the clock was striking the half hour as Miles approached. A street-lamp marked the corner, and under the lamp stood Flossie Palmer with her hands linked about the arm of a very large young man in a dark overcoat. She displayed complete self-possession, introduced Mr. Bowden, and got down at once to business.

"I've told Ernie how you're looking for a young lady, Mr. Miles, and of course he says anything we can do to help he's only too willing— aren't you, Ernie?"

Mr. Ernest Bowden did not convey the impression that he was bursting with a desire to be helpful. Flossie went on without waiting for him to speak.

"I've told Ernie about the letter from the lady that signed herself 'Yours truly Agnes Smith,' and its being her rooms that the baby was born in, so he knows all that. And only last Saturday Aunt let me have him to tea, and there we sat looking at her old photograph album, and coo—if some of the people weren't a scream! However they could have worn the things they did! Well, there was one I'd forgotten who it was, so I took it out and turned it round, because most of them are wrote on, and sure enough this one was. And when I saw what was wrote on it I remembered what you said, because there it was, just the same, 'Yours truly Agnes Smith.'"

"*What?*" said Miles.

Flossie was enjoying herself very much indeed. Two young men were hanging on her words, Ernie just about as jealous as he could be, and Mr. Miles regular worked up.

"'Yours truly Agnes Smith,'" she repeated. "Wasn't it, Ernie?" She pinched Mr. Bowden suddenly and hard on the inside of the arm. The monosyllabic grunt which he emitted *might* have been taken as corroboration, but the only thing it really conveyed was that Mr. Bowden was in a very bad temper.

"You're sure?" said Miles. "What an extraordinary thing!"

"Ooh! Isn't it?" said Flossie. "And I said to Aunt at once—she was there all the time, never left us a minute, did she, Ernie?—I said at once, 'Aunt, who's this?' And she said, 'Why, that's your Aunt Ag.' Didn't she, Ernie?" She pinched his arm again and he withdrew it, this time in sulky silence.

"Your aunt?" said Miles.

"Aunt Ag," said Flossie. "And Smith was her first husband's name, and I s'pose I must of heard it, but it had gone clean out of my head. And she's my mother's own sister and a nearer relation than Aunt, who was only a sister-in-law, her and my mother being married to brothers, and my father killed in the war so Aunt brought me up."

Palmer—Palmer... Light broke in on Miles. Miss Collins, the little dressmaker, had mentioned a sister of Mrs. Smith's called Flo Palmer. He said the name out loud.

"Flo Palmer—is that your mother's name, Flossie?"

"Ooh—yes, Mr. Miles! I'm Flossie after her. Short for Florence, you know, same as Flo. Only I think Flossie's prettier—don't you?"

If Ernie was going to make a show of himself and forget his manners, she'd give him something to be jealous for. She giggled a little consciously and raised her large blue eyes to Miles' face. It was perhaps fortunate that he was at the moment much more interested in a previous generation. He asked quickly,

"Is Mrs. Smith alive?"

Flossie nodded.

"Mrs. Syme she is now—26 Dawnish Road, Ledlington. Her husband's verger in one of the churches there, and she lets apartments, which is a thing I wouldn't do if it was ever so."

Miles scribbled down the address on Flossie's own pale blue envelope, little knowing that the sight, and perhaps the scent, of this ornate piece of stationery was having a highly inflammatory effect upon Mr. Bowden. The paper, the scent, the winking gold forget-me-not, had been Ernie's Christmas present. The pale blue box had been tied up with a length of gold cord. He had snatched a kiss, and if Flossie had not actually returned it, she had undoubtedly turned the other cheek.

And now this Mr. Clayton just takes one of the envelopes out of his pocket and scribbles on it. Flossie needn't think she could play fast and loose with him, and she needn't think he wasn't going deeper into how she had come to meet Mr. Clayton at all. A friend of Mrs. Gilmore's was he? Well, then she ought by rights to have told Mrs. Gilmore whatever she had to tell, and not go meeting him at street corners.

"26 Dawnish Road, Ledlington. Thank you ever so much, Flossie."

"Oh, that's nothing, Mr. Miles. I brought the photograph if you'd like to see it—picked it out of Aunt's album when I was home, and let's hope she won't find out, but I thought if you saw the writing you'd know if it's the same as on the letter, because of course there's hundreds of Smiths."

Miles looked at her admiringly.

"That was clever," he said.

"Ernie's got it," said Flossie. "Ernie, where's that photo?" She came up close to him, slipped a hand into his pocket, and whispered, "*Ernie!* What's the matter? *Behave, can't you!*" Then with a little push she left him and put the photograph into Miles' hand.

He looked at it under the street-lamp, seeing at first only the high-shouldered coat and heavily trimmed hat. Under the wide brim there were two eyes and a nose, and rather a flat round face. The mouth was straight and hard. He wondered whether it would have anything to tell him. He turned the photograph over and read, in the same angular handwriting which had announced Mrs. Macintyre's death, the selfsame signature:

"Yours truly Agnes Smith."

Chapter Sixteen

MILES BORROWED a car from Ian Gilmore and drove himself down to Ledlington next morning. It was one of those days which is not exactly foggy, but which you feel may at any moment spring a fog upon you. The hedgerows had a limp, discouraged look, and a low mist clung about field and valley.

Ledlington looked damp and dirty. He had never been there before, and he didn't think he ever wanted to come back again. He had not, of côurse, seen the statue of Sir Albert Dawnish which is the pride of the town. It is a very large statue indeed. From its pedestal Sir Albert in rigid marble trousers gazes proudly upon the scene of his first triumph. Here in this very square stood the first of the long line of Quick Cash Stores which have made him famous. It has passed into the realm of history, its place knows it no more; but the statue of Sir Albert is good for some hundreds of years. Miles missed the statue because he missed the Market Square. It is the only way you can miss it.

He asked for Dawnish Street, and presently found it. It was not quite so new a street as the name would imply. Once upon a time it had been Bismarck Avenue, but in 1914 the name went into the melting-pot with a good many other things, and in due course the street had Sir Albert for a godfather. The trees which had constituted it an avenue were first lopped and then cut down altogether, and it became, and had remained, Dawnish Street. The houses are of the genteel type, high and narrow, with a small garden in front of each.

Miles rang the bell of No. 26, and presently Mrs. Syme opened the door. He knew her at once from the photograph in spite of more than twenty years difference in age. The same round, flat face. The same hard mouth. The light eyes looked at him exactly as they had looked from the photograph. Miles was the most friendly of creatures, but he didn't really feel drawn to Mrs. Syme. She had a pale auburn front which looked as if it had been dead for years. She had a brooch containing somebody's else hair at the collar of her black stuff dress. Her house smelt of cabbage-water.

He said, "Mrs. Syme?" and when she inclined her head without speaking he continued, "My name is Clayton, but you won't know it. I wonder—"

Mrs. Syme interrupted.

"Will you come in? I've my second-floor bedroom and front sitting-room vacant—twenty-five shillings a room and extras."

She threw open a door on the right and followed him into a dark narrow room encumbered with heavy mahogany furniture. Over a black marble mantelpiece there hung one of Doré's gloomier illustrations to *Paradise Lost*. Upon the shelf stood two cheap Italian vases in imitation bronze which imparted a funerary air. As much of the wall-paper as could be seen was olive-green.

"And would you be wanting the rooms immediately?" said Mrs. Syme.

With an inward shudder Miles explained that he would not be wanting them at all. He would not have lodged at No. 26 Dawnish Street for anything in the world. Or would he? All the time he was explaining to Mrs. Syme, a quirky imp was firing off questions in the back of his mind: "Come, come, you'd do it for double your salary."—"I wouldn't!" "Three times—four times—five times?"—"I tell you I wouldn't!" "I put it to you that you'd do it for five thousand a year." "Oh, shut up!" said Miles to the imp. And high time too. Mrs. Syme was looking at him very coldly indeed.

"I must explain. Your niece, Miss Palmer, gave me your address."

Mrs. Syme did not sniff; Miles could have sworn to that. Yet he received the impression that she might have sniffed if she had not been brought up to know her manners and behave like a perfect lady.

"Perhaps if we could sit down—" he said.

Mrs. Syme drew one of the chairs an inch or two away from the wall and sat down on the edge of it. It was an imitation Hepplewhite chair with a shield-shaped back and an imitation leather seat in rather a bright shade of brown mottled with black. Miles took another of the set and sat down too. The width of the room and of a mutual dislike at first sight separated them.

Miles made a manful effort.

"Mrs. Syme, I've come down here to ask you to help me." He saw her mouth tighten, but he went on. "Your niece thought you would be willing to help me. I've been trying to find you, but the only address I had was under your old name of Smith, at Laburnum Vale, Hampstead."

She was looking at him now with attention. She did not speak. He went on.

"I think you let rooms there?"

"High-class apartments," said Mrs. Syme, looking past him at one of the funerary bronzes.

"Damn this woman!" said Miles to himself. "Well, Mrs. Syme," he said aloud, "the fact is, I want to ask you some questions about a Mrs. Macintyre who, I believe, lived in your house for some months in 1914. You remember her, don't you?"

"Yes," said Mrs. Syme.

"She died in your house a week after her baby was born—"

"And had every attention," said Mrs. Syme.

"I'm sure she did. Well, she died, and you wrote to her husband in America. That was at the end of July."

He opened a letter-case, took out and unfolded a sheet of cheap white paper, and brought it over to her. Her eyes rested indifferently upon the words written nearly twenty years ago. Miles watched her as she read them, and thought that she had not changed. He had always wondered what kind of woman had written that letter. Now he knew.

DEAR SIR,

Your wife died this morning. Please send money for funeral expenses and my account enclosed and oblige

Yours truly

AGNES SMITH

"That was what you wrote?"

She said "Yes", and gave him back the sheet with a look which dismissed him to the other side of the room again.

"Mrs. Syme, did you ever hear from the husband?"

"No."

"Then your account wasn't paid?"

"Her sister paid it."

"Whose sister?"

"Mrs. Macintyre's sister."

"Mrs. Syme, Mrs. Macintyre had no sister."

"She said she was her sister. It was no business of mine. She settled my account."

"Yes," said Miles—"and I want to know why. She settled your account, and she paid for the funeral, and she took away the baby, didn't she? And I want to know why."

Mrs. Syme said nothing. She had said that it was not her business. Now, without a word, she conveyed to Miles that it was not his business either. He reacted vigorously.

"I haven't explained why I'm asking you these questions, but I'm going to. Mrs. Macintyre's husband is dead. I am his brother's secretary, and he has sent me over here to try and find his niece—the baby who was born in your house. We don't know anything at all about the person who called herself Mrs. Macintyre's sister, and we don't know what happened to the baby after she took it away. We want to find out."

"It was no business of mine," said Mrs. Syme.

Miles lost his temper a little.

"It might be," he said. "Mrs. Macintyre had some very valuable jewellery."

"And what there was her sister took away, and I can't be held responsible," said Mrs. Syme, and shut her mouth tight.

All the same he had made her speak. He went on quickly.

"Had Mrs. Macintyre ever spoken of this sister?"

Her eyes rested on him for a cold second.

"She wasn't one for gossip, and no more am I."

"Nice and matey, aren't you, darling?" said Miles to himself. Then aloud, "Meaning she didn't mention any sister?"

That went by default.

It would have given him the greatest pleasure to throw one of the sham Italian bronzes at her. He wrenched himself away from the idea and ploughed on.

"Can you tell me what this 'sister' was like?"

"I can't say that I can."

"Tall? Short? Dark? Fair?"

"Not so that you'd notice," said Mrs. Syme.

"What was her name?"

"I don't call it to mind."

"Won't you try?"

She sat there. It was quite evident that she hadn't the least intention of trying. Her face was exactly like a flat, well floured scone. Miles had never disliked anyone more.

"Mrs. Syme, can't you tell me *anything*?" he said.

"It's twenty years ago," she said with a flat finality, and with that she got to her feet and opened the dining-room door. "I've a pie in the oven spoiling, so I'll wish you good-morning, Mr. Clayton."

Miles got up too. There was a pause while he put away his letter-case and collected his hat, and as he did these things he was thinking, "Why is she like this? Why won't she talk? Why is she in such a hurry to get rid of me? Is it just plain natural disagreeableness, or is there a nigger in the wood-pile?" He cast back in his mind, and thought he had pricked her twice—once over the jewellery and once when he mentioned Flossie. He didn't want to stress the jewellery, because he hadn't a leg to stand on there, and she knew it. But why had the mention of Flossie produced that I-could-sniff-if-I-would atmosphere? Why should she sniff at Flossie? He thought he would see if he could prick her again.

"Well," he said, "I am sorry to have taken up your time. Your niece Miss Flossie Palmer thought you might be able to help me. Have you seen her lately? She's your sister's daughter, isn't she?"

Mrs. Syme's cold anger got the better of her. She opened her mouth and said what she had never intended to say. She said, "No, she isn't!" and shut her mouth again, but too late, because the words were out.

Miles felt a little tingling shock of surprise.

"I thought Florence Palmer was your sister."

Mrs. Syme stood silent.

"Isn't Flossie her daughter?"

"No, she isn't! And what business it is of yours, I don't know, Mr. Clayton!"

The wildest suspicion flashed into Miles' mind. Suppose the story of this supposititious sister of Mrs. Macintyre's was an invention. Suppose Mrs. Syme and Florence Palmer had themselves disposed of the jewels and the baby. But no, if Mrs. Syme had any criminal knowledge she wouldn't have let out that Flossie was not her sister's child. He judged it a commonplace piece of spite and no more. But he meant to find out all he could.

"If Flossie wasn't your sister's child, who was she?"

"Adopted," said Mrs. Syme, and held the door a little wider. "And I'll say good-morning, Mr. Clayton. This way, if you please."

He got no more out of her than that. What a woman! And she had had two husbands. Over beef and bread and cheese at the George, Miles wondered at his sex. Imagine swearing to love, honour and obey Mrs. Syme! No, it was the other way round, but he was prepared to bet his boots that that was the size of it. He drank confusion to all scone-faced women with auburn fronts, and proceeded to try and get Flossie on the telephone. It was rather a ticklish business and almost certainly one of the things that isn't done. He didn't know quite what he was going to say if Lila Gilmore answered the telephone, but on the other hand he did want "Aunt's" address, and with any luck he might get Flossie herself straight away.

Luck was in. He recognized her voice at once, and her "Ooh!" told him that she had recognized his.

"Look here, Flossie," he said, "I want your aunt's address—the one you lived with. There's something I want to ask her. Mrs. Syme's a wash-out."

"Then she's nothing to what Aunt'll be!" said Flossie with a giggle. "Not half she isn't!"

"Have a heart, Flossie!"

She giggled again.

"Ooh—I'm sorry for you—I am reelly. She's a terror Aunt is, and she don't like men. You should have heard her with Ernie when she let him come to tea. Ooh, Mr. Miles—Ernie isn't half wild! Wants to know how we met and all that. You should have *heard* him go on! I didn't know he *could*! What do you think I'd better do?"

"I should tell him the truth."

"What—all of it?"

"Why not? I say, let me have that address. Is it all right your talking to me like this?"

He thought himself she was being a little rash. He would have preferred that she should not address him by name. Her delighted giggle did not at once reassure him.

"Ooh—that's all right. They're out to lunch, and it's Gladys' afternoon, and Cook's having a nice lie-down. She's a *scream*."

Miles began to feel that the conversation had lasted long enough. He said,

"O.K. And now for that address."

"Mrs. Palmer, 18 Potter's Row, Islington," said Flossie. "And don't I just hope you'll enjoy yourself, Mr. Miles!"

Chapter Seventeen

MILES FOUND Mrs. Palmer a formidable person, but she aroused none of the dislike he had felt for Mrs. Syme. She struck him as shrewd, honest and dependable, and if she had a tongue and a temper, well, so much the better. A practical person Mrs. Palmer. She asked his business at once, and he stated it in the fewest possible words. Then—

"I have just been seeing Mrs. Syme. I am making inquiries about the baby who was born in her house in July 1914."

"And did Agnes Syme send you on to me?" said Mrs. Palmer.

"Well, no, she didn't. The fact is Mrs. Syme didn't seem at all willing to help me, and that is why I have come to you."

"And if Agnes Syme didn't send you, who did?"

"Well, I know your niece Flossie, and she very kindly—"

"Girls talk a deal too much," said Mrs. Palmer.

He felt rather as if he had come to a dead end.

"Mrs. Palmer," he said, "I'm over here on my employer's business, as I told you. He's anxious to find his niece. Mrs. Syme wouldn't help me—she wouldn't help me at all. She wouldn't answer my questions, but just as I was coming away she told me one thing, and that's what I want to ask you about. She told me Flossie wasn't her niece."

Mrs. Palmer's high colour became a little higher. She said sharply,

"And that's Ag Syme to the life—shuts her mouth like a trap when you want her to speak, and opens it when she ought by rights to keep it shut! And what more did she tell you, if I may ask?"

"She said Flossie wasn't her sister's child. She said Florence Palmer had adopted her."

Mrs. Palmer looked very angry indeed.

"Anything else?"

"Nothing," said Miles. "She wouldn't. So I've come to you."

They were sitting in Mrs. Palmer's parlour. Miles could have wished it had been the kitchen. The recently lighted fire had as yet made no impression upon the cold of a room which was only used on formal occasions. There was a bright green Brussels carpet on the floor and an aspidistra in the window. The furniture consisted of a three-piece suite upholstered in grey velvet with a pattern of black streaks and pink and green splodges. Mrs. Palmer sat on one side of the hearth in the lady's easy chair, and Miles on the other in the gent's ditto. The sofa stood with its back to the wall, and a small round table with a good deal of yellow inlay on its polished top supported a fine fern in a bright blue china pot. A green woolly mat protected the polish.

On a second table by the door lay a photograph album with gilt clasps, and a large family Bible. Above the mantelpiece, handsomely framed, hung two photographic enlargements upon which a certain amount of colouring matter had been imposed. The one on the left represented Flossie at the age of five, and the one on the right represented Sid at approximately the same age. Flossie had a white muslin frock, a blue sash, and yellow ringlets, and so had Sid. They made a perfect pair of little girls. No one could possibly have guessed that Sid was a boy. He looked if anything the more girlish of the two, and the picture, like himself, was the pride of Mrs. Palmer's heart. Even her house took second place. Yet it was plain that she was a notable housewife. Everything in the room that could be made to shine shone. The cleanness and tidiness were of the kind which arouse in the male breast a sinful longing for disorder.

Mrs. Palmer sat up very straight, an indignant gleam in her eyes.

"And what call had Ag Syme to be going out of her way to tell you anything at all about Flossie? Downright unkind, I call it, and no thought for anyone."

Miles had a flash.

"Doesn't Flossie know?"

"No, Mr. Clayton, she doesn't. And no need she should. Palmer she's been brought up, and Palmer she'll stay till she marries. And I'm sure I've cared for her like a niece, and poor Flo thought a deal more of her than a lot of mothers do. And then for Ag Syme to go telling a stranger what we've kept all these years!"

"I won't tell Flossie," said Miles, "if that's what you're afraid of. Not unless—Mrs. Palmer, will you answer me just one or two questions before I make any promises?"

Mrs. Palmer folded her hands in her lap and sat back a little.

"I'm not one to say beforehand what I can do," she said. "You'll have to ask your questions before I tell you whether I can answer them or not."

Miles considered. Then he asked,

"Why did your sister-in-law adopt a child?"

Mrs. Palmer answered him without hesitation.

"Because she lost her own baby, poor thing—and her husband that was my husband's brother killed the same week. If ever I've had trouble with Flossie, I've thought to myself, 'Well she saved poor Flo from going off her head,' and that's gospel."

"When was that? What year?"

"1915," said Mrs. Palmer slowly—"July 1915."

"And your sister-in-law's baby was how old?"

"Six months."

"And Flossie, when she adopted her?"

"Somewhere about a year."

"Mrs. Palmer, where did Flossie come from? Whose child was she? Where did your sister-in-law get her from?"

She looked at him, a steady look from under frowning brows.

"The name was Moore," she said. "I don't think I can tell you any more than that."

"But, Mrs. Palmer—"

"I'm telling you what poor Flo told me, Mr. Clayton. She told me just so much and no more. There was this Mrs. Moore with a child on her hands, and she was willing enough to part with it. And it saved poor Flo's reason having the child to look after, for she was dearly fond of her husband—though what sort of husband he'd have been if he'd come back from the war I wouldn't like to say, for he'd been a drinking man ever since I knew him, and once a drinker always a drinker is my experience—and what their poor wives go through! Well, there it is—Flo died when Flossie was five years old, and I've brought her up ever since. You haven't told me how you got acquainted with her, Mr. Clayton."

Under that grey eye Miles lapsed from the stricter ways of truth.

"She's living with the Gilmores who are friends of mine, and when I spoke of a letter signed Agnes Smith she was very kind and helpful and sent me down to see Mrs. Syme."

Mrs. Palmer rose to her feet.

"I'm afraid I can't tell you any more."

"You don't know who this Mrs. Moore was?"

She shook her head.

"Or where she lived?"

She shook her head again.

"Or even whether Flossie was her own child?"

"I'm afraid there's nothing more I can tell you, Mr. Clayton."

Miles departed. He didn't seem to have achieved anything. Flossie hadn't been adopted until a year after the Macintyre baby had disappeared. At the time of its disappearance Flo Palmer was expecting a child herself. It was inconceivable that she should have been in any way interested. Threads kept coming into his hands, but they were all odd. They ran into broken ends and led nowhere. Flossie was the right age, and so were thousands of other young women. For that matter, Kay was the right age too.

It was pleasant to let his thoughts go back to Kay. It would have been pleasanter if he had not felt anxious about her. He had been very fond of Kay, and in the very moment of their meeting this old fondness had sprung to life again. It had a warmth and vigour which would have surprised him had it not seemed so natural. He had been feeling that this return of his was rather a bleak affair—a home-coming with no home to come to; his mother gone; and George and Kitty in India. And then Kay had seemed to bring his mother close, and the old days, which had been very happy days. Kay was all that was left of them. He found himself thinking a great deal about Kay, and always with a touch of responsibility, as if she had been really one of the family instead of a little bird of passage coming from no one knew where and vanishing into the dark again. How his mother had hated letting her go off with that unpleasant woman Mrs. Moore... And suddenly, like an echo, he heard Mrs. Palmer saying the same name—"Mrs. Moore." The voice sounded so distinctly in his mind that he was startled. It was a Mrs. Moore from whom Flo Palmer had adopted Flossie. He laughed the impression away. Thousands of children had been born in 1914, and there were probably thousands of Mrs. Moores.

When Mrs. Palmer had shut the door upon Miles Clayton she went back into the parlour and began to tidy up. If a chair was an inch out of its accustomed place, it must be set back again. Where a hand had rested upon a polished surface, that surface must be repolished. The fire would be allowed to burn itself out because it was good for the room. She even put on a little more coal in view of the foggy weather and its possible effect upon the new suite, which had a value above that of ordinary furniture, being a present from Sid bought out of the earnings which he had carefully saved up for the purpose.

When she had put on the coal, Mrs. Palmer straightened herself up, stood back a little from the hearth, and looked long and earnestly at one of the pictures which hung above the mantelpiece. For once in a way it was not Sid's picture which she looked at but Flossie's. Presently she said out loud, "'Tisn't always for happiness." And then, after a long pause, "Too fond of dress and wants steadying. That Ernie Bowden seems to be a good-living young man." She went on staring at little Flossie's pink cheeks, blue eyes, and yellow ringlets. At the end she said, "I don't see my way clear." And with that she turned round and went over to the table on which the photograph album and the family Bible lay.

Standing in front of the Bible, she shut her eyes, opened the book at random, and then with grave deliberation lifted the index finger of her right hand and pressed it down upon the page. All this while her eyes had been shut. Now she opened them and looked at the verse upon which her finger rested. It read:

"It is easier for a camel to go through the eye of a needle than for a rich man to enter into the Kingdom of God."

A look of solemn triumph crossed her face. She closed the book and went out of the room.

Chapter Eighteen

AT NINE O'CLOCK that night Miles was knocking at the area door of No. 16 Varley Street. After his interviews with Mrs. Syme and Mrs. Palmer the only thing that he himself felt sure about was that he must see Kay, and the more he thought about this, the more certain he felt. He was therefore knocking at the area door and wondering what he should say if by some malevolent stroke of luck Nurse Long should answer it. This, of course, was guilty conscience. Reason informed him that nurses do not answer tradesmen's knocks, and that a fat old cook would certainly not come to the door herself if Kay were there to send.

Kay opened the door. She had on a dark red dress with a little bit of a cream apron and a little bit of a frill which did duty for a cap. The frill was tied on with a piece of red velvet ribbon, and it was quite terribly becoming.

She said, "Oh!" and then, in a hurried whisper, "Miles, you mustn't!"

Miles had a distinct recollection of his mother's parlourmaid slipping out in the evening to meet the red-headed young man who delivered the fish. He and George used to chaff her about it.

He said, "Can't you come out? I must see you."

"Oh, Miles!"

"Kay, I really do want to see you. Isn't your work done?"

"Yes, but—"

"Well, go and ask your fat old Mrs. Thingummy if you can go out to the post." That had been Rose's formula.

"Oh, Miles—I can't."

"Yes, you can. Step on it, Kay!"

She shut the door, and he wondered whether she would come back. And then she was out in the dark beside him and they ran up the area steps together. Kay said "'Ssh!" in his ear, and neither of them spoke till they were three or four houses away in the direction of the Square. He had slipped his arm through hers, so they were very close together. There was a sense of escape and adventure. They kept their voices low.

He said, "Is it all right?"

And she, "Oh, Miles, she says I can stay out till ten!"

"That's a bit of all right. I say, where are we going?"

"Into the Square. It's nice and quiet there."

"Kay, how are you getting on?"

"Oh, all right. Tell me about you. Why did you want to see me?"

He began to tell her all about his day—borrowing the car from Ian Gilmore—going to Ledlington—interviewing Mrs. Syme—interviewing Mrs. Palmer... It took quite a long time.

The Square was not very plentifully provided with lamps. There was enough mist in the air to make the lighted patches shimmery and dim. There were long stretches of darkness. The trees in the middle of the Square were black and formless.

Kay had slipped her coat and skirt over her uniform. She had taken off the bit of red ribbon and the frill and covered her dark hair with the grey cap she had worn yesterday. Whenever they came into one of those misty patches of light, he looked down at her and she looked up at him. He wasn't in any hurry to finish his story, but in the end he came to the crux of it. Flossie Palmer was an adopted child. She had been adopted by Mrs. Palmer's sister. She had been adopted from a Mrs. Moore.

"And of course I've been saying to myself ever since that there are thousands of Mrs. Moores, but all the same it seems a bit of a coincidence. I shouldn't have thought of it if I hadn't just met you again, but—Kay, what sort of woman was your aunt really? You said yesterday—" He broke off.

"What did I say?"

"You said she had some horrid friends."

"Yes, she had. I hated them. Miles, I think she hated them too. I think she was afraid, and that's why we were always moving on."

"Who were these friends?"

"I don't know. It sounds stupid to say I hated them, because I never really saw them—she used to send me into the garden or up to bed. There was a man who came."

"The man who spoke to you in the street?"

She pressed a little closer to him.

"I don't know. I was in the garden—he looked out of the window at me. And once when I was in bed Aunt Rhoda opened the door, and she said 'What a suspicious mind you've got! Look for yourself—she's there all right.' She had a candle—and it dazzled—and there was a strange man standing there—looking in. Then they went away. But it frightened me. I used to dream about it. I didn't like it."

Miles didn't like it either. Fear went through his mind like a cold wind blowing. Who had been watching Kay? Whose concern was it to watch her? How had she come to the house of shady people like her first employers, the Marstons? And by what underground manœuvring had she been transferred to Varley Street?

He said abruptly, "How did you come to be with the Marstons? That was the name, wasn't it?"

To Kay the question seemed quite inconsequent. She laughed a little.

"How sudden! We were talking about Aunt Rhoda."

"And now we're talking about the Marstons. How did you come to go there?"

She laughed again.

"Well, it was rather funny. Someone sent me a paper with a marked advertisement, and I never knew who it was."

So she had been shepherded there, and then moved on to Varley Street... Why? There was a dark answer to that, but it didn't seem to him to be the right one. He had a sense of something deeper. And yet it might be.

He said, "Kay, look here—I want you to leave this place you're in. I don't like the way you came here. I don't like any of it. I want you to leave at once."

"Miles, I *couldn't*!"

"I don't like your being there at all. I'd like to take you away to-night, but anyway you've got to leave to-morrow—you've really got to."

Kay pulled her arm away and set her hand on his sleeve.

"Miles, I couldn't really. I haven't any money."

"I want you to let me lend you some."

"Oh no—I couldn't! And it's not at all a bad place—really it isn't."

He could not shake her. She stuck to it that the place was all right. He elicited that she slept in the basement, and that Mrs. Green slept there too. Mrs. Green sounded respectable and good-natured. The house, as described by Kay, sounded as dull and respectable as any house in London. An invalid old lady—a hospital nurse—a cook who had been there for years—the ordinary routine of such a household. But it was from this house that Flossie Palmer had run out into the fog shaken with terror because she had seen a hole in the wall, and the head of a wounded man, and cruel eyes watching her.

Kay slipped her arm through his again.

"You know, Miles, we really were talking about Aunt Rhoda. I don't know how we got off on to me, and it's no use, so let's go back. I was just going to tell you something when you switched off like that—something—well, something very odd, Miles."

"About Mrs. Moore?"

"Yes, about Aunt Rhoda. But I want to ask you something first."

Miles gave up for the moment. He wasn't going to give up altogether and she needn't think it, but just for the moment he didn't mind talking about Aunt Rhoda again, especially if Kay had something to tell him. He said,

"Go ahead."

"Well, this girl Flossie—what did you say her surname was?"

"Palmer."

"I thought so. And her mother? I mean the woman who adopted her. Do you know what her name was—her Christian name?"

"Florence. She was called Flo—Flo Palmer."

He felt her squeeze his arm.

"Oh, Miles!"

"What is it? You don't mean to say—"

"Yes, I do—Miles, I *do*! Aunt Rhoda said it."

"Said Flo Palmer's name? To you?"

They stood still in the dark between the lamps. She clasped his arm tightly.

"Not to me—not to anyone. It was when she was ill, before she died. I don't think she knew what she was saying."

"And she talked about Flo Palmer? Will you tell me just what she said? The exact words, if you can remember them."

"Yes, I can. It's very little. You see, she was talking all the time, only you couldn't make out the words. And then all at once she said quite clearly, 'Tell Flo Palmer.' And then she seemed to wake up. I was sitting there, and she looked at me and asked for something to drink, and while I was getting it she said, 'What did I say just now?' So I told her, and she said, 'Flo's dead. I don't know what's happened to the child. It doesn't matter—I've got *you*.' Then she drank some milk, and she asked me to promise not to leave her."

"Kay, you're sure she said that?"

"Quite sure."

He felt her tremble a little against him.

"Because if you're sure, it means that Flo Palmer did get Flossie from your aunt. It means—Kay, I don't know what it might mean. I must go home and try and sort it all out."

The clock in the church tower of St. Barnabas' struck with three heavy strokes. Kay started.

"That's a quarter to ten!"

"Well, you needn't be in till ten—you said so."

"I've got to put my cap and apron on again and be ready to take up the old lady's Benger. Oh, Miles, listen! What's that?"

It was a faint mewing sound somewhere in the darkness. Kay called "Kitty—Kitty!" and in a moment something warm and soft brushed against her ankles. She stooped and picked up a small wailing kitten.

"Miles—look! No, you can't look here. Come down to the lamp. It's the dearest little soft thing. Feel it! And the milkman was telling us about it this morning. The people at No. 10 have just turned it out. Isn't it a shame? And Mrs. Green said if it came to us, she'd take it in because the mice are dreadful. But the milkman said it was so wild it wouldn't let anyone catch it. But it came to me at once—didn't you, Kitty? Look—isn't it a darling?"

She stopped under the lamp and showed him a little grey ball of fur cuddled up against her cheek.

"Miles, it's purring. Listen! Will you come home with me, Kitty, and have bread and milk and a lovely smell of mouse? Oh, Miles, you don't know how our basement smells of mice! And Mrs. Green says there are rats in the cellar, but I hope it's not true. She never goes down there, and she says they don't come up, so I don't see how she can possibly know—do you? Miles, I must run!"

He held her. Under the misty light with the kitten against her cheek she was the sweetest thing in the world. It was monstrous to have to let her go back to that house again.

"Kay—meet me to-morrow!"

"I can't."

"You've got a most damnable habit of saying you can't. You said you couldn't *to-night*, but you did. I'll be up at the corner of the Square at nine o'clock, and if you're more than five minutes late, I shall come and fetch you."

"Oh, Miles!"

"Oh, Kay!" said Miles. Then he put his arm round her shoulders and gave her something between a hug and a shake.

She laughed, a little soft, shaky laugh, and ran away. The lamp under which they had been standing was the next one beyond the corner of Varley Street. He watched her cross the patch of light at the corner still holding the kitten with both hands. Then he lost her in the shadows.

Chapter Nineteen

Miles went back to his hotel and got down to sorting things out. He took a block and a fountain pen, and wrote:

Mrs. Syme:—

Was Mrs. Agnes Smith in whose house the Macintyre baby was born, July 1914.

Says Mrs. Macintyre's sister paid all expenses and removed baby, also all Mrs. Macintyre's belongings.

Says she has no idea where she went or what she did with them.

N.B. There is no sister.

Further, Mrs. Syme says Flossie Palmer isn't her niece. Says Flo Palmer adopted her.

Declines to say any more.

Very disagreeable person.

Mrs. Palmer:—

Serious, formidable person. Conscientious. Fond of Flossie.

Very angry with Mrs. Syme for letting out that Flossie is an adopted child. Flossie doesn't know.

Flo Palmer got Flossie from a Mrs. Moore in July 1915. She had just lost her husband and a baby aged six months. Flossie was about a year old.

Kay:—

Says her aunt, Rhoda Moore, spoke about Flo Palmer when she was dying. Actual words, in semi-conscious state: "Tell Flo Palmer." Then, after rousing: "What did I say just now?" and, "Flo's dead. I don't know what's happened to the child. It doesn't matter—I've got *you*." (meaning Kay.)

N.B. Ask Kay if she knows anything about her aunt having charge of any other child or children. Also her exact relationship to Mrs. Moore.

He stopped and read the notes through.

Well, he had here four different women—Mrs. Syme, formerly Agnes Smith; her sister, Flo Palmer; Flo's sister-in-law, Mrs. Palmer;

and Kay's aunt, Rhoda Moore. Flo Palmer linked the other three together. She kept turning up. That was the thing that struck him very forcibly—the way Flo Palmer kept on cropping up. He wondered whether the sister-in-law had told him all she knew. He didn't think so. He had come away from her, as he had come away from Mrs. Syme, with the feeling that a door had been shut in his face. Behind Mrs. Syme's door there might be some criminal knowledge. He wasn't sure. She might have invented Mrs. Macintyre's sister, disposed of the jewels, and farmed the baby out. Flo Palmer might have aided and abetted, and after the loss of her own child she might have adopted the baby, in which case Flossie was the Macintyre heiress. The thought tickled him a good deal. But it was the purest supposition. Flo Palmer was dead, and Rhoda Moore was dead—the woman who had adopted the child, and the woman from whom it had been adopted. That meant that the two middle links in the chain were gone. There remained at the one end of it Mrs. Syme, and at the other Mrs. Palmer. Mrs. Syme would not incriminate herself, and Mrs. Palmer struck him as being the sort of person whose motto would be "Least said, soonest mended." He had certainly got Mrs. Moore's name out of her. But then she couldn't possibly have supposed that it would mean anything to him.

He went to bed, and dreamed that he was cast on a desert island with Mrs. Syme. It was one of the most unpleasant dreams he had ever had...

Kay came in at the area door rosy and breathless with the kitten on her shoulder. It arched its back, flaunted three inches of tail, and purred a small but resonant purr.

Mrs. Green stared and exclaimed, "Well, I never! What do you call that, I should like to know."

"Oh, Mrs. Green, it's the kitten—the one the milkman told us about. It came to me at once. You said you'd keep it."

Mrs. Green laughed.

"What's the good of a little bit of a thing like that? It won't catch no mice—though they do say the smell of a cat'll drive 'em away. Here, what are you doing with my milk?"

"Only a little drop—*please*, Mrs. Green. It's so hungry—aren't you, Kitty?"

The kitten lapped vigorously. Mrs. Green chuckled.

"If you want a cat to catch mice, you've got to keep it hungry. They'd a sight rather have someone to cook for 'em. And I'm not cooking for no cats, Kay, so don't you fret yourself. If that there kitten's going to stay here, it's got to work for its living same as you and me. Down to the cellar it goes nights, and it's welcome to what it can find there."

"Oh, Mrs. Green, you *can't*! Poor little thing!"

"Poor little nothing!" said Mrs. Green firmly. "I'm not going to have my kitchen messed up, and that's all there is about it!"

The kitten crouched close over the saucer which Kay had set for it. Its little pink tongue lapped eagerly. Mrs. Green let it finish its meal. Then she picked it up by the scruff of the neck and waddled into the scullery.

There was a door which went out into the back yard, and there was a second door, rather low, set in a piece of bulging wall which rounded one of the inner corners of the room. It looked as if it might be the oven door in the story of Hansel and Gretel, for it was cross-barred with old rusty iron, and the irregular bulge into which it was set had something of the shape of a primitive stove or cooking-place. Mrs. Green lifted the latch, pulled the low door towards her, and disclosed a flight of stone steps going down into unknown mouldy depths. She leaned over, dropped the kitten, banged the door, and fastened the latch again.

Kay's colour was flaming and her eyes were wet.

"Oh, *Mrs. Green!*"

"Oh, fiddlesticks!" said Mrs. Green. "I tell you I'm not going to have my kitchen messed up! And for gracious mercy's sake don't look at me like that! There's plenty of dry straw down there, and if it can't make itself a bed, it'll have to do without! I'm not going to tuck no cats up, nor yet sing 'em to sleep! And if you don't want to be late with that there Benger's, you'd better get a move on, Kay my girl. And don't you go letting that there kitten out, or you and me'll have words, which is a thing I don't want nor won't put up with, and if it comes to one of us having to go, I can tell you right away now which of us it'll be."

"Is there *really* straw, Mrs. Green?"

Mrs. Green tossed her head. All her chins quivered like jellies.

"Haven't I said so? There's enough for a hundred cats, let alone one little misery like that. Now just you hurry along!"

Kay hurried. She took up the Benger as the clock struck half past ten. Nurse Long opened the bedroom door and took in the tray. She did not say thank you, and she did not say good-night. She just took the tray and shut the door again.

Kay went downstairs, and presently to bed. She was very sad about the kitten. She would have liked so much to have had it to sleep with her, but Mrs. Green had been dreadfully out of temper when she suggested it. Any cat she had in her kitchen would go into the cellar for the night unless it went into the yard. Kay could take her choice. It would be one or the other.

Curled up in bed, Kay cried a little about the kitten. It was so small, and it had rubbed its head against her cheek and purred. And perhaps there were rats in the cellar. She did hope not, but suppose there were. Supposing it was very, very frightened... Even Mrs. Green was frightened of rats... The kitten was so very small. Supposing a rat were to bite it... She cried herself to sleep.

Chapter Twenty

FLOSSIE PALMER had also slipped out that evening. Ernie had written her the sort of letter which a girl who respected herself couldn't be expected to take lying down, and if Ernie thought he could come it over her like that, Ernie had got to be shown where he was wrong. The Gilmores were dining out, and Cook was agreeable, so Flossie put on her bright pink dress and her beads and slipped out. Ernie was partial to a bit of colour, and as it was a mild night, she could leave the collar of her coat open. Those old beads did sort of make your skin look white. She took a final look in the glass, and was a good deal heartened by what she saw there.

Mr. Bowden awaited her at the church end of the street. His letter had announced the firm intention of having things out whether or no. Either she could come and meet him, or he would come to the house and have it out there—"And if Mrs. Gilmore hears about it, so much the better, and perhaps she'll want to know what you're doing taking up with one of her gentleman friends."

Flossie halted under the lamp at the street corner. What was the good of having pink cheeks, blue eyes, and golden hair if they couldn't be seen? And Ernie needn't think he'd only to hold up his little finger to have her come after him. She didn't mind coming as far as the corner, but she wasn't going to come any farther.

Mr. Bowden came up glowering. He missed neither the yellow hair, the bright cheeks, the angry sparkle of the eyes, nor the whiteness of the neck, which the open coat collar allowed to be seen.

Flossie wasted no time, but plunged directly into the fray.

"Coo, Ernie Bowden—if you haven't got a nerve! I shouldn't of thought you'd have dared to come and meet me, not after the things you wrote in that letter of yours! If I was to show it to Aunt, well, I dursn't think what she'd say nor what she'd do. The very least of it would be that I wasn't never to speak to you again—and perhaps that's what you're after. And I must say that if I wanted to break off with anyone I'd been going with reg'lar, I wouldn't do it in the sort of hinting underground way what you done it—no, that I wouldn't! I'd tell them open, and say good-bye, and no harm done. I wouldn't go sending them insulting letters—as good as taking their characters away. And, as I said before, if Aunt was to see what you'd wrote, well, I'd be sorry for you, Ernie Bowden!"

Mr. Bowden was a good deal shaken. He had written the letter in a tearing temper. His heart quaked at the thought of losing Flossie. It also quaked at the thought of Aunt. He said in a deep growling voice,

"You don't half carry on."

This was an unfortunate remark. Flossie pounced on it.

"And what do you expect a girl to do when you've as good as told her she's lost her character?"

"I never!" said Mr. Bowden explosively.

Flossie took no notice.

"And if anyone else had said the half or the quarter of what you done, I'd have come to you, thinking you was my *friend*, and I'd have said, 'Here's someone that wants his face pushed in,' and I'd have looked for you to do it for me—yes, I *would*, Ernie—till I got that letter!"

"*Flossie!*"

"It's no good saying Flossie one minute and taking away my character the next!"

"Flossie, I never!"

The scene ran the course which Flossie had mapped out for it. When thoroughly repentant and alarmed, Ernie was allowed to plead brokenly for pardon and reinstatement.

At somewhere about half-past ten there was a complete reconciliation and a specially tender embrace on the steps of No. 12 Merriton Street.

"Ooh, Ernie—you're not half strong!" Flossie's voice was a little breathless.

Mr. Bowden nodded.

"I could choke you with one hand," he asserted, and proceeded to demonstrate the size and strength of his hand by clasping it about her throat.

Flossie, thrilled and a little frightened, tried to twist away. She found that she could not move. Ernie's arm was like a steel bar. If his hand were to close upon her throat—A shiver ran down her spine. Instead, the hand tilted her chin, the arm lifted her. She was very soundly hugged and kissed and set down again. Mr. Bowden's submissive mood had passed. He said roughly,

"You're my girl, and don't you forget it!"

Flossie ran into the house with a beating heart. Cook had let her have a key, but she'd to give it back and not be later than half-past ten. She put on the light in the hall, and it was as she lifted her hand to the switch that she felt the sag and pull of the beads about her neck. She looked quickly down and clutched them. The string was broken. That was Ernie, when he pretended to choke her.

"Coo! He *is* strong!"

The little shiver went down her back again, and still clutching the beads, she stepped into the dining-room and felt for the switch inside the door. The lights went on, but the beads were slipping. It took her a moment to find the broken ends of the string, and in that moment some of them had dropped and rolled. She spread out her handkerchief, lowered the string carefully down upon it, and picked up all the beads she could find. It was well past half past ten, and she didn't want to get on the wrong side of Cook. She knotted the handkerchief tightly, pushed it into her pocket, and ran downstairs with the key.

Chapter Twenty-One

KAY WOKE from a dream of distress. She could not remember what the dream was about. She had been in some far empty place and had heard the wind go by. That was the nearest she could get to it. She sat up in bed and listened with straining ears. Had something really cried, or had it only been the wind of her dream? If anything had cried down there in the cellar, would she have heard it? She didn't know how far the cellar ran under the house. She thought it must run a long way, because Mrs. Green had said something about "those big old cellars." She had said they did keep the house dry and that was about all you could say for them, nasty creepy things, and as for going down into them, she'd sooner give in her notice and have done with it any day of the week.

Kay lit the candle and looked at her clock. It was half past five. She was supposed to get up at six. Mrs. Green couldn't be very angry if she were to go and let the kitten out now—she couldn't really. She could bring it in here and cuddle it for half an hour before it was time to get up.

She got out of bed, put on her shoes and the old red dressing-gown which she had had since she was sixteen and which was much too short for her, and went through into the scullery carrying her candle. The kitchen smelled of mice, and the scullery of mice and cabbage-water and the fish which Miss Rowland had had for breakfast the day before. Mrs. Green hated open windows so much that smells had no chance of escaping from the basement. They lingered till they died, and sometimes they took a very long time to die.

Kay opened the door in the oven-shaped bulge which covered the cellar stair. The smell that came up out of the mouldy dark made the smell of the scullery seem quite homely and comfortable. The cellar smelled like something forgotten time out of mind. It was a most dreadfully discouraging sort of smell, and Kay hated it very much. She held her candle up and called in a small anxious voice, "Kitty—Kitty—" There was no answer and no sound.

Kay leaned down over the stair and cried a little louder, "Kitty—Kitty—Kitty!"

The silence and the old, forgotten smell rose up out of the dark. There was no other answer.

Then she caught her nightgown and the red dressing-gown tightly about her and went down four steps without letting herself stop to think. She called again, and when again there was no answer, she went right on down to the bottom of the stair and stood there holding up her candle. It was like going down into a well. It wasn't exactly cold, but it was still.

She looked about her. The cellar was very large. It must run right under the kitchen. There were doors opening from it. The place which the steps ran down into was like a wide stone-paved hall. There were doors all along one side of it. If she turned so as to face the front of the house, the doors were on her right. On the other side there was a white-washed wall running up to the roof, and at the foot of the wall was the straw which Mrs. Green had spoken about. It was piled in a heap, and consisted partly of the straw covers in which bottles are packed, and partly of the loose straw which had doubtless been stuffed between them. There was certainly plenty of bedding for one small kitten.

Kay was getting used to the feel of the cellar. She went over to the straw and stirred it with her foot, calling to the kitten, but there was no answering rustle, no little sleepy waking mew. She went along the line of doors and tried them. Only one was locked. The others showed empty cellars with brick walls and stone floors—all except the one nearest the back of the house, which contained some empty packing-cases and some more straw, but no kitten.

Kay was beginning to feel most dreadfully worried about the kitten. Suppose the rats had killed it. She hadn't seen any rats, but they might have dragged the kitten down into a hole. There were several holes in the brick. In the cellar where the packing-cases were there was a horrid-looking one on the floor level just where the party wall of the cellar met what she thought must be the side wall of the house. She called "Kitty—Kitty—Kitty!" and tried not to think about a rat coming out of the hole and running up her bare leg. She found herself away from the hole and over by the door without quite knowing how she had got there. It mightn't be a rat-hole, but it did look most dreadfully like one.

And then she heard a sound which terrified her. It wasn't exactly a groan—or was it?

She had reached the stair and climbed half the steps before she stopped to think, and by that time she no longer knew what she had heard. There had been something, and it had frightened her very much, but she didn't know what it was.

And with that, the kitten came running out of the darkness of the last cellar. It came to her mewing, just as it had come to her in the Square the night before. She went down the steps to meet it, and as soon as she lifted it, it ran up her arm and on to her shoulder, purring loudly.

She ran back to her room and shut the door. As she turned from setting down the candle, the kitten sprang on to her pillow. Kay put out her hand to stroke it and stopped short. She stopped because she caught sight of her fingers in the candle-light, and they were smeared with blood. The kitten purred. It didn't seem to be hurt. She picked it up, and found a wet smear of blood upon its shoulder. But there wasn't any cut from which the blood could have come. Search as she would, there wasn't any cut. She washed her own hand, but there was no cut there either.

When she had cleaned the kitten's fur, she got into bed and snuggled down with it.

"Did you kill a rat, Kitty? I don't believe you could. You're too small. Yes, I know your teeth are like needles. No, little wicked thing—you're not to bite me! Did you bite a rat and run away? I believe you did. But supposing it had run after us, what would you have done? I know what I should have done—I should have run away. I'm not a bit brave about rats, Kitty. Are you?"

The kitten stopped biting and became a warm purring ball just under Kay's chin. She found it very comforting. It was a pity when it was time to get up.

Mrs. Palmer also dreamed that night. She lay awake through all the first part of the night, not fidgeting as most people do when they cannot sleep, but lying stiff and straight with her head on the one low hard pillow which was all she allowed herself. She heard all the hours strike until four, and then she fell into a troubled sleep and dreamed.

She must have been thinking about the verse upon which her finger had lighted when she opened the Bible at random after sending Miles Clayton away, because in her dream she saw Flossie riding on a camel across an open sandy waste. The camel and the sand came straight out of the picture-book of Bible scenes which her grandmother used to show her when she was a little girl, but there were additions which were due to her own disturbed imagination. There was Flossie, who sat cross-legged on the top of the camel's hump in the pink dress which was a deal too bright for a Christian young woman. And there was the needle's eye sticking up out of the sand, for all the world like a needle sticking up out of bran when you empty a pin-cushion, only the eye of this needle was as large as the Marble Arch, and the sinful thought came into Mrs. Palmer's mind that there was something wrong about the text, because the camel and Flossie would go through the eye of that needle as easily as a thread of silk through a horseshoe.

And while she was thinking this, a voice said, "Look at the text," and there, out in the middle of the desert, was her polished table with the big Bible lying on it which ought by rights to be in the parlour standing against the wall next the door. And in her dream she put her hand between the leaves of the Bible and opened it. Then the voice said, "Read!" and she looked where her finger was pointing and read aloud. But it wasn't the verse she had read before. It wasn't the verse about the camel and the eye of the needle, and the rich who cannot enter into the Kingdom of God. It was another verse altogether, and it made her heart quake within her. She read it because she had to read it, and her heart quaked so much that she woke up. And as she woke, she heard her own voice repeating the verse aloud:

"Lying lips are an abomination unto the Lord."

Chapter Twenty-Two

MILES LUNCHED with the Gilmores next day. He really thought he had better tell Freddy about Flossie Palmer being mixed up in the Macintyre case. The present situation was an uncomfortable one, and he thought he had better put it straight with Freddy.

Flossie didn't appear at lunch, which was rather a relief. The other girl, Gladys, waited on them. Lila treated him as if he were the friend of a lifetime. She wore a very simple, very expensive garment of honey-coloured wool which buttoned all the way down the front with the largest buttons Miles had ever seen in his life. She had a new shade of lipstick, and was worried because her nail-polish did not match it exactly.

"And that devil of a girl at Roselle's told me it would! Isn't it too devastating? And Freddy's no help at all! Miles darling, what *am* I to do?"

"Wash one of them off," said Freddy.

"*Freddy!* How too utterly vandal! Do you know how long my nails take to do?"

"I ought to. Why not give the lipstick a miss?"

"Darling, how can I? I should feel too *utterly* nude! Besides—Miles, do you know, I've got the most enthralling scheme—at least it isn't mine really, but I'm in it, only Freddy is being too *recalcitrant*. Fitz wants me to go into a dress business with him. Really *the* most wonderful plan! There will be just a plate-glass window, and a heavy gold curtain, and a really comfy chair. I've told him I simply won't play at all unless the chair is *really* comfy. I *mean*, Miles darling, I've got to sit in it all day—haven't I?"

"Have you?" said Miles.

"But, darling, of course—in the dresses that Fitz is going to design for me—a morning one in the morning, and so on. And sometimes I'll just walk across the floor and turn round. Fitz says I shall draw crowds. And he's designed the most *marvellous* bathing-dress for me to show, only Freddy says I'm not to."

Freddy smiled his agreeable smile.

"I should hate you to catch cold, darling."

"But Fitz says it would be *the* most marvellous draw."

"Lila," said Freddy gravely, "are you fond of Fitz?"

Lila's eyebrows rose.

"Darling, I *adore* him. You know I do."

"Then I suppose you don't want him to have a black eye?"

"*Freddy!*"

"Or a thick ear?"

"*Darling!*"

"Or a split lip?"

"My *sweet!*"

"Well, personally, I think they'd improve his appearance quite a lot. And what's more, he'll get them if he doesn't look out, and then, darling, I shall be had up for assault, and all the evening papers will have headlines like 'Husband's Vengeance. Society Beauty in the Box,' and all that sort of thing."

"How *marvellous!*" She put her elbows on the table and rested her chin upon her hands. The lipstick certainly did not match the finger-nails. Freddy told her so.

"My sweet, I *know*—too *devastating!* I shall have to do my face again—it doesn't take quite as long as my hands. Besides, I really *do* think this nail stuff is rather alluring, and it's such a perfectly *foul* day, I must have *something* to cheer me up. Freddy, I think we must have the rest of the lights on. It's getting darker every minute."

Gladys was out of the room. Freddy got up and turned on the light in the four cut crystal globes which studded the black ceiling.

"Of course, if you *will* have a black room—"

"But, my sweet, it's so becoming."

"To you and Miles perhaps—but what about me? Hallo, who's been shedding beads?" He stooped and picked up a small object which the sudden illumination had discovered. It lay against the wall under the glass slab which did duty for a serving-table, and which, he always declared, reminded him of a block of ice from the fishmonger's. He did not really consider that a black room furnished with blocks of ice was a comfortable place in which to eat your meals.

He laid what he had found upon the table in front of Lila. It was a bead of about the size of a large pea, of a dark grey colour with an iridescent bloom upon it. Against the semi-transparency of the glass it looked black.

He said, "Yours?" and went back to his place.

Lila picked up the bead.

"Oh *no*, I—Freddy, where did this come from?"

"I picked it up off the floor over there."

"But darling, how extraordinary!" She turned it between finger and thumb, feeling it, looking at it. "Freddy, where could it have come from?"

Gladys had come into the room and was handing the sweet. She said in a low voice,

"Oh, madam, it's Flossie's."

Lila looked at her, the bead in her hand. Her eyes were wide. She looked like a startled child.

"This isn't Flossie's."

"Yes, madam. She broke her beads coming in last night. She told me she hadn't been able to find them all."

Lila had turned quite pale. She looked past the dish which Gladys was holding and said,

"It can't be Flossie's! What nonsense! It's a pearl."

Gladys went on holding the dish.

"It's a pearl bead, madam. Flossie broke the string last night coming in."

"Lila," said Freddy—"suppose you help yourself. I don't see why Miles and I should have cold pancakes."

Lila waved the pancakes away. She stared at the bead. Once she looked up as if she were going to speak, met Freddy's eyes, and stopped. When Gladys had left the room, she burst out.

"Freddy, it's a black pearl!"

Freddy was squeezing lemon over the quarter of an inch of sugar with which he had encrusted his pancake.

"Darling, you've got pearls on the brain. If you're not careful you'll be thinking you're an oyster, and then where shall we be?"

"But, Freddy, it *is* a pearl! It is *really*! It can't be Flossie's—it simply *can't*!" She put it to her lips and touched it with her tongue. "I knew directly I saw it. But that's the proof—it's rough. Pearl beads are smooth, but real pearls are rough if you try them with your tongue. It's a black pearl. How *can* Flossie have a string of black pearls?"

Miles had been thinking so hard that it had not occurred to him to speak, but he spoke now. He said,

"If she's Miss Macintyre, she might have her mother's pearls."

"*What?*" said Freddy Gilmore.

Lila's blue eyes rolled helplessly.

Miles beamed upon them both.

"Well, it's this way. Flossie is the adopted child of a woman called Flo Palmer in whose sister's house the Macintyre baby was born. I'd met Flossie before she came here. I was going to tell you all about it after lunch."

"You're not pulling our legs?"

"No, I'm not. It's a fact. But that's as far as I've got. I don't know that Flo Palmer adopted the Macintyre baby. In fact there's every reason to suppose that she didn't—or, let us say, there's no reason to suppose that she did. I hadn't got farther than a suspicion, but if Flossie has got a string of black pearls, it's going to have a very stimulating effect on that suspicion."

Freddy finished his pancake.

"It can't be a pearl," he said. "It's sheer blithering nonsense. Let's go upstairs and interview Flossie, who will, (a), tell us she got the beads at Woolworth's; (b), burst into tears; (c), give notice; and (d), bring an action for defamation of character. But it's all right as long as you're happy, darling. Come along!"

Flossie, who had not changed, was entrancingly pretty in a blue print dress, a white apron, and a little white cap. When Miles showed her the bead and asked her if it was hers, she looked first pleased and then puzzled, because what were they all looking at her like that for, and why didn't Mr. Miles give her the bead and have done with it? If it had been anyone but Mr. Miles, she'd have been uncomfortable the way he looked at her—sort of excited-like and eager, and perhaps just as well Ernie wasn't there to see him. Mr. and Mrs. Gilmore too—what did they want to look at her like that for? She hadn't done anything.

"Flossie," said Miles, "I wonder if you'd mind telling us where you got those beads of yours?"

She didn't mind telling anyone. She hadn't got anything to hide, thank goodness. She said,

"I didn't get them anywhere, Mr. Miles. I've had them always. They were my mother's."

"Do you remember your mother?"

"Not to say remember. Look here, Mr. Miles, what's all this? They're nothing but a lot of old beads, aren't they?"

"I don't know," said Miles. "There's nothing for you to worry about, Flossie, but I wonder whether you'd mind letting us see the rest of the string?"

Flossie turned to the door—and turned back again. She looked from Miles to Lila, and from Lila to Freddy. Mrs. Gilmore was all worked up. Mr. Gilmore looked at her straight and gave a little nod. He said the same as Mr. Miles had said.

"All right, Flossie—nothing to bother about. But if you'd—"

Well, she hadn't anything to hide. She ran out of the room and came back with the beads still knotted up in her handkerchief—and thank goodness it was a clean one straight from the wash.

They were in the drawing-room. Flossie laid the handkerchief down on a small gold table and untied it. The loose beads and the knotted string shimmered under the light with that iridescent bloom. They weren't everyone's fancy perhaps, but there was something about them. She'd have been sorry if they'd broken in the street.

Lila was hanging on Freddy's arm and staring with all her eyes.

"Oh, my *sweet!*" she breathed. "Oh, Freddy—aren't they *too* marvellous?"

Flossie felt herself beginning to get angry. Her colour deepened. She said with some heat,

"They're my beads! They belonged to my mother! Aunt always says they did! And if there's anything wrong, I ought to be told what it is—I didn't ought to be kept in the dark!"

"We're going to tell you everything we know ourselves," said Miles. "Will you tell me just one thing more? Will you tell me how many beads there are in your string—or if you don't know, will you let me count them?"

"Course I know!" said Flossie. "There's three hundred. Leastways there did ought to be three hundred, but there was one I couldn't find when the string broke, and that's it what you've got in your hand."

There were three hundred pearls in Mrs. Macintyre's string. Three hundred black pearls, perfectly matched. And Flossie Palmer had been wearing them—not thinking very much of them—leaving them lying about...

Miles pulled himself up with a jerk, because Flossie's eyes were fixed on him in a firm, determined look. Freddy had been quite wrong about her bursting into tears. If there was going to be any nonsense about her character, she would fight. And Ernie would back her up; she made no doubt about that. She stuck her chin in the air and said,

"What's it all about? That's what I want to know."

"Well," said Miles, "Mrs. Gilmore—"

Flossie shifted a defiant blue gaze to Lila, and Lila said,

"Oh, Flossie—they're pearls—they really are."

Miles caught Freddy's eye. If Lila was wrong, what fools they were all going to look.

Flossie did not actually say "Coo!" but her lips formed the shape of that expressive word. Then she took a quick half breath and said,

"*Pearls?*" And then, "Not much! They're my mother's old beads!"

"They're pearls," said Lila—"they're black pearls. They're *too* marvellous!"

"How do you know?" said Flossie bluntly.

Freddy Gilmore came forward and put a hand on Lila's shoulder.

"Well, there it is, Flossie," he said—"we don't know. Mrs. Gilmore thinks they're pearls, but she's not an expert. It seems to me that we ought to have an expert's opinion. If you've really got a string of black pearls, it's very valuable."

Flossie's colour faded. She went up to Miles and took hold of his arm with both hands.

"Do you think they're pearls, Mr. Miles?"

"I don't know, Flossie."

"You were looking for a string of black pearls—you talked about it at dinner. You said there was three hundred pearls in the string, and I took and counted my beads to see how long that would be, and there was three hundred of mine."

He patted her shoulder.

"It's all right, Flossie—don't worry."

Her hands tightened on his arm.

"Mr. Miles—do you think my beads are what you was looking for? Is that what you think?" She released him suddenly and backed away. "Oh, it's not true! My mother *never*!"

Chapter Twenty-Three

IT WAS LILA who produced Mr. Montague. She summoned him imperiously on the telephone, and he came. Ordinarily of course Mr. Montague, who is the senior partner, is only to be seen in that inner sanctum of his Bond Street shop to which Royalties, millionaires, and customers of more than ten years' standing are admitted. You do not send for Mr. Montague unless you are a crowned head—or Lila Gilmore.

Lila was quite aware that he was her slave and treated him accordingly. He had known her since she was ten years old and considered her the most beautiful woman in the world.

He came into her gold drawing-room—a thin, ugly man with Jewish features and a pleasant cultured manner. Lila poured out her story.

"And they don't think I know. But, darling Mr. Montague, I tried the bead with my tongue like you told me, and it was *rough*, so I *must* be right, and you *will* tell them so at once—*won't* you?"

Mr. Montague looked at her indulgently. He was extremely sensitive to beauty, and Lila in her gold room rejoiced the artist in him, and the oriental. He looked from her to the others, the two young men—and the maid-servant. What a pretty girl! Not frightened—angry. What a skin when she flushed.

Lila put the knotted string into his hand, and all at once his expression changed.

"So—so—so—" he said, and ran it through his fingers. Then he looked up sharply. "How many?"

It was Flossie who said "Three hundred" in her defiant voice, and then, "They're not pearls—they're my mother's old beads."

Mr. Montague looked at her, then back at what he was holding, and then at Miles Clayton.

"Oh, Mr. Montague!" said Lila.

He gave her a fleeting smile, but spoke to Miles.

"They are pearls, of course. Mrs. Gilmore is perfectly right—as always. I think, Mr. Clayton, that I have a memorandum about these pearls. Everyone in the trade has a memorandum about them. I suppose you are the Mr. Clayton who is mentioned in the memorandum?"

Miles nodded.

"Very well, Mr. Clayton, then I will tell you that this is not the first memorandum I have had about these pearls, nor is it the first time that I have handled them. They came through my hands in—let me see— yes, two years before the war. I had an inquiry from Tiffany's, and I sent them out to America. They were bought by a Mr. Knox Macintyre. Then three years afterwards—yes, it was in the first year of the war— Mr. Macintyre wrote to me to say that the pearls had disappeared over here in England at the time of his wife's death. There were other jewels too. He asked my advice as to what steps he should take, and he offered a reward. Well, the usual things were done, but nothing came to light. Then, twenty years afterwards, I am told that you are coming over to look for the pearls. I must congratulate you."

Miles went over to Flossie.

"Look here, Flossie," he said, "there really isn't anything for you to worry about, but I think we shall have to go and see your aunt and find out what she can tell us about all this." He turned to Lila. "If you can spare her."

They went off together in a taxi, Flossie pale and silent, Miles wondering whether his mission had come to an end. He liked Flossie enormously, but what would old Boss Macintyre think about her for an heiress? And what about Ernie? And what about Flossie herself? It looked as if a good many apple-carts were likely to be upset.

Mrs. Palmer received them with a severe calm of manner. Even when Flossie said, "Ooh, Aunt!" and rushed into the story of the beads that were pearls—"And Mrs. Gilmore said as how they were, and I didn't credit her, but she fetched a gentleman that's got a jeweller's shop in Bond Street and he says so too"—even then Mrs. Palmer's composure was unshaken. She opened the parlour door, checked Flossie's outpourings by bidding her put a match to the fire, and having advanced the gent's easy-chair six inches for Miles, she took an upright seat upon the lady's ditto and said in a resolute voice,

"I'm glad to see you, Mr. Clayton. It's not three hours since I posted a letter asking you to come, but you won't have got it yet. I've got something to say to you, and to Flossie too. And now what's all this about her beads?"

Flossie turned round from the fire with the spent match in her hand.

"He says they're not beads at all—he says they're pearls. Ooh, *Aunt*! He says they're Mrs. Macintyre's pearls! But they was my mother's beads—Aunt, you know they was!"

"*Were*," said Mrs. Palmer with decision. "And I don't know how often I've got to tell you not to talk so careless—a grown girl like you!"

"Mrs. Palmer," said Miles—"will you tell us anything you can about the beads?"

She did not answer for a moment. Sitting there in her black afternoon dress with her high colour and stern eyes, and her neatly brushed grey hair, she seemed the very embodiment of respectability. Her brows frowned a little and her lips were pressed together. Then she said,

"I've got things to tell you, Mr. Clayton, but not about the beads. And you've got to hear them too, Flossie, so you'd better take a chair and sit down. As for the beads, they're neither here nor there so far as I know. Flo's sister, that was Ag Smith in those days, found them in the back of a drawer when she was clearing out her house. They'd got caught up between the drawer and the back, and the string was broken. Flo took a fancy to them, and she brought them along and strung them, and if they were pearls, there was no thought of it in her, nor in anyone else so far as I can say. Just old beads was all we thought, but Flo fancied them."

Miles drew a breath of relief. He had no doubt at all that Mrs. Palmer was telling the truth. Chance had saved Mrs. Macintyre's pearls from the woman who had taken the baby and the other jewels. He knew the type of cheap drawer which does not quite meet the back of the chest. He said,

"Mrs. Palmer, the beads are Mrs. Macintyre's black pearls. They have been identified by Mr. Montague who sold them to the American jeweller from whom Mr. Macintyre bought them."

Mrs. Palmer took this with unbroken composure. She said,

"That's neither here nor there, Mr. Clayton. You'd better listen to what I've got to tell you."

Flossie had seated herself on a small upright chair beside the centre table. She stared at whoever was speaking, her face brightly flushed and her eyes wary. How did she come out of this, and what was it all about? She didn't mind about the beads, not anything to speak of, but what made Aunt look at her like that? She didn't like it. It wasn't natural.

And then Miles said, "Please go on," and Mrs. Palmer began to speak.

"You'll think I ought to have told you yesterday, and I could say I wanted time to think it over, but that wouldn't be true. I'm going to tell you the truth. I wasn't going to, but I had a dream last night that I took for a sign, and I'm not going to fly in the face of it. Flossie, my girl, you've got to hear something you won't like, but there isn't any call for you to be upset about it neither. If Flo Palmer wasn't your mother, she loved you just the same as if she was, and no one's ever felt any different to you than if you'd been Palmer born as well as Palmer bred."

Flossie gave a startled cry and dropped on her knees beside Mrs. Palmer's chair.

"Aunt!"

"Now, Flossie, there's no need to take on, nor to forget your manners in front of Mr. Clayton. Get up and sit properly in your chair. An adopted child's just as good as a real one as far as I can see, provided it's cared for the same." Her tone was dry and bracing.

Flossie went back to her chair. She felt as if an earthquake had shaken all the accustomed foundations of her life. If she wasn't Flossie Palmer, who was she? It was just as if she wasn't anyone at all. Out of the confusion of her thought Ernie loomed up like a rock. Ernie wouldn't care who she was—*Ernie*... Then Miles' voice saying,

"Well, Mrs. Palmer?"

Aunt went on speaking.

"What I told you yesterday was all of it quite true, Mr. Clayton. I told you just exactly what poor Flo told me at the time, neither more nor less. Flo lost her husband and her child in July 1915 like I told you, and we were afraid she was going off her head. Then one day she came in to see me, and she told me she'd adopted a child. She said she'd got to have something. Well, I asked her where she'd got the child. She said from a Mrs. Moore. Then she pulled herself together and asked me not to repeat the name, which she needn't have done, seeing I'm not given to talking. Well, there it was—the child was a little girl about a year old, and Flo gave her her own name. That was all I knew about it for the best part of five years. And then when Flo was dying she told me some more."

Mrs. Palmer paused. It went very much against the grain to speak, but she'd got to speak. Flossie had slewed her chair round. She had her arms resting on the back of it, and she was staring at her very bright and hard as if she was trying not to cry.

Miles said, "Won't you please go on? What did Flo tell you?"

"I was sitting up with her," said Mrs. Palmer in her measured voice, "and she called to me and said, 'I want to tell you about Flossie. Someone ought to know.' I said, 'I'll look after Flossie—don't you fret.' But that wasn't what she wanted. She asked me if I remembered her sister Ag having a lodger that died when her baby was born, just before the war. And I did remember something about it, but not much. Flo was in Hampstead staying with her sister when it happened. Her husband was a sailor and he was at sea, and she was expecting a child, but she didn't know it then. Well, it seems that she took such a fancy to this Mrs. Macintyre's baby that she couldn't rest for thinking about it—it takes young women that way sometimes. But when the sister came and fetched the baby away and no address left nor anything, Flo said she didn't feel to be able to bear it, and when the cab drove away she jumped on her bicycle and went down to the station after it. She said she felt as if it was her own child being taken away and she'd got to know where they took it. Well, they went to London, and Flo went too. She put her bicycle in the cloakroom and got into the last carriage of the train. When they got to London they took the Underground out to Ealing, and so did Flo. She found out where they went, and she waited and saw them come away without the baby. She went home with the address, but she didn't tell her sister nor anyone."

"What was the address?"

"Mrs. Moore, The Laurels, Kempton Road," said Mrs. Palmer. "Flo used to go once a week and watch to see if she could see the baby. She got into talk with the tradespeople, and she found out Mrs. Moore was a widow that took in children. There were two or three of them there, all babies. And then she heard Mrs. Moore's maid was leaving—she only kept the one—and she had the crazy idea that she would offer for the place, but just about then she found she was going to have a child herself—and if she hadn't been in such a queer state of mind she'd have known it before. Well, her sister Ag Smith was breaking up her house and leaving Hampstead, and she'd a maid called Ada Mills that Flo was friendly with. What does she do but get this Ada to go after Mrs. Moore's place so that she could keep an eye on the baby for her. Well, it seems Ada took the place, and her and Flo used to meet and she'd tell her how the baby was getting along, and sometimes Flo would get a sight of it and sometimes she wouldn't. But when Flo had her own baby she stopped going. It was just a craze, and it went off like they do. And then she told me that when her husband went and the baby too, her craze for the Macintyre baby came back stronger than ever. She went down and she saw Ada, but she didn't see the baby. And she went again, and this time she saw Mrs. Moore. And Mrs. Moore told Flo she'd got the child left on her hands and no money being paid for it, and she as good as asked her would she take it away, because she couldn't afford to go on keeping it with nothing coming in. So Flo took the baby, and I shall always say it saved her reason. And nothing for you to cry about, Flossie, that I can see, for if she wasn't your mother by her flesh and blood, that's not everything, and she loved you a sight more than a lot of flesh-and-blood mothers love their children."

There was a silence, broken only by Flossie's sobs.

"Oh, my hat!" said Miles to himself. "That's torn it!"

He hadn't the very slightest doubt that he had arrived at the end of his search. Nobody could have listened to Mrs. Palmer without being sure that her statements were statements of sober fact. Flo Palmer had adopted the Macintyre baby. Flossie was Flossie Macintyre. He wondered what old Boss Macintyre would think about it all.

Mrs. Palmer had risen from her chair and was dealing firmly with Flossie's tears.

"Here's a clean handkerchief. Dry your eyes and take a hold of yourself or you'll be having hysterics, which is a thing I don't allow, and don't you forget it. And then up you go and wash your face. There's nothing to cry for that I can see. I'll put on the kettle for a cup of tea, and while it's hotting you can run around to the Hodges and see Ivy for five minutes. She came out of hospital last night, and the way Mrs. Hodge goes on about her looks, and her appetite, and what a lot she's changed is enough to send the poor girl melancholy. You go round and see her, and I'll have a word with Mr. Clayton when I've put the kettle on."

It was Ivy's name which arrested Flossie's tears. She sniffed, gulped, and ran out of the room. Mrs. Palmer followed her, and presently returned with a purposeful air. As she seated herself, the door banged and Flossie ran past the window.

"Now, Mr. Clayton," said Mrs. Palmer—"you've found what you were looking for. What I want to know while Flossie's out of the way is just what it's going to mean for her."

"And that's just what I can't tell you," said Miles. "Mr. Macintyre sent me over here to find his niece, and it looks as if I'd found her. What happens after that depends on him. I'm going to be perfectly frank with you. As things stand, as far as the Macintyre side of the family is concerned, Flossie gets a name, and her mother's pearls—at least

I should think she gets the pearls—but she doesn't get anything else. Her father, Mr. Knox Macintyre, left everything to his brother, and his brother can do anything he likes with it. He can play the markets, throw it into the sea, give it away in charity, or leave it to anyone he fancies."

Mrs. Palmer fixed him with her steel-grey eyes.

"You said, 'as far as the Macintyre family is concerned.' I'd like to know just what you meant by that."

"I meant what I said."

"I think you must have meant something more than you said, Mr. Clayton."

Miles laughed. After all there was no secret about it. Old Miss Basing's will had been in the papers. They had all had headlines like "Is The Macintyre Baby Alive?" and "Where is Miss Macintyre?"

He said, "Well, I did. You must understand that I'm only acting for Mr. Macintyre. But as a matter of fact an aunt of Mrs. Macintyre's left a lot of money to her or to her children if she had any."

Mrs. Palmer continued to look at him.

"It's getting on for twenty years since Mrs. Macintyre died."

Miles nodded.

"This old Miss Basing only died a few months ago. She made a will in Mrs. Macintyre's favour at the time of Mrs. Macintyre's marriage twenty-two years ago, and about a year later she went out of her mind. She was a certified lunatic until her death, so nothing could be done about getting her to make a new will after Mrs. Macintyre died and the baby disappeared."

"I see," said Mrs. Palmer. "And all that would come to Flossie?"

"If she's Miss Macintyre."

"Is it a lot of money?" said Mrs. Palmer very composedly.

"Yes, it's a lot of money," said Miles.

"And the most of it's vanity and vexation of spirit," said Mrs. Palmer.

Miles grinned suddenly. He couldn't help it.

"Nobody worries very much about that," he said.

Mrs. Palmer's glance reproved his levity.

"You can speak for yourself, Mr. Clayton. Money's not always a blessing. There was my own sister that was married to a man with a nice little cycle business, and he came in for five thousand pounds from an aunt that no one would have thought had a penny to leave to anyone.

And what was the fruits of it? First thing, he bought a motor-car and went riding all over the country lunching at public houses and getting a taste for the drink. And the next thing, he took up with going to horse-racing and playing cards—and worse than that—and all my poor sister could do was to keep the business going as well as she could. And in the end he ran off with another woman and left her with four children to bring up, and I'm thankful to say they all turned out steady. But that's all that five thousand pounds did for my brother-in-law—led him into drink and riotous living that he hadn't got neither time nor thought for when he had to work. And if I hadn't had what I took to be a sign, I'd have held my tongue about Flossie. If you'll excuse me, Mr. Clayton, I'll go and have a look at that kettle."

The tea was excellent. The cups were old cottage Worcester, though only Miles knew it. An old cousin of his mother's had some. To Mrs. Palmer they were her grandmother's tea-set, produced when occasion warranted. They had not been produced for Ernie. They lived in the oak corner-cupboard which was not considered good enough for the parlour. It hung on the dark side of the kitchen, and Mrs. Palmer had always refused to part with it, because she remembered it in Gran's cottage when she was a little girl.

Flossie came back in the middle of tea. She was white and silent, and she wouldn't eat anything, though she kept on passing up her cup to be filled. She said, in response to direct questions, that Ivy was all right, and yes, she'd got the bandages off. And then she was up out of her chair and saying she must be getting back, and Mr. Miles would be coming too, wouldn't he, because what was she going to say to Mrs. Gilmore? She passed behind Aunt's chair as she spoke, and fixed an imploring gaze on Miles' face. Her lips formed words, but the fact that they were trembling said as much as any words could have done. Miles was being implored to come with her. He responded by thanking his hostess and making his farewells.

As soon as they were out in the street Flossie clutched at his arm.

"Ooh, Mr. Miles—I *am* frightened!"

"What's frightened you, Flossie?"

She looked over her shoulder nervously. The dusk was gathering, but there would be daylight of sorts for another twenty minutes or so.

"Ooh, Mr. Miles—they know that it wasn't Ivy!"

For the moment Miles had forgotten all about Ivy Hodge. He felt slightly bewildered. Flossie's clutch tightened on his arm.

"Ivy, Mr. Miles—Ivy Hodge that I went to 16 Varley Street instead of because of her making it up with Billy and wanting to get married. I told you I took her name and all. And when she got pushed in the river, I got a most awful turn, because she never done it herself—reely she never—and it come to me like a flash that it was me they were trying to get rid of."

Miles remembered all about Ivy Hodge. He said,

"All right, I've got there. What's happened?"

"They know it wasn't Ivy that was at 16 Varley Street."

"How do you know that?"

"Because Ivy told me. She said there was a nurse came to see her in hospital, and the way she described her it was Nurse Long. And so soon as she saw Ivy she looked at her awful straight, and she said, '*Your* name isn't Ivy Hodge.' And Ivy said it was. And after that she asked her a whole lot of questions about her last place, and whether it was a good one, and why she left. And in the end she got Ivy so tied up that she let on about its being a friend that had gone to Varley Street to oblige her—only she didn't tell her the name because of getting me into trouble for using her character. And she wouldn't have said what she did only for being muzzy in the head—poor Ivy! But there, Mr. Miles— they know, and 'twon't be long before they find out that it was me that took the job. And I'm frightened, Mr. Miles—I'm *frightened*!"

Miles did not speak at once. He had never felt at all clear in his own mind about Flossie's tale of what had happened on the night she ran away from Varley Street. The whole thing was so—the word *disconnected* slipped through his mind—that he couldn't really bring himself to believe in it. He thought Flossie was frightened, but he inclined to believe that she was frightening herself. It might have been her own face she had caught sight of in the mirror—she had said there was a mirror—and some trick of the light or of her imagination, or both, had startled her into panic flight. She might have dreamed her blood-stained head and her man with the cruel eyes looking out from the hole in the wall. She might have had a momentary vivid memory-picture of something seen at the cinema or read about in a book. Any of these things was more probable than that she had actually seen what she said she had seen. If he believed her, it was his bounden duty to make her go to the police with her story, but quite frankly he did not believe her. As to Ivy Hodge having been pushed into the river, it was all nonsense.

He spoke soothingly to Flossie, and she lost her temper with him.

"Might as well call me a liar at once and have done with it!" she declared.

Chapter Twenty-Four

AT TEN MINUTES to nine that evening Miles knocked on the area door of 16 Varley Street and Kay slipped out to him. He so very nearly kissed her that he spent the next five minutes in wondering, first, why he hadn't, and after that, what she would have said if he had. It had seemed such an extraordinarily natural thing to do that he had nearly done it without thinking at all. Kay and he—he and Kay. There was a belonging feeling between them. That was it, they belonged. He didn't know whether he was in love with her, but they belonged. He hadn't felt in the least like that about Angela. Being in love with Angela had been a heady, exciting sort of affair. He had been all strung up—everything working at top speed—a restless, racing fever in his blood. No, it wasn't at all like that.

He heard Kay saying in a reproachful voice,

"You know, you're not listening, Miles."

He laughed. He didn't quite know why, but it was nice to laugh at Kay.

"No, I wasn't. But I was thinking about you."

Kay laughed too.

"I don't believe you were."

"Oh yes, I was. I was thinking you were a comfortable person to be with."

"It sounds like a sofa cushion."

"And very nice too."

"Mushy!" said Kay.

"Reposeful," said Miles.

They both laughed. Kay tugged at his arm.

"You didn't listen—and I was telling you about rescuing the kitten from the cellar. Wasn't it dreadful of Mrs. Green to make it sleep down there? And oh, Miles, there *must* be rats. I think it must have bitten one, the little brave thing, because first of all I thought it had been bitten itself, and then I found it hadn't, and—oh, Miles, do you think Mrs. Green could possibly find out if I waited till she was asleep—it's quite easy to tell, because she snores—and *then* fetched the kitten and had it in my room? Because in the morning she wouldn't know I hadn't just let it out—would she? Or do you think it would be very deceitful? It's so tiny and young, and I can't sleep when I think of its being down there with the rats."

Miles put his arm round her and gave her something between a hug and a shake.

"Oh, Kay—you little funny thing!" he said.

"I'm not! Miles, *do* you think it would be very bad of me?"

He burst out laughing.

"I should chance it. If the kitten got eaten, you'd probably never forgive yourself."

"No—I shouldn't. Oh, Miles, I've got something to tell you."

He still had his arm round her. It seemed a good place for it to be. If Kay minded, she didn't say so. The Square was dark and unfrequented.

"Miles, you're not listening. Do listen! You know that man who spoke to me in the street—I've had a letter from him... No, it's quite a polite letter, and I don't think you ought to say things like that, because perhaps it was silly of me to take it the way I did. He really did know Aunt Rhoda and—my mother. Come under a lamp-post and I'll show you what he says."

Under the next lamp Miles took the sheet of stiff white paper and looked at it curiously. It was one of the more expensive makes of paper, but it was not stamped with any address. Instead there was a typed heading with yesterday's date. The body of the letter was also typed. It ran:

"DEAR MISS MOORE,

I fear I startled you yesterday, and I fear I offended you by using your name. I will not repeat my offence without your permission, but I saw you often as a child and it is natural for me to think of you as Kay. Your aunt, Mrs. Moore, was a very old friend of mine, but it is as your mother's daughter that I feel, and always have felt, the deepest interest in you. Some day, if you will give me the opportunity, I should like to talk to you about your mother. You are quite right to be careful about what acquaintances you make, but I happen to know your present employer, and if you will ask Miss Long, she will, I am sure, tell you that I am to be trusted. It would give me great pleasure if you would have tea with me on Sunday. I understand that you will be free then. There is not much time to get an answer, so I will call for you at four o'clock.

Yours sincerely,

A. HARRIS.

"It's Sunday to-morrow," said Kay. "How did he know I was going to have an afternoon out? He must have asked Nurse Long. I don't really want to go."

Miles stared at the letter. The signature was typed too. That was unusual. He said,

"I don't want you to go, Kay."

"But he's coming for me at four."

"And I'm coming for you at half-past two," said Miles firmly.

Kay gave a little gurgling laugh.

"Oh, Miles—how lovely! But won't it seem rude?"

"Let it! You've got a previous engagement. You can tell him so. You can tell him you've got a young man who walks out with you, reg'lar, as Flossie would say."

Her colour brightened and her eyes shone.

"Oh, Miles—but—"

"But what?"

"I do want to hear about my mother."

"Then he must ask us both to tea. You're not going without me. I want you to promise you won't."

Kay said "All right," with a sigh of relief. It was bad of her to dislike poor Mr. Harris, but she couldn't help it. The thought of having tea with him gave her a little cold shiver down her back. She put the letter away in her pocket, and they walked on.

"Kay," said Miles—"who was your mother? What exact relation was Mrs. Moore to you? If you were her own niece, your name wouldn't be Moore—would it?"

Kay said, "I don't know. Miles, isn't that funny? I don't know anything at all about my father or my mother. Aunt Rhoda always got very angry if I asked. She said wasn't she enough for me? And—oh, Miles, you know what she was like when she was angry."

Miles did know. He had a vivid recollection of Rhoda Moore's white face and burning eyes, and the abuse which she had poured out during that odious scene in his mother's hall when Kay was saying good-bye to them all. It was plain enough that the woman would tolerate no claim on Kay but her own. Poor little Kay...

He said, "Yes, I know. Never mind, darling."

Kay pressed closer to him. His arm came round her again.

"Kay," he said, "some rather odd things have been turning up. Do you know if your aunt ever had charge of any other children besides you?"

"I think so. She told me once that she knew all about babies because she used to take charge of them. She said she had a baby whose mother was in India, and another whose mother had died. She said it was a lot of trouble and people didn't pay. And then she said what she was always saying, that she didn't want anyone but me and I oughtn't to want anyone but her."

What a woman! Flossie had been lucky to be adopted by Flo Palmer. His poor little Kay! He held her close to him, but he did not speak. He did not feel as if there was any need for him to speak.

After a minute Kay said, "Miles, I want to tell you something. Aunt Rhoda was ill for some time. I think she knew she was going to die. She said she hadn't any money to leave me, because what she lived on was an annuity, but she said I would be all right. She said some very funny things."

"What sort of things?"

"Well, sometimes she spoke as if I was going to have a lot of money. Once she said, 'Nobody will ever love you like I have. That's better than money. Don't you ever dare to look back and reproach me.' It—it was—rather frightening, Miles."

He felt her quiver.

"Darling—don't!"

"No, I won't. It was only for a moment. And another time she said, 'You'll be rich, but you needn't think that's everything.' And she always ended up with, 'Nobody will ever love you like I have.' I—I've never told anyone else. I never felt I could."

Miles was thinking more of Kay than of what she was saying. Rhoda Moore was probably wandering. Her jealous love for Kay had always had something crazy about it.

Kay went on speaking.

"And then she began to write. She wasn't in bed all the time, you know. She used to sit up in a chair, and she made me fetch her old desk and put it by her, and then she wrote and wrote. She said, 'I'm putting it all down, but you're not to dare to read it till I'm gone.' "

Miles' interest woke up. If Rhoda Moore had really left a statement of some kind, there might be something about Flossie Palmer in it. He said,

"She *wrote*?"

"Sheets and sheets," said Kay. "I couldn't stop her. And when she had finished she put them away in the secret drawer of her desk. It was a funny old thing with a secret drawer, and she showed me how to open it, only I had to promise that I wouldn't as long as she was alive. She died about a week later."

"Kay, what had she written?"

"I don't know."

"You don't know? Didn't you read it?"

"No. That's the odd part. I was going to, but I thought I'd wait till the funeral was over. I was so tired. I had been sitting up with her. I just wanted to lie down and go to sleep. I didn't care about anything else. But afterwards when I thought about the desk and went to open it, it wasn't there."

"The desk wasn't there?"

"No. Wasn't that extraordinary? It was gone—just vanished. So I never knew what Aunt Rhoda had written."

"But, Kay—who could have taken it?"

He felt her come a little closer.

"Miles, I couldn't tell anyone else, but I do think Aunt Rhoda had some very queer friends. She said things when she was ill—bits of things, but I couldn't help putting them together. Once she said, 'It's no good threatening me.' And another time she woke suddenly with a dreadful start, and she said, 'Is he here?' I said, 'Who, Aunt Rhoda?' and she said, 'It's not his real name. He won't tell anyone that.' And then she said, 'Don't let him in. I know too much. It's not safe to know too much, Kay. That's why I never told you anything, but you'll know all about it when I'm gone.' She went on saying that sort of thing. And I don't know, but I think perhaps someone came down and took the desk when they knew she was dead. It was quite an easy house to get into, and I'm sure I shouldn't have heard anyone those first two nights, I was so tired."

"Kay—you weren't there alone!" his tone was a horrified one.

"Oh yes—I didn't mind that. Mrs. Ellery didn't know, or she wouldn't have let me. She'd been away, and as soon as she came back she made me come to them, and I stayed on as mother's help. She was the Vicar's wife I told you about. She was very kind to me."

They walked on for a little while in silence. Rhoda Moore's statement seemed to have been effectually disposed of. Kay's explanation sounded likely enough. Her odd friends had doubtless considered it safer to make sure of her papers. He had a horrid vivid picture of the house that was "quite easy to get into," with Rhoda Moore lying dead in her room and Kay sunk deep in an exhausted sleep, while some unknown criminal went soft-foot up and down. Perhaps he had ransacked the dead woman's drawers and boxes. Perhaps he had stood looking in on Kay in her sleep. In the end he had taken the desk and gone. But why take the desk? Perhaps he had been disturbed. Perhaps... What was the good of speculating? The desk was gone, and Rhoda Moore's statement with it. She might have saved herself the painful, fevered effort of writing those lost sheets. Her secrets, if she had any, had died with her. After all it didn't matter very much. Kay was Kay. He didn't need Rhoda Moore to tell him that. Let the dead past bury its dead. With every look, and word, and tone of her voice Kay was telling him about herself. With every passing moment his own heart was telling him about Kay. There was a living present and a living future. He didn't give a damn for the past or Rhoda Moore.

He said, "Kay, do you mind?"

Kay didn't mind anything in the world just then. To have a friend, and for that friend to be Miles, to be able to tell him all the things she had never been able to tell anyone before, was to feel a happiness and a security which were beyond words. She said with a little laugh,

"How do you mean, *mind*? There just wasn't anything to mind."

He laughed too.

"I'm afraid your riches have taken wings."

"I don't want to be rich."

"I've got about six hundred a year besides my salary. It's something to put one's back against."

To Angela it had seemed grinding poverty. To Kay it appeared to be a most impressive income. She said with a little gurgle of laughter,

"I haven't got six hundred pence. But I don't mind—not now."

They were getting into deeper water than either of them had intended. The ground had shelved suddenly beneath their feet and the current ran strong. Miles had not meant to say what he had said, but when he had said it he did not wish to take it back, because it was the most natural thing in the world that he and Kay should be talking like this. He said,

"Why don't you mind—now?"

Her answer was as quick and spontaneous as if she had still been only twelve years old.

"Because I've got you. Oh, Miles, it's so lovely to have a real friend! I've never had anyone to talk to or to tell things to. You know, I couldn't talk to Aunt Rhoda. She used to come in sometimes after I was in bed, and she used to sit on the edge of the bed and say, 'You don't tell me things. Why don't you confide in me? I want to know your thoughts, and you hide them.' But you know, Miles, when she talked like that I simply hadn't got any thoughts to tell. She just made me feel all hollow and dry and empty. It's dreadful to feel like that when someone is loving you and wanting you to love them."

"Don't let's talk about Rhoda Moore," said Miles.

"What shall we talk about?"

"You and me."

Kay laughed. She didn't quite know why.

"All right—you begin."

"Kay—"

"Miles—"

"Kay—"

"Yes?"

The current took Miles off his feet.

"If—if I asked you to love me, would it make you feel all cold and hollow and empty?"

It made Kay feel the exact opposite. There was an astonishing warmth, a feeling of being fed and comforted.

"Oh, Kay, *would* it—would it?"

Kay didn't answer, because something seemed to have happened to her voice. The breath fluttered in her throat, but it did not make any words. They were between two lamp-posts and the darkness closed them in. She turned with a childish unconscious movement and lifted her face to his. Her hair brushed his cheek, and in a moment he had his arms round her and was kissing her.

Chapter Twenty-Five

THERE WAS a letter waiting for Miles Clayton when he got back to his hotel. It had a neatly typed address and he took it to be a circular of the more exclusive kind, but on opening it discovered an enclosure addressed in violet ink to the box number which he had given in his advertisement. This second envelope contained a sheet of ruled paper upon which he read in an untidy handwriting:

"DEAR SIR,

I was formerly Ada Mills as per your advertisement and beg to inform you I am now Mrs. Gossington and quite willing to oblige in any way at the Horse and Groom, Lea Hill Road, Perry Green, Essex.

Yours truly

MRS. A. GOSSINGTON."

Well, she was a day after the fair, but it would be just as well to have Mrs. Palmer's statement corroborated by someone else. He had better go and see this Gossington woman to-morrow morning. Ian's car would come in useful again if he didn't happen to be wanting it himself. He would have to fix that up in the morning. But whatever happened, he must be back in time to meet Kay at half past two, and on Monday at latest she must leave that house in Varley Street. If he had had anywhere to take her, she wouldn't be there now.

He considered his plans. Three hours should cover this Gossington business. If he was back in town by half-past twelve, that would give him two hours to find somewhere for Kay. Now that they were engaged, he could appear in the matter. If necessary Lila must give a hand— there were hostels, and people who took in paying guests. Then at half-past two he would call for Kay, tell her what he had arranged, and if possible get her to come away with him then and there. If this wasn't possible—and he had a feeling that Kay might be obstinate about it— then he would give her until Monday morning, but not a moment later.

Having settled all this, he let himself go back to thinking about Kay—just Kay herself. A few hours before he had not known whether he was in love with her or not. Now he was most humbly, triumphantly, and gloriously sure of it. It wasn't in the least like being in love with Angela, because of course he had never really been in love with Angela at all. He had been miraculously preserved from a marriage which would have wrecked his happiness. Horrible to think that he might have married Angela and never met Kay at all, or that having married Angela, he might have met Kay too late. He was made for Kay, and Kay was made for him. She was romance, but she was also home, the home of his heart. Everything about her was as dear and familiar as if the years that had separated them had been lived out side by side, and yet the glamour and the dream were there too.

He passed a night almost entirely without sleep, planning with a good deal of enthusiasm the future which he and Kay would share. He would probably have to find another job, but that didn't matter in the least. He felt in himself a complete ability to achieve any one of fifty jobs. Nothing was difficult. Nothing was impossible. In such a mood it would be sheer waste of time to sleep. The night was all too short for his dreams.

It was something of a come-down to drive through miles of East End streets with a small public house as his objective.

Perry Green still boasted a green, but the pear trees from which it had once taken its name were now no more. Street upon street of small new villas and small new shops obliterated the very site of what had been green fields not so long ago. He discovered Lea Hill Road somewhere in the middle of this eruption of houses. The Horse and Groom, which had begun life upon an open country road, stood about half way up the rise. It had taken to itself a new front hung with mustard-coloured tiles, but the old sign still swung shabbily in the wind.

Miles found himself presently in a parlour behind the bar shaking hands with Mrs. Gossington. She was a large, hearty woman with a high colour and a rolling eye. Her hand was warm and rather damp. She wore a bright blue dress that might with advantage have been a size or two larger and an inch or two longer.

Miles began to explain why he had come, and was most hospitably pressed to take a seat.

"I thought as much," said Mrs. Gossington; "As soon as ever I saw the advert I said to my 'usband, 'You mark my words, Henery, it's that there old business a-cropping up—you see if it isn't. I've always had a feeling in my bones about it, and if anyone's going to make trouble, well, it wasn't nothing to do with me.' And my 'usband says to me, 'You leave it alone. What's it got to do with you anyway?' But as I says to him, 'That's all very well, but suppose someone's been and left me a fortune—what about it then?' So I answered the advert."

She had a jolly, fat voice, and was, as she had stated in her letter, quite willing to oblige. He could see her twenty years ago as a buxom, good-natured girl with a roving eye. He wondered what she was going to tell him.

"Well now, Mrs. Gossington," he said—"you were with Mrs. Smith in Laburnum Vale when Mrs. Macintyre had her baby and died in July 1914. And afterwards—some months afterwards—Flo Palmer persuaded you to go to Mrs. Moore at Ealing because she had discovered that the Macintyre baby was there."

"That's right," said Mrs. Gossington. "I went to oblige her—and not so sorry to leave Mrs. Smith neither. Funny how set Flo was on that baby. I won't say it wasn't a pretty little thing, because it was, but I can't understand anyone wanting to clutter 'emselves up with someone else's kid. 'Tisn't natural to my mind. But there—there's all sorts in the world."

"Yes," said Miles. "Now, Mrs. Gossington, would you mind just telling me in your own words what happened to the Macintyre baby?"

Mrs. Gossington's rolling eyes came to rest upon his face in an odd half hesitating look. He thought it meant "How much do you know already?" He smiled encouragingly and said,

"I'd be most awfully grateful."

"Oh well," said Mrs. Gossington, "you might as well have it. I can hold my tongue when there's a reason for it, but I'm not one of your close sort and never was. You may believe me or you may not, but I'd sooner tell the truth any day of the week. I only done it to oblige Mrs. Moore, and I don't see where the harm came in, and as I said to my 'usband last night, it's twenty years ago or getting on that way, so I don't see how anyone's going to make trouble about it now."

Miles reassured her.

"There won't be any trouble, Mrs. Gossington. If you would just tell me what happened—"

"Well, Mr. Clayton, it was this way. I went there to oblige Flo Palmer like I said. I always liked Flo—different as chalk from cheese to Mrs. Smith she was. Did you say you'd met her? She's Mrs. Syme now, isn't she? And what two men wanted to marry her for passes me. But Flo was different."

"You were going to tell me what happened to the Macintyre baby," said Miles.

Mrs. Gossington laughed a jolly laugh.

"So I was, and so I am. Well then, I went to Mrs. Moore, and it was the funniest place I ever lived in, I can tell you."

"In what way?"

"Well, there was Mrs. Moore, that wasn't the sort of woman you'd expect to look across the road at a child, and she'd got three of 'em there to look after, all babies. And why she was doing it, goodness knows, for it wasn't for what she earned by it. Time and again I had to wait for my wages and we'd be living on porridge and odds and ends of stews and things, and she told me right out that the people who had left the children with her weren't paying."

"There were three children?"

Mrs. Gossington nodded.

"Three babies—all girls, and all about the same age."

"Did you know which was the Macintyre baby?"

"Know? Of course I knew! That's what Flo got me to go there for, to keep an eye on it. Besides she was the prettiest little thing I ever saw. In a way you could understand why Flo was so crazy about her."

"Won't you go on?" said Miles.

"All in good time, Mr. Clayton. Well, there I was, and not best pleased with my place. Flo stopped coming, because she had a baby of her own, and I'd have left only for my wages being held back. And then in July—July '15—Flo started coming again. She'd lost her 'usband and her baby, and she was pretty near out of her mind pore thing. She told me she was, and she said if there was one thing that would stop her going right off her head, it was the baby of Mrs. Macintyre's that she'd always had such a fancy for. And when she found that no one ever come to see it or wrote, and how short the money was, she got me to say I'd speak to Mrs. Moore and find out whether there was any chance she'd let Flo have the baby to adopt."

This was Mrs. Palmer's story over again. Miles felt a little bored and a good deal relieved. He didn't know why he should have felt relieved, but he did. It was ridiculous that he should have had any misgiving as to what Mrs. Gossington would say.

She went on in her comfortable, leisurely manner.

"It happened money was as short as short just then. There was one of the babies—her mother was in India. She'd left her with Mrs. Moore from the month and gone out to her 'usband right at the beginning of the war, and the 'usband was killed in Mespot, and sometimes she'd send a cheque and sometimes she wouldn't, and after a bit she didn't write but to say she was going here and going there, and it was all heathen names as long as your arm."

"Mrs. Gossington, how do you know all this?" said Miles firmly.

She laughed with enjoyment.

"How do you think? I read the letters of course. I'd my wages to think of, and a duty to find out whether there was any money coming. But this Mrs. Lestrange, she was one of the sort that'll send you a hundred pounds one time and then forget about you for a year on end. When she sent a cheque it was a fat one, but the people that had planted Mrs. Moore with the Macintyre baby they never sent nothing at all, so I thought maybe Flo had a chance of getting what she wanted."

"And she did?"

Mrs. Gossington winked.

"In a manner of speaking," she said.

"Do you mind tell me what you mean by that?"

"All in good time, and no need to be in an 'urry. I put it to Mrs. Moore, and she went all stiff and haughty which she'd no call to do, and she said, '*Impossible!*' and she walks out of the room and bangs the door. But in a day or two she'd come to talking about it all in the way of how it couldn't be thought of, but I could see she was turning it over in her mind."

"And in the end she said yes?"

Mrs. Gossington winked again.

"Well, she did and she didn't. She told me to tell Flo she could come and see her, and Flo came and they had a talk, and the upshot of it was Flo came into the kitchen and sat down and burst out crying, and 'Ada,' she says—that being my name—'Ada, I've got her—I've got my baby.' And she cried fit to break her 'eart."

"And she took the baby?"

"Don't you be in an 'urry, Mr. Clayton. She sits there and cries, and Mrs. Moore she calls me into the dining-room and she puts it to me straight. She says, 'Look here, I can't let her have that baby, not for anything in the world—not if they never paid another penny. It'd be as much as my life was worth if so be they should ever turn their minds to the child again and want her. I've got to keep her whether I want to or not, but if your friend's so set on having a baby, there's one she can have and welcome.' And the minute she said that, I knew what she was up to."

Miles wasn't bored any longer. One part of his mind was saying 'I told you so,' and the other was full of a half shocked anticipation. He said rather breathlessly,

"Go on."

"As fast as I can," said Mrs. Gossington. "I told you there were three children, didn't I? There was the Macintyre baby, and the Lestrange baby, and there was the little thing that Mrs. Moore said was a niece but I'd my doubts about it. The same age as the others she was, and a pretty little fair thing with blue eyes. And as soon as Mrs. Moore said that to me I knew what was in her mind. She dursn't let Flo have the Macintyre baby, but she'd be pleased enough to get the one she said was her sister's child off of her hands. She put it to me straight, I'll say that for her, and she said, 'Your friend won't know the difference.' And I said, 'She may or she mayn't,' for it was getting on for six months since Flo had set eyes on the Macintyre baby. 'Well,' says Mrs. Moore, 'she *don't* know the difference, and that's that. I took and showed her the other one, and she cried all over the top of its head and said she'd have known it anywhere.' Both fair babies they were, with blue eyes and fair hair and a bit of colour, and this little thing was pretty enough, but the Macintyre baby beat anything I ever did see for looks."

"Mrs. Gossington," said Miles, "which baby did Flo Palmer have?"

She gave her jolly laugh.

"I'm telling you, aren't I? You're in such an 'urry, Mr. Clayton. Well, Mrs. Moore put it to me straight, and it didn't take me long to make up my mind. There was pore Flo Palmer breaking her 'eart for a baby, and there was a baby that nobody wanted, and I couldn't see any harm in bringing 'em together. It'd just about save Flo from going off her head, and the baby'd get a good 'ome. So there you are. I said yes to it, and I've never reckoned I did anything wrong."

"Oh, *Lord!*" said Miles to himself. Aloud he repeated his former question. "Which baby did Flo Palmer have?"

Mrs. Gossington rolled her eyes reproachfully.

"Haven't I told you?"

"Well, I want it in plain words."

"Hard to please, aren't you? But you can have it any way you like. Flo Palmer had the baby that Mrs. Moore said was her sister's child, and that's the truth, and the whole truth, and nothing but the truth, Mr. Clayton."

"I'll have to ask you to sign a statement," said Miles.

Chapter Twenty-Six

MRS. GOSSINGTON wrote out her statement and signed it, and Miles took it back with him to town. He drove fast, but his thoughts ran faster. He had got to get back, have something to eat, and be at 16 Varley Street by half past two to fetch Kay. Round this definite purpose those racing thoughts of his whirled like the grains in a sandstorm—hard, pelting,

stinging thoughts over which he had no control. He had come over here
to find Miss Macintyre. He had found Kay. They had found each other.
They loved each other. He had come over to find an heiress for old Boss
Macintyre. He had found Kay. *He had lost Kay.* She was Kay Macintyre.
She was Boss Macintyre's heiress. She was his employer's niece. He had
lost her. "*No, I'm damned if I have!* You've lost her. You're bound to
lose her. You can't in common decency hold her to it. She won't need
holding. Boss Macintyre's heiress. What's it going to look like, you
coming back and saying you're engaged to her? Mud—that's what your
name will be—common, dirty mud. And no one in the world is going
to believe that you got engaged to Kay when you didn't know who she
was." The thoughts went on, stinging, pelting, burning.

By and by the storm of them died away. He could order his thinking
again. He would have to write a new report for to-morrow's mail. Flo
Palmer had adopted Rhoda Moore's niece, and not the Macintyre baby.
Therefore Kay was not Rhoda Moore's niece at all. She must be Kay
Macintyre. Rhoda Moore's references to Kay having plenty of money
were now explained. It seemed clear that the woman who posed as Mrs.
Macintyre's sister had only taken the baby because she could hardly
leave it behind. She was after the jewels, and having planted the baby
on Rhoda Moore, she had vanished into the blue.

Or had she? He wasn't sure. Rhoda Moore had told Ada Gossington
that she didn't dare get rid of the child—it was as much as her life was
worth. He wondered whether Ada had invented the phrase. She had
stuck to it when she made her statement. And there was Kay's story
of the man who had looked out on her in the garden and looked in on
her when she was supposed to be asleep, and Rhoda Moore's "What a
suspicious mind you've got!" And then the odd way Kay had come to
London and to Varley Street, and the episode of Mr. Harris. It all looked
as if someone had been keeping an eye on her, never quite losing touch,
shepherding her, and just at the moment when she was on the edge of
being declared an heiress getting ready to close in. It looked like that
to him, and he didn't like the look of it. *Now*, whatever happened, Kay
must leave Varley Street this afternoon. He would take the car round
and fetch her away bag and baggage. If necessary he would interview
Miss Rowland or the nurse himself. In the circumstances, he felt equal
to bearding the stiffest aunt and demanding her hospitality for Kay.

Afterwards? He set his jaw and looked grimmer than one would have supposed possible. They must break off their engagement—but he meant to marry Kay in the end. It would mean getting another job, but it would mean getting another job without any help from Boss Macintyre. He couldn't have married as a secretary anyhow, but it had certainly been at the back of his mind that old Macintyre could very easily help him to a job which would make marriage possible. Well, he couldn't take advantage of that now. That didn't mean he wouldn't get a job. He intended to get one. And he intended to get Kay.

He snatched a hasty lunch, drove the car round to Varley Street, descended the area steps, and rang the bell. In a minute Kay would be there at the door and he would tell her that he had come to fetch her away. He wasn't going to stand any nonsense about it either. Ten minutes to pack, and perhaps ten minutes for the necessary explanations, and they would be driving away together in Ian Gilmore's car.

He woke up out of this to realize that no one was coming to the door at all. In a mood of angry impatience he put his thumb on the bell and kept it there. A faint distant tinkling encouraged him. Of course Kay might be upstairs... The tinkling continued. He wondered if Kay would hear it if she were a couple of stories up. Well, if somebody didn't come soon, he would go up the steps to the front door and see what could be done with the knocker.

He took his thumb off the bell, and at the same moment the door opened. As soon as he saw it move he knew that he had been afraid. His anger and his impatience had been fear—fear of what might have happened to Kay in this house to which she had been shepherded.

He said "Kay!" in rather a breathless voice, and then the door opened about half way and he saw it was not Kay who stood behind it, but a very fat old woman in a flowered overall. She had untidy grey hair, and she bulged in every direction. There was a black smudge over one eye, and her hands looked as if she had just been putting coal on the fire. Undoubtedly Mrs. Green. Kay must be upstairs.

He smiled pleasantly and said, "Good afternoon. I've come to call for Miss Moore."

Kay was upstairs—she must be upstairs. Once again he knew that he had been frightened, because when Mrs. Green said "She's upstairs," his heart gave a jump and it came to him that he had not known what she might be going to say. Suppose she had said that Kay had gone away, or that she was ill, or that she was—dead. Why should he have a horrible thought like that? He felt the sweat break out on his temples as he said,

"Will you tell her—I'm here. She's expecting me."

Mrs. Green looked at him with interest. As nice a young fellow as she'd seen this twelve-month, and quite the gentleman. Some girls had all the luck. She said in her soft, wheezing voice,

"Well there—she can't come out, and that's all there is about it."

Miles was angry again. It wasn't like him to be angry, but he was hard put to it to hold on to his temper. Mrs. Green, describing the scene afterwards, declared that he had right down flashed his eyes at her.

"She can't come out?" said Miles. "Why can't she? It's her afternoon out, isn't it?"

"Well," said Mrs. Green, "she's to get every other Sunday—but there's nothing to say when it starts."

"But she told me—"

"She come last Sunday, and if she took it into her head she'd get her afternoon off to-day, well, she was mistook, and that's all about it. You come back next Sunday and maybe you'll 'ave better luck."

Next Sunday! He controlled himself with an effort.

"Mrs. Green, can't I see her for a minute? I've got something most awfully important to say to her."

A faint sly smile played about Mrs. Green's chins.

"Save it up," she said. "'Twon't hurt with keeping."

"Look here, Mrs. Green—I must see her."

Mrs. Green shook her head.

"Not now you can't. She's up with Miss Rowland. Nurse is out, and she's to sit there till she comes back in case of 'er wanting anything."

Miles' heart went down into his boots.

"Mrs. Green—couldn't you send her down just for a minute? I mean, couldn't you stay with the old lady?"

Mrs. Green leaned against the doorpost and shook with silent laughter. All her chins shook too.

"Oh lor!" she said when she got her breath. "You and your 'Send 'er down'! How am I going to get 'er, do you suppose? Why, young man, I been here five years and I never been up that basement stair but once, and then I stuck at the turn. You and your 'Send 'er down'! Oh lor!"

"And what happens if anyone comes to the front door?"

"Nobody do," said Mrs. Green, still shaking.

"Well, suppose I do—suppose I go and bang with the knocker? What happens then? She'd have to come down, wouldn't she?"

Mrs. Green stopped laughing rather suddenly and shook her head. "I wouldn't do that."

"She'd have to come down," said Miles.

Mrs. Green shook her head again.

"She can't leave the old lady, not if it was ever so. Look here, you don't want to make trouble—do you? The old lady's resting. If you're all that keen on seeing the girl, you come along back about nine o'clock or so like you done last night. And now you'd best be off or you'll be getting 'er into a row."

She stepped back a great deal more quickly than he could have supposed possible and shut the door.

Chapter Twenty-Seven

ON SUNDAY MORNING, while Miles was driving down to Perry Green in search of Mrs. Gossington, Kay was busy as usual with her house work. There really was plenty to do in the tall old house. If there had been much coming and going, she could not have coped with it single-handed, but from day's end to day's end nobody rang the front door bell except the postman. She had been a week in Varley Street, and even he had only rung three times. Twice he had left a circular addressed "Occupier," and the other time he had brought the letter which Mr. Harris had written to Miss Kay Moore. Neither Miss Rowland nor Nurse Long appeared to have any correspondence. This did not really strike Kay as very strange, because she had lived for years with Rhoda Moore who hardly ever received a letter. The post, to Kay, was associated with bills, circulars, or those occasional letters which used to send Aunt Rhoda to her room in grim-faced silence.

This morning Kay thought she would spend a little extra time on the drawing-room. As she worked, she pleased herself with a game of make-believe. Supposing this was her house, and the drawing-room her drawing-room, how would she furnish it? She had just begun with a plain Axminster carpet in a sort of camel-colour, when it occurred to her in the most vivid and exciting manner that if this was her house and her drawing-room, it would be Miles' house and Miles' drawing-room too, and she hadn't the slightest idea whether Miles would like a plain camel-coloured carpet.

She sat back on her heels with her carpet-brush in her hand and her dustpan in front of her and earnestly considered this problem. Miles wouldn't want a Brussels carpet with wreaths of flowers all over it like this one. That sort of carpet was definitely dead. Even she knew that. But suppose he liked the sort which Mrs. Marston had had—jags of orange and scarlet and black like a thunderstorm gone crazy... No, he wouldn't. Eleanor Clayton's drawing-room rose before her reassuringly. Miles couldn't possibly want a thunder-and-lightning carpet after that.

By the time she had got into the L, she was trying to decide whether she would have camel coloured curtains or not. The sort of green velvet ones that look like moss would be rather nice, and the chair covers could have a pattern of vine leaves and grapes, or—she remembered a linen with a drifty pattern of autumn leaves. She wasn't sure about the autumn leaves. You might get tired of things that went on drifting.

She finished the floor and got up from her knees. There were two or three bits of furniture at this end of the room that really did need polishing—the piano, and the old-fashioned mirror with its carved and gilded frame. She wasn't quite sure what to do about the gilding. It was dreadfully dirty, but furniture polish mightn't be good for it. She thought she would try a little bit where it wouldn't be noticed and see what happened. She didn't like doing floors very much, but she really did love polishing things and leaving them bright and clean.

She put a little polish on her duster and came up close to the mirror. She had never seen one quite like it before, and she admired it very much, only she would have hung it between the windows in the front part of the room, not here in the narrow L where you couldn't see it properly. It was too big to be where it was. It must be quite six foot high. She wondered where she could try her polish. Not on the big shell at the top. Perhaps one of these curly acanthus leaves.

And then all of a sudden she saw the crack. It gave her the sort of startled shock which comes from something quite unexpected, something which doesn't seem possible. How could there be a crack all down one edge of the glass? She had done this room every day for a week, and if the crack had been there, she must have seen it, because she had dusted the glass every day. She stood with her duster in her hand and gazed at the crack. It ran the whole way down the right-hand edge beside the gilded frame. If you stood a little to the right of the mirror, you couldn't see it at all. If you stood a little to the left, it looked as if the glass had started from the frame. And she had dusted it six days running, and there hadn't been any crack...

That sense of having been rather violently startled went on. She put out her hand—not the one with the duster in it, but her left hand—and touched the crack. Until she touched it she had a little hopeful feeling that it might be just a shadow pretending to be a crack, but when her fingers touched the hard, cold edge of the glass something that was the very opposite of hope came banging and thumping into her thoughts. It confused and scattered them, and set her heart knocking against her side.

All down the right-hand side of the mirror the glass did not meet the frame by a quarter of an inch or more.

More—more—more—

She snatched her hand away and stared at the gap between the edge of the glass and the edge of the frame. It wasn't a crack now, it was a gap. When her fingers had tightened on the glass, the glass had moved. Between the brightness of the gilding and the brightness of the mirror there was an inch-wide strip of darkness.

The glass had moved. Her fingers had contracted a little, and, quite easily and silently, the glass had moved. She went on staring at it with the vague fascinated feeling that at any moment it might move again.

It did not move.

After what seemed like a very long time Kay put out her hand and took hold of the edge of the glass. She hadn't planned to do this, but she did it. She hadn't even known that she was going to do it, or that she had done it, until she felt the edge of the glass against her palm. Her fingers slipped through the inch-wide gap and felt the space behind it. That was the first clear thought that came to her—there was a space behind the glass. It ought to have had a wooden back, but there wasn't any back. There was only space.

She pulled suddenly upon the glass, thrusting at the edge with her palm, which lay across it, and this time the glass moved a foot or more, running easily, as a wheel runs in a groove. There was no weight or resistance, and there wasn't the slightest sound. Her hand moved again, and the glass went right out of sight into the wall. Only the carved and gilded frame remained, with the scallop shell in high relief and the border of acanthus leaves and twining stems. The mirror wasn't a mirror any longer, it was an open door. Kay was standing so close to it that a single step would take her over the lower edge of the frame and through this door.

It was a very frightening thing that there should be a door in the wall like that. Frightening, but terribly exciting—and romantic.

The sense of shock was passing. It was like being in a dream when things suddenly change and dissolve. It was like being in a fairy-tale and feeling that anything may happen at any moment.

She leaned forward and peered into the dark place on the other side of the wall. It was not very large, perhaps a little longer than the width of the mirror. It had a depth of about two and a half feet and a height of something over six feet.

Kay stepped over the frame with its gold acanthus leaves and looked curiously about her. The glass of the mirror ran into a slot in the wall. There was a little handle on this side with which you could pull it out again. She didn't know how you would shut it from the drawing-room. She supposed you would have to put your hand inside and find the handle, and finish up by pushing the glass with your fingers. It mightn't be easy. A tingling terror went over her. Suppose she couldn't shut the glass from the drawing-room side. It was quite easy from this side, but suppose she couldn't shut it from the drawing-room...

She stood in the dark narrow cupboard, her hand on the knob which controlled the glass, and all at once she heard a sound which made her knees feel exactly as if they were made of melting wax. Someone was opening the door which led into the front part of the drawing-room. Without stopping to think, she pulled on the knob she was holding and easily, smoothly, and silently the glass slid back until it filled the frame.

Kay stood in the pitch dark and trembled like a leaf. All the things she had ever been afraid of in all her life rushed into her thought. Aunt Rhoda when she was angry. The eyes of the man who had looked out at her when she was a child playing in the garden, and his voice—the voice which had made her quake with terror when he had stood with Rhoda Moore at her bedroom door looking, looking, always looking at her. Why should she think about these things now? It was because she was frightened, and because these were the things which sprang up in her mind when she was frightened. These things which she remembered were not just frightening things. They were fear itself.

She stood there shaking and heard Nurse Long's voice calling her.

Nurse was going out. She wanted to tell Kay she was going out. That was what it would be. Always before she went out she would tell Kay that she was going, and she would say, "Miss Rowland won't be wanting anything. Keep the house quiet and don't disturb her on any account." Kay knew the phrase by heart. But what would happen if Nurse Long couldn't find her? Would she go on looking until she discovered that Kay wasn't in the house at all? Or would she just take it for granted that she was busy downstairs and go out? She had done that on Wednesday when Kay was cleaning the silver.

Kay stood gripping the handle which she couldn't see and saying in an agonized inward voice, *"Please let her go.* Oh, please, please, *please* let her go."

That lasted a long time. Kay didn't know how long it lasted, but it was a long time. Her hand was stiff on the knob. Her whole body was stiff. She didn't know how long it went on. Then all of a sudden she heard the front door shut, and the stiffness went out of her and left her all weak and relaxed.

Nurse Long had gone out. The front door made a thudding sound when it was shut, and Nurse Long always shut it with a bang. She had gone out, and she would be gone for an hour at the very least. Most probably she wouldn't be back until one o'clock. She was supposed to have two hours' off every day. Sometimes she took them in the morning, and sometimes in the afternoon, and she always said not to disturb Miss Rowland on any account.

Well, all that Kay had to do now was to slide the glass back, step over the frame into the drawing-room, and then close the mirror door behind her. Nurse Long had gone. It was quite easy—it was quite safe.

It was *dreadfully* dull.

The weak, shaky feeling had passed and little waves of tingling excitement were running over her. The ditch-water dullness of going back into the drawing-room and getting on with her dusting made absolutely no appeal. She simply must find out where this door led to and why it was there. If she opened the glass into the drawing-room, it would let in the light, but after she had lifted her hand to the knob she dropped it again. Suppose Nurse Long hadn't really gone out. Suppose she was there in the drawing-room—waiting... This was nonsense, and Kay knew that it was nonsense, but all the same she didn't feel like sliding that panel back. She turned right round as she stood, groped for the opposite wall, and began to feel upon it for something, anything, that would tell her what kind of wall it was.

Well, it wasn't really a wall at all. It was wooden panelling. She felt up and down and on either side of her, and almost at once she found a little metal bolt, and beneath it an iron latch. The bolt was drawn back. She raised the latch and pulled. Nothing happened.

Doors don't always open towards you. With her hand still on the latch she pushed, and the wall of darkness before her split in two. She was in a cupboard with a door that opened outwards. She saw a handsbreadth of carpet and wall, and at once pulled the door towards her again.

Suppose there was somebody there... Her heart thumped uncomfortably. She put her ear to the crack and listened, but there was no sound at all. She opened the door an inch and listened again. There was still no sound. She pushed it six inches or so and looked out. What she saw was the first-floor landing of the next-door house. She was in a wooden cupboard which stood against the party wall, and she looked out at a landing which was exactly like the first-floor landing of No 16. Two doors opened upon it, one facing her and the other facing the stairs. They would both lead into the drawing-room, because all the drawing-rooms in this sort of house were L-shaped and had two doors. The stairs came up to the landing from the hall with one short turn and went on with another to the bedroom floor above. She might have been looking into No 16 if it had not been for the colour of the walls and the pattern of the stair-carpet. The walls here were yellow, and so was all the paint, and the stair-carpet was rather a bright brown with a black and orange pattern on it; whereas the walls of No 16 were grey, and the carpet a plain grey hair-cord, rather worn.

Kay pushed the door a little farther and listened. There wasn't a sound of any sort or kind. The silence wasn't an ordinary silence. It seemed to belong to the house and to be a part of it. She found herself wondering how long it was since anyone had made a sound there. Dreadful to be the person who broke a silence like that.

It came to her with the most complete conviction that the house was empty, and in the strength of that conviction she opened the door quite wide and stepped out upon the landing. She had not made the least sound. The carpet was soft and thick under her feet.

Who lived in this house? And why was there a door through the wall into No 16?

She took a step forward and turned. And then she saw the stain. The carpet was good, and thick, and new, but there was a stain upon it just where she had been standing outside the cupboard door. It wasn't a very large stain. It was about the size of her hand, and it had been rubbed and sponged, but it showed. The bright brown was discoloured, and the orange of the pattern had gone dull. She wondered what had been spilled there, and thought what a pity it was.

She crossed the landing and looked down over the stairs. There were six steps and a little bit of passage, and then a sharp turn, exactly like No 16. Only the walls and the stair-carpet were different—and the stains. As she stood looking down, she could see three or four more of those odd dull stains. If Flossie Palmer had seen them, she would have thought with a shudder of the head, and the clawing desperate hand which she had seen for a moment framed in the gilt acanthus leaves which ought to have been framing a mirror. Flossie was quick, and she did not lack imagination. She might have guessed at a wounded man crawling painfully—step by difficult step—half fainting—with the blood running down and making those stains which would never quite come out. Kay only thought how careless someone had been, and what a pity it was about the new carpet.

The sense of the house being empty grew stronger and stronger. She began to feel excited and adventurous. If the house was empty, why shouldn't she explore it? The Kay who had been brought up by Aunt Rhoda and always made to do exactly what she was told gave a sort of gasp and said, "*You can't!*" But another Kay who had been getting the upper hand more and more ever since Aunt Rhoda died said in tones of the most dreadful scorn, "Yes, that's you all over, you horrid little coward! People who are afraid never get *any*where or do *any*thing. You might just as well be dead and have done with it." And with that a bright, flaming colour came into Kay's cheeks and she ran upstairs without giving herself time to think, because she knew she would despise herself for ever if she didn't. The only way to keep Aunt Rhoda's Kay in her proper place was instantly to do the thing which she said you couldn't possibly do.

She ran without stopping round the bend and up the remaining steps to the bedroom landing. Her feet made no sound, because the carpet was so very soft and thick. She arrived a little breathless, not because she had run upstairs, but because of the struggle with the Kay who was a coward. She had downed her, and that gave her a pleasant don't-careish sort of feeling.

She stood still and looked about her. Not that she needed to look, because she knew already that there would be two doors, and the stairs going on up to the top floor. The only thing she hadn't known about was the cupboard. It was a twin cupboard to the one below, and it stood against the party wall in exactly the same position. Kay stared at it, and all sorts of thoughts came into her mind. Was it a real cupboard, or had it just been put there to hide a secret door like the one on the floor below? And if a door was a secret door, why didn't they keep that cupboard locked? There was an easy answer to that. They wanted to be able to come and go from either side.

Kay didn't like this answer very much. It gave her a most horrid creepy feeling all down the back of her neck. *They*—who were *They*? She didn't know. She didn't want to know. It came to her very quick and sudden that it would be dreadfully dangerous to know. And sharp on the heels of that she knew that it was very dangerous to be here in this empty, silent house.

She turned and put her hand on the balustrade, and as she did so, the house was empty and silent no more. Someone was coming up the stairs.

Chapter Twenty-Eight

KAY'S HEART gave such a frightful jump that she felt for a moment as if she were going to faint. It was only for a moment, but she hadn't any moments to spare. She looked down over the banisters and saw a man's black coat sleeve—just the bit of it between the shoulder and the elbow, foreshortened. And then she didn't wait to see any more. She ran to the cupboard door and opened it, and stepped inside and shut it after her, and then with desperate fumbling fingers she began to feel for the knob which would be somewhere in the back panel if the cupboard was like the one on the floor below. *It might be a real cupboard, and then she would be lost.* This wasn't reason; it was terrified conviction. If it was a real cupboard, why was it empty?

Her fingers found the knob, and her heart gave another jump, but this time it was a jump of joy. But the knob wouldn't slide. *It wouldn't slide.* The knob downstairs slid sideways, and the glass of the mirror went into the wall. This knob wouldn't move. It wouldn't move at all.

And then all at once it moved a little. It didn't slide, but it moved. It turned in her clutching fingers as a door-handle turns. That was it, it was a handle with a catch like the handle of an ordinary door. She turned it as far as it would go, and the panel at the back of the cupboard came swinging in. There was only just room for it. She had to squeeze against the side of the cupboard to let it pass her. And there wasn't any light. There was an open door in front of her, but there wasn't any light.

She felt with her foot and went forward, groping for the door and pulling it to behind her. It shut with the faintest little click, and there she was. Yes, but that was the trouble—where was she? She ought to be in Miss Rowland's bedroom, but she was in something like another cupboard, dark, and close, and stuffy. That bewildered sense of not knowing where she was swept over her like a cloud racing before the wind. It was hardly there before it was gone again. She *was* in Miss Rowland's bedroom, but she was inside the big dark wardrobe which faced the door. The wardrobe and the cupboard in the next-door house had only one back between them, and this back had hinges and opened like a door. She was inside Miss Rowland's wardrobe, and these soft stuffy things which smothered her were Miss Rowland's dresses.

What on earth was she going to do next? If Miss Rowland was asleep and she could creep out very, very quietly... If... Something in the back of her mind said with dreadful distinctness, "*There's someone on the landing behind you. Perhaps they're coming through.*"

Just half way through those dreadfully distinct words Kay had opened the wardrobe door. She only opened it an inch, and it encouraged her very much to find that her hand was steady. If Miss Rowland was asleep, she could get out of the room and no one would know. She put her eye to the crack and looked out.

Miss Rowland's room was just like the drawing-room, and the wardrobe occupied exactly the same position as the mirror did in the room below. There were two doors, one of them in the front part of the room and the other immediately facing Kay as she looked through the crack. The bed stood between this second door and the back window. The head was away from Kay and the foot towards her. There was a light Japanese screen between the bed and the door.

Kay had forgotten the screen. She had only once been inside the room, because Nurse Long kept it in order, and she had forgotten the screen. It almost hid the bed, and she couldn't tell whether Miss Rowland was asleep or not. All that she could see was the brass foot-rail and a wedge-shaped piece of Miss Rowland's crimson eider-down. She could see about two feet of this on the far side of the bed, but on the near side it narrowed to a point and the screen interrupted her view. It was a red screen with golden storks and bullrushes. There was a crimson carpet on the floor, and crimson curtains were drawn quite across the windows in the front of the house and partly across the window by the bed, so that the room was not really light, but full of shadows and of an odd warm twilight.

Kay saw all this as one picture. She didn't think about it or disentangle the details. It was just there in her mind as a picture, and there was nothing in the picture to tell her whether Miss Rowland was asleep or awake. The drawn curtains suggested that she was trying to sleep—but even Kay didn't always go to sleep when she wanted to.

She got as far as that, and turned giddy with fright. Behind her, but not so very far behind her, a footfall sounded upon wood. She knew exactly what that meant. It meant that someone had just opened the cupboard door on the bedroom landing of the next-door house and, having opened it, had stepped inside. And that could only mean one dreadful, terrifying thing—the man she had seen on the stairs was coming through the wall after her. Miss Rowland, either asleep or awake, was nothing to this—

Kay did not hesitate at all. The instant she heard the sound she was out of the wardrobe and running for the door. She had enough presence of mind to shut the wardrobe door behind her. She gave it a back-handed push as she jumped out. She had only to run a few steps and she would be safe. She would be safe if she could get out of the room without being seen.

And then she was at the door, and the door wouldn't open. It wouldn't open. Kay had a sick moment of terror. The door was locked, and the key wasn't there. She threw a desperate glance over her shoulder and saw the closed wardrobe in all its Victorian respectability. But as she looked, she saw something else. The screen didn't meet the wall by a foot, and what she saw was the bed head, and the crimson eiderdown drawn neatly up to meet the untumbled pillows. *And the bed was empty.*

This too was a picture. At the moment it meant nothing, because her mind had stopped working. She was dominated by the primitive instinct of the hunted. Escape—she must escape before the wardrobe door opened.

She ran into the front part of the room and round to the other door. It was locked, but the key was in the lock. She heard a sound behind her. She turned the key and opened the door, and ran as Flossie Palmer had run, taking the stairs at a flying break-neck speed and never stopping until she was safe in the basement. She sat down on one of the kitchen chairs and felt the kitchen heave and rock.

Mrs. Green was standing over the range with her back to her, stirring something in a saucepan. Her hand went round and round, and the kitchen went round and round, and Kay's thoughts went round and round...

Presently the kitchen stopped. Mrs. Green went on stirring. And Kay tried to order her thoughts. As far as she could make out, Mrs. Green was telling her all about a proposal she had once had from a fishmonger in a very good way of business—"And only two things against it, and maybe I was a fool not to know which side my bread was buttered, but if there's a thing I can't abide it's raw fish, and thank goodness they're not much struck on fish here, though cooking a nice bit of sole now and again is one thing, and living with marble slabs and blocks of ice and cold dead fish all around is another and what I didn't feel as I could put up with, let alone that I 'ated the man with all 'atred."

It seemed quite a good reason for not having married him. Kay made the sort of vague acquiescent sound which you make when you can't think of anything to say. She was too busy with those pictures in her mind to have anything to say to Mrs. Green.

The bed was empty.

As she turned her head to look at the wardrobe, she had seen round the screen, and the bed was empty. It wasn't only the bed that was empty. The room was empty too. Miss Rowland wasn't there. She wasn't in her bed, and she wasn't anywhere else. Kay had seen the whole room as she ran to the other door, and Miss Rowland wasn't there.

These were her first conscious thoughts about the pictures in her mind. There had been two pictures, a picture of Miss Rowland's room as she had seen it from the wardrobe, and a picture of Miss Rowland's room as she had seen it from the door. In this second picture the bed was empty and the room was empty. But now the two pictures slid together in her mind and became one picture, so that when she looked at it she could see the whole room at once. She could see the bed with the eiderdown drawn up to meet the unruffled pillows. She could see a chair with a chintz cover and crimson cushions, and the washstand, and a little table with books on it, and in the front part of the room an old-fashioned couch, and a desk, and the drawn curtains with the light coming through them in a red glow. She could see a dozen details that she hadn't consciously seen at the time. The picture showed her the room and all its furnishings. But it didn't show her Miss Rowland, because Miss Rowland wasn't there.

Chapter Twenty-Nine

"AND MY ADVICE to you," said Mrs. Green, "or to any other young girl for the matter of that, is don't you be too picksome, or you may find you've got left. Not but what there's worse things than living single. If it's for the name of the thing, you can clap on a Mrs. as soon as not and keep yourself to yourself and not have the clutter and upsettingness of a man about the place, which if he doesn't drink you're lucky, and if he does your life is 'ell. So when I turned forty-five I called myself Mrs. Green and 'ad done with it, and nobody's business but my own that I could see. It wasn't only the forty-five, you know, but when you come to fifteen stone and over, Mrs. do seem more suitable as you may say."

Kay made that vague sound again. Mrs. Green's soft throaty voice was like running water. It made a background for her thoughts. It went on and on, and it made her feel safe enough to think about the things that she had got to think about.

The picture in her mind was fading. She couldn't see the details any more. And with this fading there came a reaction, and the whole experience took on a dream-like quality. It was a most horrid dream, but she was waking up. It couldn't really have happened. She hadn't really gone through the drawing-room mirror like Alice through the Looking-glass and come back by way of Miss Rowland's wardrobe. Put like that, it was the sort of thing you couldn't possibly believe. *But it had happened...* It couldn't have happened. And if it *had* happened, she had frightened herself for nothing. If someone had walked upstairs in No 18, that wasn't anything to be frightened about. People could walk upstairs in their own house, couldn't they? And as for Miss Rowland not being in her room, that was just nonsense. The curtains were drawn and the room was nearly dark.

All at once Kay over-reached herself. The picture she was calling up was more terrifying than the picture she was trying to destroy. It was less frightening to think that the room was empty than to believe that Miss Rowland had been there all the time watching her from the red shadows.

Mrs. Green turned round from the fire.

"Aren't you doing no work this morning, Kay?" she inquired. "Somebody left you a fortune or something? You can't have finished upstairs, not in the time you can't. And Nurse called down the stairs afore she went out, wanting to know where you was, so I said you'd just stepped out into the yard, and she says 'All right.' What you been up to?"

Kay's cheeks burned.

"Nothing, Mrs. Green."

"Then suppose you do get up to something and get on with your work, my girl!" said Mrs. Green.

Kay went out of the kitchen and stood on the steps leading up from the basement. It was no good having cold feet and wobbly knees. She had got to finish her work. She had got to finish dusting the drawing-room, or at the very least she must fetch away her dust-pan and brush. If she didn't it was as good as a confession that she had seen what she hadn't been meant to see, and *that*—yes, *that*—would be dangerous. She was sure that she had got out of Miss Rowland's room without being seen. She told herself very firmly about this. But she had had to unlock the bedroom door and leave it open. They couldn't be sure about the door being locked. They might have forgotten to lock it. They hadn't seen her. They couldn't have seen her. *They*—who were *They*?... She mustn't think about that. It was much too frightening. She must just go on as if nothing had happened, and in less than three hours Miles would come and call for her, and she would let him take her away. She wasn't going to be proud about it any more. They would tell Nurse Long that she was going to leave at once, and Miles would take her away.

She went upstairs to the drawing-room feeling a good deal fortified. She wasn't going into the back part of the room where the mirror was except to pick up her cleaning things and her dust-pan and brush. After that she would finish dusting, but with one eye on the mirror, so that if the glass began to move, she could run helter-skelter downstairs to Mrs. Green.

She finished her dusting, and did a little more polishing too. The glass behaved as a looking-glass should. It reflected what was there for it to reflect, and seemed to be as incapable of movement as the solid wall.

When she had finished the drawing-room she went downstairs and did the dining-room. Every single minute was bringing Miles nearer, and as soon as he came she would ask him to take her away.

Nurse Long came back at one o'clock. She was in her nurse's dress—Kay had never seen her without it—and she came and stood at the dining-room door and looked coldly in.

"You are going out this afternoon," she said.

"I'm going away," said Kay to herself, but she hadn't the courage to say it out loud. She simply must wait for Miles, and Miles would be here in an hour and a half. So she coloured a little and didn't speak.

Nurse Long didn't seem to expect her to say anything, for she went straight on.

"I met Mr. Harris when I was out. He tells me he is very kindly taking you out this afternoon. He seems to have known your aunt rather well. And by the way, he asked me to tell you that he would call for you at two o'clock, so you'd better hurry up and get Miss Rowland's tray."

Kay's colour fairly flamed.

"I'm not going out with Mr. Harris!" she said.

"He seems to think you are."

"That is because he didn't give me time to answer his letter. I'm certainly not going out with Mr. Harris. I don't know him."

Nurse Long looked at her with rather an odd expression. It was cold, but behind the coldness Kay had an idea that she was amused—and angry. She said,

"I think you'd better go. He is calling for you at two."

Kay was now so angry that she had stopped being frightened. She was too angry to speak. She pressed her lips together and shook her head.

"You'd better," said Nurse Long.

Kay shook her head again.

"Do you really mean it?"

"Of course I mean it!" said Kay with her chin in the air.

Nurse Long turned round and went out of the room.

Kay went down to get the tray. She was still angry, and she was very glad to be angry, because being angry stopped her being frightened, and what had been frightening her more than anything else was knowing that she would have to take up Miss Rowland's tray. It was like a dreadful shadow across the path, and she would have to go through it before she could get to the place where Miles was waiting to take her away. If she could only keep on being angry, she might be able to do it. But as she propped open the basement door and went down for the tray, she felt the anger beginning to drain out of her, and when she got to the kitchen Mrs. Green wasn't ready with the cutlets.

Miss Rowland had a very good appetite for an invalid, and so had Nurse Long. Very little that was sent upstairs ever came down again, and they both liked their meat well done. There were cutlets and mashed potato and a vegetable, and a shape of calves-foot jelly.

"And another ten minutes I'll be at the very least of it. Better say quarter of an hour," said Mrs. Green.

Try as she would, Kay couldn't go on being angry for a quarter of an hour. She ran along the passage to her own room and finished her packing. When she had put her out-door things ready on the bed and locked her box, she began to feel that she really was going away with Miles. It was a quarter past one, and he would come and call for her at half-past two. If Mr. Harris chose to call at two o'clock, he would get no for an answer, and that was that.

She went back into the kitchen and found Mrs. Green dishing up.

All the way upstairs she had to fight against a cold, sick feeling of fear. It was no use telling herself that there was nothing to be afraid of, because what she wanted to do was to drop the tray and run for her life out of the front door and down the street. You may want to do things like that, but you can't really do them. Kay wasn't twenty yet, but she had often had to do things that frightened her, and she had never yet run away from what she had to do. Life with Rhoda Moore had at least taught her self-control. As long as she was in Miss Rowland's service she must do the work that she had been engaged to do, and it was part of that work to carry up Miss Rowland's tray.

She went up the last flight holding tightly on to the thought of how lovely it would be to be coming down again. She had only to knock at Miss Rowland's door, give the tray to Nurse Long, and run, run, run downstairs again to the basement where her box was locked and her coat and hat laid all ready for her to go away with Miles.

Between the two doors on the landing there was a small table. Kay rested the tray upon it and knocked on the nearer door, and at once it was opened, and there was Nurse Long, still in her outdoor things. She took the tray, and it was just as if she was lifting a cold, heavy weight from Kay's heart. Now it was over. Now she could run down the stairs.

She turned to go, and Nurse Long said,

"You'd better hurry and have your lunch if you're going out. You can come up for the tray as soon as you've finished." And with that she went back into the room and Kay ran down.

It was frightfully stupid of her, but she had forgotten that she would have to fetch the tray. She wasn't running down the stairs for the last time after all, because she would have to go up for the tray. Perhaps Miles would be early. If she knew he was waiting outside, she wouldn't mind going up again. Perhaps...

She and Mrs. Green had rabbit stew and a suet pudding. Mrs. Green ate so heartily herself that she didn't notice whether Kay ate anything or not. Kay couldn't eat. She put a little gravy on her plate and kept the potatoes between herself and Mrs. Green, and when it came to the suet pudding she said she wasn't hungry. Mrs. Green didn't mind who ate, or who didn't eat, as long as she had plenty herself. She put away two helpings of the stew and an incredible amount of suet pudding, and she talked all the time.

But in the end Kay had to go upstairs for the tray. She ran, because the quicker she went, the quicker it would be over. When she came to the last turn she had to stop and get her breath. It was new for her to be out of breath after running upstairs. She stood still for a moment, and what must she think about horridly, suddenly, and vividly, but the stains on the next-door stairs—stains where something had been spilt and the carpet had been rubbed and rubbed but the marks had never quite come out. *Bloodstains never quite come out.* It was such a dreadful thought that Kay ran away from it.

She ran up six steps to the bedroom landing and knocked on the door as she had knocked before. This time it didn't open, but Nurse Long's voice said, "Come in." There was nothing in that. Only two days ago the same thing had happened, and Kay had gone in and fetched the tray. She went in, and there was the wardrobe facing her, and the Japanese screen on her right, only now it was drawn up close to the wall so that she couldn't see the head of the bed.

Once she was actually in the room, she wasn't so much afraid. Everything looked very comfortable and old-fashioned. The crimson curtains were drawn across the windows towards the street, but plenty of light came in through the window which looked out at the back.

Kay went round the screen and saw Miss Rowland sitting up in bed propped with pillows. She wore an old-fashioned night-cap with a frill, and she had a big white cross-over shawl about her shoulders. Nurse Long was at the window, and as Kay came round the screen, she pulled the right-hand curtain so that the light no longer fell upon the bed. The tray was on a little table which had been pulled out from the wall. But before Kay could take it up Miss Rowland spoke to her in her deep quavering voice.

"You are going out this afternoon."

Kay said, "Yes, madam."

Miss Rowland looked at her out of the red shadow cast by the curtain, and Kay had again that odd feeling of recognition. She didn't like it. It frightened her. She stooped to take up the tray, but Miss Rowland spoke again.

"Nurse tells me you are going out with Mr. Harris. It is very kind of him. I am pleased that you should go."

Kay stood up straight. Why did they want her to go out with Mr. Harris? They couldn't make her go. She said politely but firmly,

"I can't go out with Mr. Harris, because I'm going out with a friend."

"Better go with Mr. Harris," said Miss Rowland.

There was a funny smell in the room like the smell of a chemist's shop. Kay loathed it with a sudden passionate loathing. She said, "I'm afraid I can't," and she stooped again to pick up the tray.

As she did so, Miss Rowland nodded, and Nurse Long turned quickly round from the window with something white in her hand. The smell which was like the smell of a chemist's shop became overpowering, and all at once, and before Kay could touch the tray, there was a thick soft pad over her nose and mouth, and two very strong hands were holding it there. She tried to scream, and she couldn't scream. She put up her hands and tried to tear the pad away, and as she did that she saw Miss Rowland throw back the bed-clothes and jump out of bed. Her cap fell off, and her woolly shawl fell off, and she had a close-cropped head of dark hair, and she had on a man's striped shirt and a pair of grey tweed trousers. Kay saw this, and then she stopped seeing anything at all, but she heard Miss Rowland say in a man's deep voice which seemed to come from a long way off, "Mind you don't give her too much." And then she went down, and down, and down into a deep place where she could neither hear nor see. Fear went with her, but in the end there wasn't even fear. There wasn't anything at all.

Chapter Thirty

HALF AN HOUR later Miles Clayton was being sent away by Mrs. Green. He was a good deal more disturbed and disappointed than the occasion seemed to warrant. He couldn't very well force his way into the house and burst into the bedroom of an invalid old lady to insist that Kay should leave with him at once. One of the disadvantages of being brought up in a civilized society is that it gives you tiresome inhibitions about this sort of thing. The natural man in Miles was all for shoving Mrs. Green out of the way, finding Kay wherever she might be, and removing her with a strong hand and no damned nonsense about it. Had he followed this impulse, it is just possible that he might have surprised Miss Rowland in those incongruous grey tweed trousers, and everything might have happened a little differently. As it was, the inhibitions were too much for him, and he went away in a state of champing impatience. He hadn't the slightest intention of waiting till nine o'clock. Nurse Long would be bound to be back by half past four or so to give the old lady her tea. Meanwhile he had better go and see the Gilmores about Flossie. Since it now seemed that she was not Flossie Macintyre but Rhoda Moore's niece, the sooner this was made quite clear the better it would be for everyone.

Flossie opened the door, and it was perfectly plain that she had been crying. Her eyelids were swollen and pink, and so was her pretty little nose. As Miles walked in, she sniffed a most woe-begone sniff and said,

"Mrs. Gilmore's out, Mr. Miles."

"Good Lord, Flossie—what's the matter?"

Flossie shut the door and burst into tears.

"I'm sure I wish I was dead!" she said, and dabbed her eyes with a handkerchief already sodden.

Miles took her by the arm and marched her into the dining-room.

"You'd better tell me all about it. Mrs. Gilmore won't mind. What's been happening?"

Flossie sat down on one of the dining-room chairs and looked up at him through her long, drenched eyelashes.

"I don't care if I never see Ernie again!" she declared.

Not a very tactful fellow Ernie. A bit class-conscious too. He had probably been renouncing the Macintyre heiress with plain-spoken scorn. From Flossie's rather incoherent remarks this appeared to be the case, and it had naturally incensed her very much. If there was any breaking off to be done, she was the one to do it. Furthermore it would have been one thing to be nobly renounced in the humble adoring manner so popular on the stage and in romantic fiction, and quite another to be scornfully discarded as belonging to a class detested by the true Marxian. Ernie, it seemed, was Red, and though not averse from a partnership in a garage with the giddy height of proprietorship in view, yet drew the line quite firmly at everything else of a capitalist nature.

"Him to have the neck to talk about bloodsuckers, and exploiting wage-slaves, and all the rest of it! And to say he wouldn't demean himself to marry a girl out of a capitalist family! Which I said to him, 'Ernie Bowden,' I said, 'you may think yourself lucky if you ever get married at all,' I said. 'And it won't be me,' I said, 'not if it was ever so,' I said, 'and not if you went down on your bended knees and begged and beseeched me till you was black in the face,' I said. 'And I'm sure whoever she is, I'm sorry for her, pore thing—I am reelly—for she won't know what a bargain she's getting till it's too late! And I'm sure I've reason to be thankful as I've found you out in time, for a more miserable girl there won't never be than the one that's got to call herself Mrs. Ernest Bowden—which it isn't me and never will be!" I said. The words came pouring out, accompanied but not impeded by dabbings, and sniffs, and gulps.

When she stopped for breath, Miles said,

"Poor Ernie! But you wouldn't have married him if you'd been an heiress, would you, Flossie?"

Flossie was sharp. Flossie was uncommon sharp. The handkerchief dropped from her eyes, and her first angry stare gave place to a look which combined intelligence and relief.

"What do you mean, Mr. Miles?"

"Well, you wouldn't—would you?"

Flossie brushed that away. It wasn't any of his business anyhow—not whether she married Ernie it wasn't.

"You said *if*, Mr. Miles. And I'd like to know what you mean by that."

Miles told her. He took another of Lila Gilmore's backless glass chairs and sat down upon its scarlet velvet cushion. Then he told Flossie all about his visit to Mrs. Gossington, and about half way through she got so interested that she stopped sniffing and put her handkerchief away.

"So I'm afraid you're not Miss Macintyre after all," he finished up.

Flossie heaved a sigh.

"Well, I don't think that I was all that struck on it," she said. "You see, Mr. Miles, it's this way. I didn't sleep last night—not what you might call sleep. And when you can't sleep, you do a bit of thinking, and it come over me pretty strong that a bit more than what you've got is what everybody'd like to have. There's things I've planned to do and things I thought I'd save up for, and got a lot of fun out of it. But when it isn't just a little more, but an awful lot that you hardly know what you'd do with, why it makes all the things you've been planning for look kind of silly, don't you think? And then look how it's upset Ernie—right down made him forget himself. And what Aunt would have said if she'd heard him, I *don't* know."

Miles felt a good deal of admiration and respect for Miss Flossie Palmer. He said,

"I think Ernie's a very lucky young man."

The colour came into Flossie's cheeks. She tossed her head.

"Oh—*Ernie*—" she said. "If he thinks he can treat me the way he done and not hear no more about it, he's got to hurry up and think again!"

Miles laughed.

"Don't be too fierce with him!"

Flossie stuck her chin in the air, and then spoilt the effect by giggling.

"Fact is, Ernie's got a temper, and so've I, and when he goes all on about capitalists and that Marx that you can't understand a word of it feeds me up—it does reelly. And when it come to saying as how he wouldn't marry a capitalist's daughter, well, I did think it was the limit and no mistake. And mind you, Mr. Miles, he's right down fond of me Ernie is, so how he'd the nerve, I don't know. And look what a sight he's made me make of myself!" She tossed her head again. "Pore Ernie indeed! If he's half as miserable as what he's made me, it's no more than what he deserves—and I only hope he is!"

Miles waited until the Gilmores came in, and informed them that Flossie wasn't Miss Macintyre after all.

"She's done nothing but cry her eyes out ever since you told her she *was*," said Lila plaintively. "I can't think why, but she has. You know, Miles darling, if you were to tell *me* that I was a simply enormous heiress, and that those divine black pearls were really mine, I shouldn't cry. But Flossie's done nothing but cry. It's too unbalanced of her—isn't it?"

"Ah, but then you see her young man cut up rough, and she thought she'd lost him."

Lila hung on Freddy's arm.

"Freddy *darling*, you wouldn't leave me if I was an heiress, would you?"

"I don't know," said Freddy. "If you began to come it over me, I might."

"But, darling, I *shouldn't*, and I'd simply *love* to be an heiress. Fitz says he's got *the* most marvellous investment if I've got any spare cash—and of *course* I haven't, but it would be simply *bound* to make my fortune if I had. And I do think Freddy might listen about it even if he *won't* do anything—don't you, Miles? It's either a gold mine or a coal mine, and I can't remember whether the name of the place is Yukon or Yucatan, but I'm practically certain it begins with a Y. And Fitz says it's the most wonderful offer that's ever been made and he's putting his shirt on it, and Freddy simply won't *listen*."

Freddy looked up from Mrs. Gossington's statement, which he had been reading.

"So you've got to start all over again and look for this Mrs. Moore."

"She's dead," said Miles.

"Oh, you know that? Well then, you've got to find her niece. I suppose if she passed off her niece as the Macintyre child, she probably just changed them over and said the Macintyre child was her niece."

"Freddy *darling*, I don't see that at all."

"Well, as a matter of fact—" said Miles.

"Miles darling, you're blushing!" said Lila. "He *is*, Freddy—*isn't* he? I didn't know anyone could—especially not anyone who's been to America. I believe he's found her! Have you really, Miles?"

"Yes, I've found her," said Miles. "Her name is Kay Moore, but I think she really is Kay Macintyre. If you don't mind, I think I had better begin at the beginning and tell you all about it, because there's more in it than meets the eye, and I want your help."

The telling took a little time, and Miles found it a great relief. All the time that he was talking Lila sat leaning forward in one of her gold chairs. She remained quite silent, and sometimes she looked at him, and sometimes she looked at Freddy, with a small puzzled frown between her eyes.

When Miles had finished telling them about Kay, Freddy said, "You'd better bring her here—hadn't he, Lila?" and Lila gave a start and said,

"Oh yes, Miles darling."

But presently, when Miles had gone away and she still sat on and didn't speak, Freddy came and put his arm round her and said,

"What's the matter, darling?"

"I don't know. When he said that girl's name, I thought—" She broke off and looked up at him. "Freddy, I didn't like it."

"Silly old goose! What didn't you like?"

"I don't know. Freddy, say it again."

"Say what?"

"What you said—'Silly old goose!' It makes me feel safe."

Freddy hugged her heartily.

"Oh, Lila—you mug! You—you silly old goose! What's it all about? Why have I got to make you feel safe?"

She had one of his hands, and was holding it very hard.

"Because I *didn't*."

"Didn't feel safe?"

"No. Freddy, it was *horrid*. Freddy, I don't think I want that girl to come here."

"Oh rubbish, darling!"

She held him harder still.

"Freddy, it was when he said her name—I *didn't* like it. I thought I was going to remember something, and then I *didn't*."

Freddy said, "Kay Moore?" and she gave a little cry.

"Oh, Freddy—*don't*!"

"But, my darling idiot—"

"Yes, I am, aren't I? Freddy, *say* I'm an idiot!"

"My darling, you are."

She snuggled up to him.

"Freddy, you're a very comfortable person. You do love me, don't you?"

Freddy said, "Yes."

Lila put up her face to be kissed.

"Then I don't mind about Kay Moore," she said.

Chapter Thirty-One

MILES CAME BACK to No 16 Varley Street at half past four. Mrs. Green took a long time to answer the door, and when she saw him she looked very much surprised and not best pleased.

"Back again, are you?"

"Yes," said Miles. "Mrs. Green, I really must see her at once."

Mrs. Green stared.

"*Must?*" she said, and then she gave a little angry laugh. "You and your *must*! Well, you can't see her, and if you don't know that already, well, you've been sold a pup same as what I was, and I'd be sorry for you if I wasn't a deal too taken up being sorry for myself, for I come 'ere as a cook and not a general servant, and if they can't keep their girls more nor a week, well, they won't keep me, and so I took and told Nurse Long! And she says, 'Oh, Mrs. Green, I'll be sure and get someone in to-morrow,' she says. And what I felt like saying was, 'What's the good of getting 'em if you can't keep 'em?'"

Miles felt a cold horror. If words meant anything, then Mrs. Green's words meant that Kay had gone away. But when—and why—and where? He said,

"Mrs. Green!"

His voice sounded loud and strange. He saw her take a step back as if it frightened her, and when he saw that, he was afraid that she was going to shut the door, so he put his foot across the threshold and kept it there.

"What do you mean? You must tell me what you mean!"

And all the time he knew very well what her meaning was. She meant that Kay was gone.

Mrs. Green went back another step.

"'Ere, what d'you think you're doing, coming pushing in like this? Come now, young man—you take your foot out of that and be off! If she's let you down, she's let you down, and talking won't mend it."

Miles stayed where he was.

"Do you mean she's gone?"

"Acourse she's gone. And what girls are a-coming to I'm sure I don't know."

"Why did she go?"

"Just took and went, and no rhyme nor reason."

"But you said she was upstairs with Miss Rowland."

"And so she was. I don't tell lies, young man."

"Mrs. Green—when did she go?"

Mrs. Green relaxed a little.

"Well, she was up with the old lady like I told you, and by-and-by Nurse Long come down the stairs. I 'eard her go along the passage to Kay's room, and I thought, 'What's up?' And she couldn't 'ave done no more than look inside the door, for she come straight back to the kitchen and she said angry-like, 'I see she's got her box all ready packed. I s'pose you know she's going?' Well, I didn't know nothing of the sort and I up and says so, and she shrugs her shoulders the way she's got, and she says, 'Cab'll be here in five minutes,' and she goes back into the room and she comes along with Kay's 'at and costume over 'er arm. Well, I was clean bowled over as you might say, but I wasn't going to let 'er go like that. 'Here, Nurse,' I says, 'what's all this? The girl's just had 'er dinner, and not a word said about leaving.' And she shrugs 'er shoulders again and 'Take a look into 'er room,' she says. 'There's 'er box packed and locked, and 'er coat and 'at laid ready, so she'd got it all planned. She's upset Miss Rowland something dreadful,' she says— 'waiting till my back was turned and telling the pore old lady as she was going to leave without notice! It's a shame!' she says, and she goes on up with Kay's things. And then the taxi come, and the man fetched out 'er box and off she went."

Miles tried to collect his thoughts. What could have happened to make Kay go off like that? She must have known that he would come back. What could possibly have happened to make her go off without waiting for him, and why had Nurse Long come down for her things? Why hadn't she come down for them herself? Flossie Palmer's story came back to him. Had Kay seen something that she wasn't meant to see, and had they just turned her out of the house then and there so that she shouldn't have any chance of talking to Mrs. Green? That was what it looked like to him. It looked like that, but the cold, horrible thought went through his mind—if Flossie's story was true—if Kay had seen what Flossie had seen—would they dare to let her go? He thought Mrs. Green was honest. He said,

"Didn't you see her to say good-bye? Didn't she tell you why she was going?"

"Tell me?" said Mrs. Green. "How could she tell me when I never seen 'er?"

"You didn't see her before she went?"

"Aren't I telling you I didn't?"

"And you didn't see her go?"

Mrs. Green tossed her head.

"Oh, she went all right—you needn't fret about that! The man came and took 'er box, and I went out after 'im and she was just a-getting into the taxi."

Miles turned round where he stood and looked up the area steps. If Kay had been coming down the steps of the house, Mrs. Green would have seen her all right, but if the driver had been going up with Kay's box, Mrs. Green couldn't have seen very much, and she couldn't possibly have seen her getting into the taxi, because the area wall came in the way.

"Look here," he said, "I wonder if you'd mind coming here a minute and telling me just where she was when you saw her, and just how much of her you saw?"

Mrs. Green came out to the doorway and looked up the steps.

"I don't know what you're getting at," she said. "But I saw 'er go all right. Coming down the steps she was, and I'd have called out to 'er, only the man was between us with the box."

"Did you see her face?"

Mrs. Green stared at him.

"See 'er face? No, I didn't—and good reason too, for from what I could see she'd 'er angkercher up to it crying. And if you ask me, I should say there'd been a row upstairs and no mistake about it. I don't know what she said and I don't know what she done, but it's my belief they just sent for the taxi and bundled 'er out of the house, or why did Nurse come down for 'er coat and 'at 'stead of letting the girl come down 'erself—though that don't account for 'er box being packed ready. But there—girls is past me, and I've no patience with their goings on."

Miles went back to his hotel profoundly disturbed and dissatisfied. Where had Kay gone, and where was she now? She had his address. She was bound to ring up. Perhaps there was a message waiting for him. Perhaps Kay herself would be waiting for him...

There was no message, and there was no Kay. Hour followed hour, and still no message came.

Chapter Thirty-Two

KAY BEGAN to come back to consciousness. She didn't come back all at once. It was like coming up out of a fog. She got a little above it, and then it closed down upon her again. Presently it didn't close down any more. She was awake, but she didn't know where she was or how she got there. She opened her eyes upon thick, unbroken darkness. It is very difficult to keep your eyes open in the dark. She shut them again, and just as she shut them, she remembered. She had gone into Miss Rowland's room. Oh, why, why, *why* had she gone? And Nurse Long had held some thing over her face, and she had fallen down and down into this darkness. She had been free to go, and she hadn't gone. She could have put on her hat and coat and walked out of the house, and she hadn't. She had walked into Miss Rowland's room, and Miss Rowland had jumped out of bed in a pair of grey tweed trousers. Miss Rowland wasn't Miss Rowland at all. *She was Mr. Harris.*

Kay took a long breath and opened her eyes again. The darkness was the unbroken darkness of a closed-in place. She was lying down in it. She moved, and felt the rustling of straw. She put out her hand, and it fell upon cold, damp brick. A most dreadful terror swept over her. Where was she? Where was this dark place that was damp and cold to the touch and without the least faintest glimmer of light?

The wave of terror ebbed. She became aware of her body and of her own control of it again. She was lying on a pile of straw, but she could move, she could sit up. Could she? The terror came back in a drowning wave. Suppose she was in a place where she couldn't sit up. Suppose the cold, damp roof came so low down over her that she couldn't sit up. For a moment she saw the darkness starred with fiery sparks. The solid floor lifted and fell beneath her. Then, with a sort of desperate courage, she thrust upwards with her right hand and felt a most blessed relief. As far as she could reach there was a free space over her.

She lay still for a moment, panting a little, and then sat up. She felt giddy, but that passed. In a minute or two she was on her feet, and now when she stretched upwards she really could feel the roof with her hand. She began to move very cautiously along the wall.

Four steps brought her to a corner, and six more to another one. There was a door in this wall. It wasn't until she felt the door under her hand that she knew how much afraid she had been. The shadowy corners of her mind had been full of terrifying whispers, echoes from stories about people who had been buried alive, walled up in a living tomb. That was what the stories always called it—a living tomb. But as soon as she felt the door under her hand the whispers stopped. She *wasn't* walled in or buried alive. There was a door, and doors can be opened. The walls were of brick—she could feel the joins—but the door was of wood, with a heavy iron lock. There was no key in the key-hole, and there was no handle, but a little way above the lock there was a latch. She lifted it and pulled, but the door wouldn't move. It must be locked upon the outside.

She came to the third corner, and felt her way back to the heap of straw and sat down upon it. The place must be a cellar—a small cellar about eight feet by six. The door was locked. There wasn't any window. The air was heavy and damp, but not very cold. She thought she must be in one of the cellars of the house next door—only it wasn't next door any longer, because she was in it. Yes, that was it, she was in one of the cellars of No 18, and no one—no one would know where she was or be able to find her.

She thought of Miles not being able to find her. It was a very desolating thought. He was coming at half past two to fetch her away, and he wouldn't be able to find her. But it must be much, much more than half past two, and Miles must have come and gone again, perhaps hours ago. She didn't know how long she had been unconscious, or how long it had taken her to come round. Sometimes it seemed to her that she had lain there for a long time, rousing a little and then slipping back again into something that wasn't quite sleep.

The comforting thought came to her that Miles would come back, and just as she thought of that, she heard a sound from the other side of the door—footsteps, and then the turn of the key in the lock. The door moved on grating hinges. A streak of light broke the darkness, and there came in Mr. Harris with a bedroom candle in his hand. He still wore the grey tweed trousers and the blue striped shirt, but he had put on a collar and tie, and the coat which belonged to the trousers. He left the door wide open, turned back for a moment, and then came in again with a small wooden case which he set down by the pile of straw. He put the candle on the floor, shut the door without locking it, and came and sat down on the wooden box, all very composedly and as if there were nothing in the least unusual in the situation.

Kay remained sitting on her pile of straw, because it was no use getting up or trying to run away. There was nowhere to run to. She must just sit still and hold on desperately to her courage.

"Well?" said Mr. Harris. "Feeling better? I'm sorry we had to put you out, but you really didn't give us any choice. How are you feeling? Head a bit muzzy?"

Kay shook it very slightly. Mr. Harris laughed a little.

"Well, well, well, well! You asked for it—didn't you, my dear? Ever read about Bluebeard when you were a kid—or didn't it run to fairy stories with Rhoda? Bit grim, wasn't she? I'll give you a better time than that. Oh, come along—don't look as if you thought I was going to knife you! I'm not, I can assure you." He put out a hand and patted her on the shoulder.

"Cheer up, my dear—there's a good time coming."

Kay felt cold—very, very cold. She said,

"Where's Nurse Long?"

"Where she won't interfere with us," said Mr. Harris succinctly. "Now don't you get all worked up—I'm not going to hurt you." He laughed again. "My intentions are strictly honourable, and all I want at the moment is a little talk, but if your head's too muzzy you've only to say so and I'll go away—but if I do, you'll only be worrying yourself and thinking I'm all the villains you've ever heard about rolled into one, so I think you'd better listen to what I've got to say."

Kay looked away from him. The cellar was quite empty except for the box he had brought in and the pile of straw on which she was sitting. The walls were of white-washed brick, and the floor was of stone. There must be a draught coming in from somewhere, because the candle flickered. She turned her eyes suddenly on Mr. Harris and said,

"What do you want?"

"That's what I propose to tell you," he said. "And if you're sensible, it won't take long to fix things up. I'm really sorry you had a fright, but you shouldn't have gone prying into things you weren't meant to see. And by the way, how did you get through the wall?"

It didn't matter whether he knew now. She said,

"The glass door wasn't quite shut, and when I pulled it, it slid back."

He looked at her, and all at once she knew why Miss Rowland's eyes had seemed familiar. Miss Rowland's eyes—Mr. Harris' eyes—were the eyes which had frightened her when she was a child. It was Mr. Harris who had stood and looked out on her when she had played in the garden years ago. And it was Mr. Harris who had looked in on her when she was supposed to be asleep and Aunt Rhoda had said, "What a suspicious mind you've got!" They were pale eyes—pale, cruel eyes. The lids drooped across them a little. There was something frightening about those drooping lids. If they were to lift suddenly and show the whole staring eyeball, it would be too horrible to bear.

They did not lift. His lips smiled pleasantly, and he said,

"But I found it shut."

"Yes—I shut it. I heard Nurse Long calling me." It didn't matter what she said now—it didn't matter at all.

"And what did you do then?"

"I went upstairs."

His lids drooped a little more.

"You went straight upstairs?"

Kay said, "Yes."

He went on looking at her. It came to her that he wasn't sure whether she had gone straight upstairs, and that he wanted to know. Perhaps he thought she had been in some of the rooms. Perhaps he was afraid she had. *Why?*

It was a little time before he spoke again. Then he said,

"You went upstairs. And what happened then?"

"I heard someone coming and I went into the cupboard, and then I found that it opened into Miss Rowland's room, and I thought perhaps I could get away."

He laughed.

"That was very silly of you. You never had the slightest chance of getting away. You found the bedroom door locked and you left it open. Did you think we shouldn't notice a thing like that? Now, my dear, this is where we come down to brass tacks. You've been stupid, and you've got yourself into a mess, but I don't want to be hard on you, and I'm going to see what can be done about helping you out. Now, just to clear the ground, I want to know what Rhoda told you about yourself?"

Kay thought for a minute. Why did he want to know that?... She said at last,

"She didn't tell me very much."

"Well, what did she tell you?"

"I don't know that she ever told me anything."

"Did she tell you she was your aunt?"

"I don't think she told me she was. I called her Aunt Rhoda."

"She didn't tell you anything about your father and mother?"

Kay said, "No."

His voice sharpened suddenly.

"Why didn't you ask?"

"I did—once."

"And she didn't tell you?"

"No."

She couldn't tell him what she had told Miles, but Rhoda Moore's passionate "Am I not enough for you?" rang in her ears.

His manner changed abruptly.

"Well, we won't bother about that—it doesn't matter. What matters is how we are going to get you out of this mess. You know, I haven't got a room full of murdered wives like Bluebeard, but you've butted in on some business secrets which it wouldn't suit me at all to have talked about. Now—what are we going to do about it?"

A wild hope sent the colour flaming into Kay's cheeks. If she promised not to speak—if she promised faithfully—would he let her go? She looked at him with eager, brightening eyes.

"If I promise—"

The lids lifted to show a mocking gleam. Then he said quite pleasantly,

"Nothing doing. No, there are two ways out, and you can choose whichever you please. You see, I can't just take your word that you won't talk. I've got to have a guarantee. You might promise, and then one day you might find yourself in the witness-box, and then you'd have to speak. Unless—" He paused for quite a long time.

"Unless what?" said Kay. And then she was sorry she had asked, because she felt quite sure that he had meant her to ask. It was too late now. She couldn't take her question back.

He answered her in his pleasant, reasonable way.

"Unless you were my wife. You couldn't be made to give evidence against me if you were my wife. English law has a profound respect for family ties, you see, so if you were my wife, I might let you make a promise which you wouldn't be very seriously tempted to break. You wouldn't want to put your husband in prison, I'm sure. A prisoner's wife is in a most unpleasant position—you can realise that."

Kay listened with deepening horror. He couldn't really mean that he was saying. He was just trying to frighten her. Of course he didn't know that she was engaged to Miles, but even if she wasn't, the idea of marrying someone who lived in two houses at once, and who spent half his time pretending to be an old lady, made her feel quite cold and sick. Of course he couldn't really want to marry her. And then suddenly she could hear Rhoda Moore speaking as she had heard her during those last few days when she rambled on not always knowing what she said. Some of the rapid muttered sentences came back to Kay now: "They may try and get hold of you... he'll do anything for money... but I've written it all down... don't lose it... be careful and don't lose it..."

Money—but she hadn't any money. Rhoda Moore had said "You'll have plenty of money." She didn't know where it was to come from, but perhaps Mr. Harris knew. She looked up at him and said,

"You said there was another way out."

He nodded.

"Oh yes. Dead men tell no tales." His tone remained pleasant and light. "But we needn't talk about that. Just you think the whole thing over. And meanwhile I'm going to move you to more comfortable quarters. We were rather hurried, you know, so we hadn't got anything ready."

He reached for the candlestick, got up, and opened the door. Then he took Kay by the arm, pulled her up on to her feet, and took her out into what she could see at once was the cellar which ran under the house. It was just like the one at No 16. There were the steps going up in the corner, and a row of doors leading to the small cellars set against the party wall. She had been in the cellar farthest from the steps. Mr. Harris now led her towards the back of the house and opened the door of the last cellar but one. There was a mattress on the floor, and a bed had been made up on it with a pillow, blankets and sheets. There was a jug, a basin, and a pail, with a carafe of water and a tumbler to drink from. On a packing-case in the corner there was a tray with a loaf of brown bread and some butter.

"We're not pampering you, but we're not starving you," he said. "Just you think things over, and in the morning—well, I hope to hear that you've made up your mind to take the pleasanter of the two ways out."

Kay stood against the cellar wall.

"Do you think no one will look for me?" she said.

Mr. Harris laughed.

"Mr. Clayton has been making the most assiduous inquiries. He is probably now trying to trace the taxi which drove you to Waterloo Station. It's news to you, of course, but about three o'clock you upset

Miss Rowland very much by saying you were going to leave without notice—not at all a nice way to treat an old lady—and as Nurse Long found your box all ready packed, I'm afraid you and Mr. Clayton had planned it. As a matter of fact, I happened to overhear some of your conversation the night before—it's really not safe to talk secrets in a public square—and when I heard that your young man was going to steal a march on me by calling for you at half past two, I had to arrange to steal a march on him. So when he called he was told quite innocently by Mrs. Green that you were sitting with the old lady. The innocence of Mrs. Green is really invaluable. When he came back at half past four, she was able to tell him that she had actually seen you go off in a taxi. She saw the driver carry up your box, and she saw your blue coat and skirt and your grey hat come down the steps from the front door. They are a little tight for Addie Long, but she managed to squeeze into them. And of course, leaving like that after the dressing-down you had just had for upsetting a poor helpless old invalid, it was quite natural that you should be crying and holding a handkerchief up to your face. I shouldn't wonder if you hadn't cried all the way to Waterloo."

Kay put her hand behind her and pressed it against the wall. Waterloo—Nurse Long wearing her clothes and going away in a taxi—to make people think—to make them think she had gone away—if Miles thought she had gone away in a taxi, he wouldn't look for her here—that's what they had done it for—he would believe Mrs. Green, and he would think she had gone away without letting him know.

She looked at Mr. Harris, and she said,

"Miles will go on looking for me."

As soon as she heard herself saying that, she knew that it was true. Miles would go on looking for her until he found her. There are things that you are sure about, and there are things that you are not sure about. You hope, and you believe, but you are not sure. This was one of the sure things, and it comforted Kay very much.

Mr. Harris smiled. Kay did so wish he wouldn't smile at her, because a smile ought to be a friendly thing, and this one wasn't in the least bit friendly. It was sarcastic and cruel, as if he were thinking what a little fool she was, and as if it pleased him to be able to frighten her.

"Oh yes, he'll go looking for you," he said. "He's a most pertinacious young man. He'll find out that from Waterloo you took the Tube to

Victoria, and that you there took a ticket for Folkestone, and after that I'm afraid he'll lose track of you. It will take him some time to get as far as that, especially if he follows you to Folkestone, and it may put him off if he finds out that when last seen you were with a young man with whom you seemed to be on the very best of terms. So you see it's not much good your counting on Mr. Clayton."

He came forward and lighted a very small candle end which was on the tray. Then he went out of the cellar and shut the door. The key turned in the lock. Kay heard him going away.

Chapter Thirty-Three

KAY LOOKED at the candle end, and then she looked at the cellar. She had better look at it whilst she could, for that candle end wasn't going to last any time at all. If she had had some matches, she could have saved it to light for a minute or two at a time when the dark became unbearable. She could have made it last a long time like that, but it wasn't any good thinking about it, because she hadn't got any matches. She must learn every inch of the cellar and know just where everything was before the light went out. If she did that, it would give her something to think of. So many steps from the bed to the door. So many to the side wall. So many from the door to the party wall. The jug and basin here, the carafe and tumbler there. The packing-case with the tray on it in the right-hand corner farthest from the door.

The packing-case was empty. It was about three feet by two, but it was quite light, because it was empty. She pulled it a little away from the wall, and found the floor in the corner very rough and broken.

The candle end was only a rim of wax with the wick beginning to fall sideways in the middle of it. The flame flickered in an upward draught and made a monstrous leaping thing of Kay's own shadow. It was funny that there should be a draught in the corner. She remembered that there had been a draught in the first cellar. She knelt down in the space she had made between the packing-case and the wall and saw a rectangular hole in the bottom course of bricks. Right in the corner there was a whole brick missing. She put her hand into the hole and felt a wobbly grating there. That was why there was a draught. There was a ventilator in the corner between this cellar and the one at the end of the row. Perhaps there were ventilators between all the cellars. No, there didn't seem to be one on the other side. Perhaps there was only one between every pair of cellars.

She had got as far as this, when the light flared and went out. The crowding shadows rushed together and made an impenetrable blackness. Then, just as Kay was going to get up from her knees, she heard a sound which set her heart knocking against her side. In the end cellar of all, on the other side of the wall against which she was leaning, someone moved—and muttered—and groaned.

Kay's hand was on the wall. It seemed to shake and tremble. After a moment she knew that it was she who was shaking. The brick was cold against her palm. The brick didn't move. It was her hand that was shaking. The groaning came again and the low muttering. She took her hand from the wall and bent down to the ventilator. The groaning was louder, and she could hear the sound of someone or something moving. It was a slow, dragging sound, and all at once she remembered how the kitten had come back to her out of the cellar with a smear of blood upon its fur.

She leaned against the packing-case with her heart beating wildly. She must stop it. She must be calm. She must try and think... The kitten had gone through a hole in the wall between the two houses. It wasn't a big hole. If the kitten had been any larger, it wouldn't have got through. It was such a tiny little thing, all fur. There had been blood on the fur. It had gone into the end cellar at the back of the house and she had lost it there, and when she went to look with a candle, there was a hole in the party wall, and the kitten had come back through the hole with blood on its fur.

Everything began to straighten out in her mind. The kitten had gone into the end cellar at the back of the house at No 16. 18 came next to 16, because the odd numbers were on the other side of the street. The groans came from the end cellar at the back of the house in No 18. She herself was in the end cellar but one.

But who was it that was groaning on the other side of the wall? It was dreadful to crouch there in the dark and hear those groans. There must be someone there who was hurt. Just then Kay saw a picture in her own mind. It was a picture of what she had seen when she came through the wall on to the first-floor landing of No 18. In this picture she saw the new stair carpet and its bright garish pattern, and she saw the odd marks where something had stained it—and it had been rubbed—and the stain hadn't quite come out. She had been afraid of what might have stained it then, and she was more afraid now, because she knew that the stains had been blood, and blood never quite comes out.

The groaning had stopped. The wild knocking of Kay's heart had stopped. In some curious way it gave her courage to know that there was someone in the next cellar. She stooped down again, put her lips against the hole, and said in a whisper,

"Who is there?"

There wasn't any answer to that.

The sound of her own voice had frightened her again. Suppose Mr. Harris hadn't really gone away. Suppose he was listening. Suppose he suddenly opened the door and caught her kneeling here... Well, suppose he did—

She said again, "Who is there?" and this time she said it a little louder.

There was a groan, but no other answer.

In a quick revulsion of feeling she scrambled up and pushed the packing-case back against the wall. One or two groans came to her faintly. Then they ceased and a dead weight of silence settled down.

Time goes very slowly in the dark. She felt rather sick and not at all hungry, so she did not touch the bread, but she found the carafe and drank a tumbler of water. Then she lay down on the mattress bed and tried to think that Miles would come and find her. Presently she slept.

Mr. Harris went up through the house, unlatched the door of Miss Rowland's wardrobe, and stepped out into the bedroom. The room was lighted, the curtains were drawn, and the fire burned brightly. Two chairs were pulled up to the hearth, and on the table between them stood a well filled tray. Nurse Long sat in the farther chair. She still wore Kay's coat and skirt, but she had taken off the little grey hat and thrown it on the bed. She was pale and frowning as she looked up and said,

"I thought you were never coming. Everything's getting cold."

Mr. Harris shrugged his shoulders.

"I didn't ask you to wait for me," he said, and helped himself to chicken stew. He was getting a little tired of chicken, but Miss Rowland's character as an invalid had to be considered.

Nurse Long helped herself when he had done. She took a few hasty mouthfuls, eating as if she were famished, and then suddenly dropping her knife and fork, she demanded,

"What are you going to do?"

"Have my supper," said Mr. Harris equably.

"I must know what you're going to do." Her tone was sharp and exasperated.

Mr. Harris raised his eyebrows.

"Oh, I'm going to marry her. I told you so."

"And suppose she won't?"

"This is very good stew. You might tell Mrs. Green I enjoyed it," said Mr. Harris. "Well, I'd rather suppose she will."

"Oh, chuck it!" said Addie Long. "What have you done to her? I've got to know!"

"I haven't done anything—yet—except move her into more comfortable quarters."

She looked startled.

"You've moved her? Where have you put her?"

"Next to the Yank."

Addie Long put down her plate and jumped up.

"Damned fool! She'll hear him! He makes the hell of a row."

Mr. Harris went on eating stew.

"My dear Addie, I do wish you'd believe that I know my own business. Kay's probably listening to the Yank's groans at this very minute. I hope she is. I expect them to have a very persuading effect. You see, I want her to marry me of her own free will."

Addie Long stood over the fire and kicked at it with her foot.

"What do you want to marry her for? I tell you it's much too risky. You've got to prove that she's Kay Macintyre—and when you've done that, what have you got? The off-chance that Boss Macintyre will leave her his wad. And what is he—sixty—sixty-five? He might hang on for another twenty years. It's not worth it. And if he knew who she'd married, it wouldn't take him long to make another will—would it?"

Mr. Harris took another helping of stew.

"Come and sit down, can't you, and eat your supper. Restless—that's what you are—and a nagger. And if you know anything that feeds a man up worse than that, I don't."

Addie Long came back to her chair, and got an approving nod.

"That's better. Now I don't mind telling you something you don't know—and something I didn't know till the other day. Kay's mother would have come in for all old Miss Harriet Basing's money if she'd lived. She was the favourite niece, and Miss Basing left the whole wad to her and her children—tied it up tight on them. Miss Basing only died a few months ago, but she couldn't alter her will after Mrs. Macintyre died, because she was a certified lunatic. The will she made twenty-two years ago before she went off her head is good in law, and it means that Kay gets the Basing millions. That, my dear, is why I began to take an interest in her again. As you say, the off chance of her coming in for anything from Boss Macintyre wouldn't be worth running any serious risk for. But the Basing millions are another story, and they're hers—there's nothing problematical about them."

Her face sharpened. After a moment she looked away.

"You'll have to prove who she is."

"Rhoda's letters will do that. They're all together in that old desk of hers."

"Where is it?"

He nodded towards the wardrobe.

"Next door. Well—now are you on?"

He watched the struggle in her averted face. After a minute she said sulkily,

"I suppose so."

Chapter Thirty-Four

KAY WOKE UP. She had been dreaming that she and Miles were walking in the Square just as they had really walked there. Only in her dream there were no lamp-posts, and no pavements, but soft green grass under foot and trees shining with blossom and very sweet to smell. Some of the blossom was pink like almond, and some of it was white like plum, and some of it was green like lime. They walked in a bright dusk, and there was a great happiness and content between them. And then all at once she heard the kitten mew. She couldn't see it, but she could hear it crying with a tiny insistent cry which troubled her and broke in upon her dream. She began to wake, and the dream began to recede. The colour and the brightness faded from the blossoming trees. She couldn't see Miles any more. All her comfort went. But the cry of the kitten still sounded in her ears; she woke to the dark loneliness of the cellar, and as she woke, she heard it still.

It took her a moment to find herself. The mattress low on the floor, the heavy stuffy air, the cold weight upon her thought—it took her a moment to remember why these things were as they were. Then when she was fully awake and herself, there came again that faint insistent mew. She sat up and listened with all her ears, but this time the sound that filled them was one of those deep and dreadful groans. And then it flashed over Kay that the groan and the kitten's mew both came from the same cellar, the cellar that was next to hers.

In a moment she knew what had happened just as well as if she had seen it happening. Mrs. Green had shut the kitten into the cellar for the night. It wouldn't matter how much it mewed or clung to her hand, she would push it down the steps and bang the door, and go into the warm lighted kitchen and have her supper just as if it wasn't a frightfully cruel thing to shut a poor baby of a kitten into a horrid cold cellar where there might be rats.

The kitten was a very brave little thing—Kay had seen that from the first. It really was an Example. It didn't let itself be frightened. It started looking for adventures. She could just see it dancing up to a bit of straw and patting at it, and dancing away again all sideways like a crab. Kay didn't feel herself to be nearly as brave—but of course the kitten could see in the dark, and that did make a difference. Well, after it was shut up it would play little pouncing games and pretend there were mice in the straw. And then it would get bored with that—kittens never played any game for more than a minute or two on end—and that was when it would remember the hole in the end cellar where it had got through before. Perhaps it had a game about catching something that lived in the hole. Perhaps it knew that there was someone in the cellar through the party wall. Perhaps it was lonely. Perhaps it was only curious. Whichever it was, one thing was certain—the kitten was in the next cellar.

Kay jumped up, pulled the packing-case away from the wall, and crouched down by the ventilator with her head almost at floor level. She put her lips to the hole and called, "Kitty—Kitty—Kitty—" Then she remembered that the kitten couldn't come to her because the hole didn't go all the way through. She had felt the grating which blocked it. It was a very wobbly grating. It had wobbled when she touched it. If she could get it out of the way, the kitten would be able to come to her. It would be very, very comforting to have the kitten for company.

She put her hand into the hole, which was just the size of a single brick, and pulled sharply at the grating. It was quite loose, and the brick to which it was fastened had crumbled away on the right-hand side. She kept on pulling and working it to and fro until the crumbly brick broke away and left one end free. Then she found that the whole grating was loose in her hand and could be bent back like an opening door. She called "Kitty—Kitty—Kitty—" again, but the answer she got was a groan that frightened her. It must have frightened the kitten too, for it shot through the hole she had made and came clawing and scrambling to her shoulder, where it mewed, and purred, and nuzzled against her cheek as if it was as glad of company as she was.

The kitten did make all the difference. Kay blocked the hole so that it couldn't get out, because it soon got tired of being on her shoulder and went prancing off into the darkness. They played at hide-and-seek together, and sometimes Kay caught the kitten, and sometimes the kitten pounced with a growl upon the handkerchief which she trailed across the floor as a bait. Once it was so fierce that the handkerchief was torn and Kay's hand scratched.

It was when she was sucking the blood from the scratch that Kay thought of the Plan—or rather it seemed to think of itself. The kitten, and her scratched hand, and her torn handkerchief all rushed together in her mind, and the Plan was there. If she tore a strip from her handkerchief, and wrote on it with her blood, and tied it round the kitten's neck, someone might see it and come and help her. *Someone...* Mr. Harris or Nurse Long? "No, no—please don't let it be them— *please!*"... Mrs. Green? It was more likely to be Mrs. Green than anyone. But if Mrs. Green found it, what would she do? Kay didn't know. She didn't know whether to say "Please don't let Mrs. Green find it!" or not. She didn't know about Mrs. Green... Miles? "Oh, please, please, *please* let Miles find it!" He *might*. He would come and look for her. "Oh, Miles, you *will*—won't you? Oh, Miles, *please* come quickly!" And if he came to look for her, he might see the kitten. He *might*. There wasn't anything impossible about that. And if he saw the kitten, he would remember that she was fond of it. And if he saw a bit of her handkerchief tied round its neck... *If—if—if—if—if.* She saw those ifs like five barred gates all standing up shut and locked between her and Miles. The tears came hot and stinging to her eyes and ran down over her cheeks, and as they ran, that groaning came again.

Ten minutes later she had cried some of the hopelessness away. Anyhow if you didn't try, you deserved to go down. Only cowards didn't try. Kay was afraid of cellars, and darkness, and Mr. Harris, but she was still more afraid of being a coward. If you could keep your courage you could get through anything—only sometimes it was so difficult.

Well, she could do what she had planned. She was going to do it now. She wasn't going to cry any more. She tore a narrow strip from her handkerchief. That was the first thing, and that was easy enough. But how was she going to write in the dark? There was no name on the handkerchief. She could have written in the dark with a pencil upon paper, but to write with a pin dipped in blood upon cambric was something altogether different. The pin was too thin. It wouldn't do. She had thought of a pin because she had one in the band of her apron. She had kept on her apron to take the tray upstairs. The head of the pin would be thicker than the point. She couldn't think of anything else. Her hand was still bleeding. The kitten had scratched deep. She could feel the blood trickling down.

She found the pin, and holding it by the point, she did her best to scrawl a capital K on the strip she had torn from her handkerchief. She couldn't do any more than that—it was no use trying without a light—but if Miles saw that K scrawled in blood, he would know that something had happened to her in this house. "Oh, please, please, *please* let him find it!"

She tied the strip round the kitten's neck. It had to be seen, but it mustn't look like a message. At least it must look like a message to Miles, but not to Mr. Harris or Nurse Long. She tied the ends in a little bow—you often saw a kitten with a bow round its neck—and then she pulled the packing-case away again and kissed the kitten, and told it to be careful, and put it through the hole, shutting the ventilator after it and pushing the packing-case back against the wall.

Chapter Thirty-Five

At about half past seven Miles managed to get on to Ian Gilmore. Ian, as usual, was dining out. He listened to what Miles had to say, and was extremely discouraging.

"My dear man, if you go to the police, they'll think you're batty. You'll probably hear from her in the morning. You say yourself that you've been urging her to leave. Now she's done it, and you've got the wind up. It sounds a bit unreasonable to me."

It sounded unreasonable to Miles himself, but that didn't make any difference. The hot, stuffy telephone-box in the hotel was full of his unreasoning, unreasonable fear. He said in a hard, strained voice,

"She knew I was coming to fetch her away."

Ian at the other end of the line sounded rather impatient. "You've just told me you went at half past two, and you were sent away because she was with the old lady. Well, after that she wouldn't know whether you were coming back or not. She probably flared up, had words with them, and walked out of the house."

This, of course, was a perfectly reasonable explanation; Miles' brain told him so. But it wasn't his brain which was in charge just now. He was afraid for Kay, and fear had nothing in common with reason.

"Sleep on it," said Ian Gilmore, and rang off.

Miles came out of the telephone-box. He would wait a little longer, and then he would go round to Varley Street again. He might be able to find out where the taxi had come from. Mrs. Green would probably know. He was a fool not to have asked her. The prospect of having something to do made him feel better. Waiting for news is of all things in the world the most damnable. Well, he would wait till half past eight, but not a minute longer. Meanwhile he was probably all the sorts of fool that Ian Gilmore was thinking him.

Flossie Palmer slipped out to the post that evening about nine o'clock. It was Gladys' afternoon and evening out, but you could always go round to the post. Ernie *might* be hanging around on the chance of her slipping out. It wasn't very likely because of the row they'd had, but if they hadn't had a row, he'd have been there sure enough, walking up and down and waiting for her to slip out for half an hour. Flossie hoped passionately that he was going to be there, because now that it was all over and she wasn't an heiress, she was going to enjoy herself letting Ernie Bowden know exactly what she thought about him and his trampling ways. She'd got it all mapped out. First she was going to tell him that she wasn't Miss Macintyre, and then when he tried to make it up with her, she'd just show him. Ernie Bowden was going to learn a thing or two about the way a young lady that *was* a young lady expected him to treat her. She looked forward to this a good deal. And then, when Ernie was properly humble and crushed, perhaps she'd think about making it up with him.

She got down to the pillar-box and walked past it round the corner. When she had gone a little way, she heard a footstep following her. Her heart beat a little faster, but she wasn't going to look round. Ernie needn't think she was looking out for him. Oh no—she was going to be ever so surprised when he came up with her.

The footstep came nearer. Insensibly her pace slackened a little. And then, in the darkest place between the lamp at the corner and the lamp at Western Terrace, the step came up beside her, and a perfectly strange man's voice spoke her name.

"Miss Palmer—"

Flossie was so startled that she hadn't anything to say. She had made sure that it was Ernie who was following her. She could have cried with disappointment. And then all of a sudden she was afraid. There wasn't a soul about, and it was very dark. She turned round to go back to the corner, and a hand took her by the arm.

Flossie caught her breath.

"Look here, let go, or I shall scream!" And as she said it, she wondered whether anyone would hear her, because there were two empty houses just here, and then the long blank side of the corner house.

The man said, "I shouldn't do that. I only want a word with you."

He stopped, and she had to stop too. She couldn't see his face. She couldn't see anything except a dark figure. She thought he had a muffler about his neck, and a hat with a turned-down brim. His voice had no ring in it. It was just a whisper.

She said, "What do you want?" and had so little breath to say it with that she felt quite sure she could never scream loud enough for anyone to hear.

"Listen to me," said the whispering voice. "You've just missed getting into serious trouble."

"I don't know what you mean."

"Don't you—Miss Flossie Palmer Ivy Hodge?"

Flossie felt a stab of terror.

"Ooh! It's *Them*!"

She must have made some uncontrollable movement, because he laughed a little. There is something horrid about a whispering laugh.

"So now you know what we're talking about," said the man. "And what I want to know is, why did you do it?"

Flossie was frightened, but she had her wits about her. She thought there was no harm in pretending to be even more frightened than she was.

"Ooh! What do you mean?"

"Why did you call yourself Ivy Hodge?"

"To oblige Ivy."

"But why did you run away?"

"Oh, I dunno—I come over queer. Must have been a bad dream or something. P'raps it was a ghost."

Her arm was shaken a little.

"A bad dream, was it? And how many people have you told this dream to?"

Flossie burst into tears.

"Ooh—I *never*! Do you think I want people to think I'm batty? Why, if I was to say I see someone staring at me out of a looking-glass, they'd be bound to think I was batty—wouldn't they?"

"I should think so," said the man. "Was that what you thought you saw?"

"I come over queer," said Flossie. "I'm not batty—honest I'm not. I come over queer and I run away."

There was a pause. Was he going to believe her or wasn't he? And if he didn't believe her, what was going to happen next? A cold shudder ran all over Flossie from her head to her feet. Then the hand on her arm relaxed its grasp. It didn't let go altogether, but it held her less tightly. The man said,

"I certainly shouldn't talk about it if I were you. You wouldn't like to be put away in a lunatic asylum, would you? It might happen if you talked—or you might find yourself in the river or under a car some dark night. No, you'd better not talk."

"Ooh—I *won't!*" said Flossie with heartfelt terror. And with that a car turned out of Western Terrace and she pulled her arm away and ran for it into the light of the corner lamp, and round the corner and up Merriton Street to No 12.

Chapter Thirty-Six

MRS. GREEN was in a very bad temper. She was an easy-going woman as a rule, but she didn't like to be put about. She considered that she had been put about something cruel. The lunch things to wash and the tea tray to get ready, and then the tea things to wash up, and then the supper tray and the supper things—all of which was the girl's work and not to be expected of a cook that *was* a cook. Then that there kitten of Kay's must needs get under her feet, the dratted little beast, so that it was going on for a miracle she hadn't come down smack and as like as not broken something. Well, she'd shut it up safe enough now, and without giving it its supper either, and perhaps now she could have her own supper in peace—a plate of the stew, very good and tasty it was, and surprising how much Miss Rowland and Nurse had put away between them, but still there was plenty left.

Mrs. Green had a sound, solid appetite. She sat down to a good plateful of stew with a hunk of bread, a slab of yellow cheese, and a bottle of beer. If she'd got to do all the work, she'd got to keep her strength up. She began to eat, slowly and with relish, but instead of feeling soothed her anger kept on mounting in a steady, sluggish tide. She would have the trays to see to and all the washing up on her hands—and Kay off gallivanting with that young man no doubt. Supper things to wash, breakfast things to wash, and that there dratted kitten to clean up after and to feed—and getting in anyone's way just to spite them, the dratted little toad.

Mrs. Green stopped munching and called herself a regular right-down fool. What did she want to go putting the kitten in the cellar for? What she did ought to have done was to throw it out neck and crop into the street, where it belonged. So she would too, just as soon as ever she'd finished her supper. A sight too easy-going she'd been, letting Kay bring it in, and she wasn't going to keep it, not another day she wasn't. Out it would go, and lucky if it didn't get its neck twisted. All her anger against Kay became directed towards Kay's kitten. She would finish her supper, and then out it would go. She cut a thick slice of cheese and ate it with enjoyment.

Downstairs in the cellar Kay was tying the strip of her handkerchief round the kitten's neck.

Mrs. Green's supper was a protracted affair. Washing up or no washing up, she wasn't going to be hurried over her food. She finished the stew, and then she finished the cheese, and then she finished the beer. And then she got heavily to her feet and went into the scullery, where she opened the cellar door and called down the steps to the kitten. She didn't put on the scullery light, because she didn't need it. After five years in the house she didn't need a light to find her way across her own scullery. She just opened the low door and called down into the darkness.

"Here, you dratted little nuisance—come along with you! Puss—puss—puss—"

The kitten had returned through the hole in the party wall between the houses. Curiosity, and a faint smell of food, had taken it into the cellar next to Kay's. There was a hole that it could squeeze through, and it was hungry, having had nothing to eat since breakfast time. The cellar had been disappointing. There was no food. There was a faint mousy smell, but there were no mice. There was a large, alarming, groaning creature lying on a bed in one corner. It wasn't at all a nice bed. The kitten had wailed its disapproval. And then, miraculously, there had come Kay's voice, calling it. But Kay had been disappointing too. The kitten associated her with milk, but there wasn't any milk. Highly disgruntled, it found itself back in the cellar with the groaning creature. There was something round its neck, something that tickled, something that wouldn't come off in the maddest scampering rush.

With a little growl of rage, the kitten squeezed through the hole by which it had come and emerged into the large cellar under the kitchen of No 16. The thing round its neck wouldn't come off. Neither scratching, rolling, twisting, nor flying round in circles would get rid of it. The only thing that happened was that the bow which had stuck up at the back of its neck slipped round under its chin where it tickled worse than ever.

And then the door at the top of the cellar steps opened noisily. A delicious smell of stew came rushing down, and Mrs. Green's voice called, "Puss—puss—puss!" With a loud ecstatic mew the kitten ran, tail erect, towards that lovely satisfying smell. Mewing, purring, and trembling with ecstasy, it reached the top step, to be instantly snatched up and carried at arm's length across the kitchen, along the passage, and out of the door into the area. Mrs. Green's hands were large and nubbly. The one that held the kitten left its head and tail visible, but not much else. If Kay's cambric bow had still been sticking up on end, it is just possible that Mrs. Green might have noticed it as she passed through the lighted kitchen—possible, but not probable, because her mind was of the sort which admits but one idea at a time, and that one slowly. At the moment what she wanted to do was to get rid of that dratted girl's dratted kitten, and the sooner the better. She actually mounted the area steps, and, flinging the kitten across the pavement into the gutter, she slammed, first the area gate, and then, breathing heavily but triumphantly, the area door—"And if the next girl tries bringing livestock in on me, I'll soon let 'er know as this is a kitchen and not a menagerie!" With this to support her Mrs. Green addressed herself to the washing-up.

It was not an auspicious moment for Miles Clayton to put in an appearance. Mrs. Green came to the door with "Drat!" written all over her, and when she saw who it was that had knocked, she would have banged the door on him if he hadn't been too quick for her and got his foot across the sill again.

"Mrs. Green, I won't keep you a minute."

Mrs. Green stepped back heavily in order to glare at him the better.

"Here, young man, I've had about enough of this! You take your foot out of here, or I'll send for the police!"

"Miss Rowland would like that—wouldn't she?" said Miles. "No, look here, Mrs. Green, I really won't keep you. And I know you've got extra to do and all that, but if you would just tell me where that taxi came from—the one Kay went off in—I'd be most awfully obliged to you—I really would." He put out his hand as he spoke, and Mrs. Green saw a Treasury note in it.

Next moment the note was crackling between her fingers. Very free with his money, the young man. Better to walk out with than to get married to, that sort. She put the note into her apron pocket and said,

"What do you want to know for?"

"Well, I do. *Please*, Mrs. Green."

"Well, they mostly has their taxis from the garridge round at the back."

"What name?"

"Well, I don't rightly know the name. You can't miss it. You go up into the Square and you turn right, and it's the first on the right again— Barnabas Row—and the garridge is right at the back of us here, though what you want with it is more than I know."

Miles took a step towards her.

"Mrs. Green—you did see her go?"

Mrs. Green made a snorting sound. The Treasury note was safe in her pocket.

"What do you think I am, young man—a liar? Course I seen her go! Down the steps and into the taxi, like I told you. And if you 'aven't got nothing better to do with your time than to stand here gossiping all night, well I 'ave, and I'll thank you to take yourself off and let me get on with my work!"

She slammed the door as soon as Miles removed his foot, after which there was nothing for him to do but climb the area steps into the street. It was in his mind to go round to the garage, but at getting on for nine o'clock on a Sunday evening it was likely enough that there wouldn't be anyone there.

As he let the area gate fall to with a clang, something rubbed against his ankle. Looking down, he saw a small dark creature which incontinently opened its mouth and wailed. It was Kay's kitten, and as he picked it up and it rubbed itself against him mewing and purring, it came to him with a sort of shock that it wasn't like Kay to have left the kitten behind her. What was he going to do about it? He blenched at the idea of knocking Mrs. Green up again. It seemed extremely likely that she had slung the kitten out. She had grumbled at Kay for bringing it in.

The sense of shock deepened perceptibly. It wasn't a bit like Kay to have gone away and left her kitten to Mrs. Green's angry mercies. Then, on the top of that, a quick thought stabbed like a knife. Kay wouldn't have done it.

He reacted against this by reminding himself coldly that kittens were a drug on the market, and that in this light, or rather absence of light, it was quite impossible to be sure that this particular kitten was Kay's.

He walked to the next lamp-post with the creature nuzzling and purring under his chin. It was a very determined kitten. It clung to his tie with all its dozens of claws, and shrieked with fury when he detached it and held it up under the light. It certainly looked like Kay's kitten. It was dark and faintly striped, and it had a singularly piercing mew. It was when it stuck its chin in the air and shrieked that he saw the draggled bow. He fingered it, and the kitten bit his finger and scratched him with its hind legs, after which it scrambled to his shoulder and sat rubbing and purring against his ear.

He thought he had better get the bow off. He'd better have a look at it. The little beast might strangle itself. Good riddance of course, but still—Kay's kitten... Who had tied this thing round its neck? Not Mrs. Green. It was a strip off somebody's handkerchief. Kay's handkerchief?... But why should Kay tear a strip off her handkerchief and tie it round the kitten's neck?...

The kitten walked up and down on his shoulder and tickled him with its tail while he smoothed out the strip of cambric and held it to the light. It might have K's name on it. What would that mean? Would that mean anything?

There wasn't any name on the cambric. There was only an odd irregular streak or smear, or rather two streaks, one straight and the other like a V set sideways. That was his first impression. And then, horribly and suddenly, he realised that the smear was blood, and that the straight streak and the V-shaped one if brought together would form a capital K. They were about half an inch apart, but if you brought them together they made a K. If you tried to write in the dark, you might make a letter like that. You couldn't do it with your eyes open and seeing.

A cold horror came over him as he stared at the strip of cambric. Why should Kay tear a strip from her handkerchief and write, or try to write, upon it in the dark? The streaks were blood, and he thought they had been made with a pin or a splinter, because the threads of the thin white stuff were dragged, as if something sharp had been used. In one place they were torn.

The cold horror gained upon him. In what desperate straits had Kay tied that stained cambric round her kitten's neck? And where was she? In the dark. That much was sure, for the two parts of her initial letter would have joined if she had been able to see what she was doing. He no longer thought of going to the garage in Barnabas Row. If a hundred to one chance came off and he were to find the driver who had picked up Kay's box that afternoon, he knew exactly what the man would say and how he would describe his fare—a blue serge coat and a grey hat. Kay's clothes; not Kay herself. And he wouldn't have seen a face, only a hand holding a handkerchief to eyes that might or might not have been weeping. He ought to have guessed it at once when Mrs. Green said that Kay had her handkerchief up to her face. Kay's box had gone, and someone in Kay's clothes had gone with it, but Kay herself was somewhere—in the dark, desperately hoping that her message might be found and understood.

Chapter Thirty-Seven

FLOSSIE PALMER was alone in the kitchen when the front door bell rang. The cook had gone to bed, but it as was still only a quarter to ten, Gladys had not come in, and goodness only knew when Mr. and Mrs. Gilmore would be home. After what had happened earlier in the evening she would just as soon have had someone about while she went to the door. Cook was as good as dead once her door was shut, and Gladys wouldn't be in a minute before half past ten, so it wasn't any good shilly-shallying. A vague thought of just leaving the bell to ring until it got tired presented itself, but Aunt's upbringing had not been without its effect, and Flossie dismissed this temptation. She wouldn't open the door except on the chain though, not for nothing in the world.

Whoever it was that was ringing was in a mortal hurry, for the bell went on ringing all the time she was coming upstairs and all the time she was crossing the hall. She didn't come very quickly, but she came, and when she got to the door she made sure that the chain was fast, and then she slid the bottom bolt and pulled back the catch.

The door opened a couple of inches. Flossie's heart banged and her knees shook.

"Ooh! It's a man!" she thought. And then there he was, calling urgently through the crack in Miles Clayton's voice,

"Is that you, Flossie? Let me in quick!"

"Ooh, Mr. Miles—you did frighten me!"

She undid the chain, and he came in, jerking it out of her hand as he pushed the door.

"What's the hurry?" said Flossie to herself—"pushing in like that!" She was cross because she had been frightened. Aloud she said, "Mr. and Mrs. Gilmore is out."

"It's you I want to see," said Miles. He slammed the door, took her by the arm, and hurried her into the dining-room.

When the four ceiling lights came on, Flossie wondered what had happened. If it had been some people, she would have wondered if he had been drinking. His fair hair was rumpled, his face pale, and his voice unsteady.

"Lor', Mr. Miles!" she said. "What's wrong?"

"Look here, Flossie, you've got to give me back that promise."

Flossie's expression changed. The very first instant minute he said "promise," she knew what he was getting at. It was what she had told him in the fog, and he'd promised faithful he wouldn't go to the police about it, nor let on to nobody. She said sharply,

"What promise?"

"Flossie, you know—I can see you do. Look here—someone's life may depend on it. Was that all true that you told me about seeing a hole in the wall when you were at 16 Varley Street?"

Flossie's colour and Flossie's temper flared together.

"True? Of course it's true! I don't tell lies, Mr. Miles, nor I don't like people that think I tell them!"

He ran a distracted hand through his hair. If Flossie was going to go off the deep end, he wouldn't be able to do anything with her.

"My dear girl, I didn't mean lies. I only meant are you sure there wasn't any mistake?"

Flossie tossed her head.

"Sure enough to make me run out of the house in what I stood up in!" she said defiantly.

"Then, Flossie, listen. The girl who went there after you has disappeared. I don't know what's happened to her. I—we—we're engaged. I think she's the real Miss Macintyre, but she doesn't know about it yet. I was going to tell her this afternoon, but when I went there Mrs. Green said she couldn't come—she was up with Miss Rowland. And when I went back at half-past four she said there had been a row, and that Kay had gone."

Flossie's eyes rested upon him with a cold sparkle.

"And what makes you think there's anything wrong about that?"

He told her rather disjointedly, walking up and down the end of the room, using his hands in jerky, forcible gestures, and finally producing the strip of cambric with that faint scrawl which might be a capital K.

"You see, you've got to give me back my promise. I can't keep it any longer. I've been to the police, and they pooh-pooh the whole thing. I can't make them listen to me. You see, it sounds too thin—I know it does. When I simply wouldn't go away, they sent a man round to the house and the garage. Mrs. Green told him just what she'd told me, and at the garage they said their driver had picked up a young lady and her luggage at No 16 Varley Street and driven her to Waterloo. After that it was no use saying anything more, but if you will come round there with me and tell them what you saw—"

"Not much I won't!" said Flossie in the loudest voice he had ever heard from her. It was loud because she was afraid—afraid that Mr. Miles would make her go to the police, and quite dreadfully afraid of what would happen to her if she went.

"*Flossie*—"

"I won't, I tell you! Why can't you believe what Mrs. Green and the garridge man had to say? Seems to me you think everybody's telling lies to-night! Why shouldn't she have had a row with them and cleared out same as Mrs. Green says she did? It's a house as any girl 'ud want to clear out of, I should say. If you go home and go to bed, you'll be getting a letter from her in the morning, telling you all about it."

Miles turned at the end of the room and came striding down upon her.

"I wish to heaven I could think so, but I can't! Flossie, think of what you saw—*think*! Look back and make a picture of it in your mind— see it again, and then *think*! Suppose you hadn't got away. Suppose you hadn't been able to open the door. Suppose the man you saw had caught you up on the stairs. You said you saw him looking at you— suppose he had caught you up—where would you be now? And what would you think of someone who knew where you were and wouldn't move a finger to help you out?"

Flossie had turned very pale. She said, still in that loud defiant voice,

"I'd be past helping all right if he'd caught me, Mr. Miles."

He cried out, "Don't!" and then, "Flossie, you can't say that and then refuse to help her!"

Flossie clenched her hands.

"Now look here, Mr. Miles—it's no use your talking, and it's no use your carrying on. My life's as good as hers, isn't it? And I'm not throwing it away along of stirring up a lot of trouble and going to the police. I told you what happened to Ivy, and no later than this very evening I got my warning of what 'ud happen to me if I didn't hold my tongue."

"What do you mean?"

"I'm not saying, thank you, Mr. Miles. And I'm not going to the police, not for you nor for no one, and if you bring them here, I'll say and swear, and stick to it, that I didn't see nothing—so *there*!"

She was panting a little and her heart was thumping. He shouldn't make her speak—no, he shouldn't. She wanted to marry Ernie and live comfortable. If he made her speak, she'd never do that—no, never. It'd be a hand at her throat round a dark corner and the breath strangled out of her, or a cold dreadful plunge into the river some black night same as Ivy. She wasn't going to think about that other girl and the hole in the wall. She wasn't—no, she *wasn't*. She'd got herself to think about.

Miles had gone grey in the face. He said,

"You said you'd been warned. Who warned you?"

"I *never*! No one."

"You said you'd been warned—you can't get away from that. You said it, and you've got to tell me."

"Got to nothing, Mr. Miles!"

"*Flossie!*"

"I *dursn't*!" said Flossie with a choking sob. And then all of a sudden she was stamping her foot and telling him to go away. "I'll call Cook if you won't—I will reely! And I won't say another word, not if you was to stay here all night, and you did ought to be ashamed of yourself, coming here and carrying on like this, and as likely as not getting my character took away, and Ernie as jealous as he can be without any more trouble being made! And whatever Aunt would say, I don't know nor I don't want to! And are you going, or have I to go down for Cook? And I think it's a *shame*, I do, coming here like this and trying to make me say things! And I won't *never*, so it's no use your going on!"

It wasn't any use.

He said, "All right, I'm going," and went.

The slamming of the door relieved Flossie's terror. She shot the bolt and put up the chain with shaking hands. The tears were running down her cheeks. He hadn't made her speak—he *hadn't*. She wasn't going to speak—not never, not for no one. She stood in the hall behind the bolted door and cried. There wasn't nothing to cry about. "Gladys'll be home any time now." She couldn't help it. She couldn't stop crying, and her legs had all gone funny.

She got to the bottom step of the stairs and crouched there in a heap, and still she couldn't stop crying. She knew where that girl had gone all right—through the hole in the wall. She hadn't been quick enough, and *They* had got her. Mr. Miles wouldn't get any letter from her in the morning. Ooh! He did look awful! Same as if he'd been ill for a month. "I dursn't speak—I dursn't! They'd do me in if I did. And Ernie"—a choking sob—"Ernie 'ud break his heart!" But he wouldn't go on breaking it— men didn't. And presently he would go walking out with someone else—and marry them—and have the little house they'd planned. And it wouldn't be Flossie's house, because she'd be in the river.

"I dursn't! Ooh—I *dursn't*!" said Flossie.

She got out her handkerchief and tried to stop crying. Gladys would think she was batty. If she could stop seeing the hole in the wall and the way Mr. Miles looked, it would be all right. That Kay Moore wasn't any business of hers. . . . Wasn't she? . . . If she were to speak now, at once, there might be just time to save Kay Moore. . . . The picture of the black hole rose vividly before her. The man with the wounded head lifted that clawing hand of his and gazed at her with a desperate appeal in his eyes. She might have saved *him* if she had spoken. He wasn't dead *then*. Perhaps the girl wasn't dead now. She was Mr. Miles's girl. If she spoke at once—

"Ooh—I dursn't!" said Flossie, and felt the tears gush out again.

Chapter Thirty-Eight

KAY HAD BEEN sitting in the dark for a long time. She didn't lie down, because she didn't want to go to sleep. It frightened her to think of going away into a dream. She wanted to be here to listen—to pray desperate prayers that Miles might find the kitten and read her message. She must be awake, so that she could call out at once if she heard him coming. She told herself fervently that he would certainly come.

The groans from the next cellar had stopped, but presently she heard something that frightened her even more. It was a slow dragging sound. It seemed to come nearer, and then there was a low tapping. Kay got to her feet and stood there listening. Someone was tapping on the ventilator between the two cellars.

She pulled away the packing-case, got down on her trembling knees, and whispered, "Who's there?"

One of those groans came back to her. It sounded most terrifyingly near, and as she recoiled a voice said, "Who are you?" It was a man's voice. It was very low and weak, but it was unmistakably an American voice.

Kay said, "I'm Kay Moore. Who are you?"

"A blamed fool, or I wouldn't be here. Say, has there been anything about me in the papers? Are they looking for me? That's what I want to know. Cal Morgan—that's me, and I used to think myself a pretty smart detective." He gave an odd faint laugh that caught half way. "I came over here hunting trouble, and I sure found it."

"Are you *hurt*?" said Kay in a small fluttering voice. She wasn't frightened of him any longer, but she was afraid for them both.

He groaned again.

"I sure am. They knocked me on the head to start with. They knew I was after them, and they'd have bumped me off, only they think they can do a deal." He broke off, panting. "Don't know how much longer they'll think so. I'd get out of here easy enough if I wasn't so weak. I'm real handy at picking a lock. I thought I'd got away once—played 'possum—tripped Harris up and left him stunned. But it took me too long to crawl up the stairs, and he came round, and fetched me back. Gee, Miss Moore—it's good to talk to someone again! I didn't dare before for fear of his coming back. I don't talk to *them*, you know—only groan, and act as if I was out of my head. Did you say there wasn't anything in the papers about me?"

"I haven't seen anything."

He groaned again.

"That's tough. We're up against a pretty bad proposition. I heard what he said to you a while ago, and don't you make any mistake, you're up against it. He's a bad man and a tough gangster. What you've got to do is play for time. There's someone who will look for you, isn't there?"

"Miles will," said Kay.

Saying it helped her to believe it. She was going to tell him about Miles, when a sound came to her from the outer cellar. Someone was coming down the cellar steps, and in the same instant Mr. Cal Morgan whispered,

"Ssh! He's coming!"

As she pushed the packing-case back again, she could hear that slow dragging sound, and through it the footsteps coming nearer. She straightened up and stood with her hands pressed down upon her breast. Suppose it was Miles. "Oh, please, please, *please* let it be Miles!" Oh, *lovely* if it was Miles!

It is the starving person who knows how good bread is. As Kay listened to the footsteps coming nearer, she knew just how good it was to love Miles, and to be loved by him, and to be safe, oh, safe with his arms round her. It was like looking into heaven.

And then the key turned in the lock, the door opened, and Miles and heaven were immeasurably far away, because it was Mr. Harris who came in with Miss Rowland's bedroom candlestick in his hand. He looked at Kay and laughed.

"Well, have you had enough of the dark?" he said.

Not Miles—Mr. Harris—

Kay took a long sighing breath and went back a step. Mr. Harris went on laughing.

"I'd have been down before, only I had to get rid of Addie. She's jealous, you know. That's what she is—jealous. So I had to wait till she'd gone to bed."

Kay could see with horror that he had been drinking. He wasn't drunk or anything near it, but he was in a mood which added a new terror to what she already felt.

"So now we'll talk."

Kay shook her head.

"It's so late," she said in a faltering voice.

"Late? Not a bit of it! Do you know what time it is? It's only ten o'clock. Now you can't call that late—you really can't. But we won't talk here, we'll come upstairs. You know, you're a lucky girl, that's what you are. You come along upstairs with me, and I'll tell you all about it, and then you'll see what a lucky girl you're going to be. I told you there was a good time coming, didn't I?"

Upstairs. Kay's heart leapt at the word. Upstairs spelt hope, and a chance of escape. Let her once get out of this cellar into a room, and there would surely be something she could do to help herself. She might be able to break a window and scream, or she might be able to give him the slip on the stairs—she was very quick on her feet.

One of these hopes died immediately, for Mr. Harris took her by the arm, holding her with a grip in which she could not move, and so brought her up the cellar steps and one flight of stairs to the drawing-room floor. It was the drawing-room floor, but the room into which they came in no way resembled a drawing-room. It was like a shop, an office and a lumber-room all run together.

Kay's other hope died too as she looked about her, for the windows had old-fashioned shutters, all securely fastened. There was half an inch of wood between her and the glass she had dreamed of breaking.

For the rest, there was a writing-table with a great many drawers. There were filing cabinets. There was a stack of old trunks and dispatch-cases, and a pile of quite new cardboard dress-boxes. The floor was dingy with a drab linoleum, and the walls with a very old stained paper whose satin stripes, once white, were now the colour of a London fog. Hanging straight and undrawn at the windows there were curtains of dark blue net, quite good and new. Kay stared at all these things and felt bewildered. The mixture was so odd.

Mr. Harris had switched on a strong unshaded light in the ceiling. There was neglected dust everywhere, but the room wasn't cold. A good fire burned on the hearth, and a couple of comfortable shabby chairs were drawn up to it. It was when Kay saw the fire that she realized how cold she was—how very cold.

She went to the hearth and knelt down, spreading out her hands to the blaze. She even stopped being afraid of Mr. Harris as she felt the warmth come into her, round her, through her. Just for a moment nothing else mattered. Then she heard him laugh behind her in the room, and the fear came back. She got up from her knees and sat down on the edge of one of the chairs. She sat down because her legs were shaking so much that she was afraid she was going to fall.

Mr. Harris sat on the arm of the other chair and laughed again.

"Quite a cosy family party—aren't we? Good thing Addie's gone to bed—isn't it? And now we can have a real good heart-to-heart talk and fix our wedding day."

Kay heard herself say, "That's nonsense." And then a darting stab of fear went through her, because what was she to do if she made him angry?

"Well, well—" said Mr. Harris. He didn't seem at all angry. "Now what I want you to do is to listen to me. I told you there was a good time coming, and now I'm going to explain. But first of all I'm going to ask you a question or two. You needn't look scared—there's nothing you'll mind answering. First of all—did you like living with Rhoda Moore?"

Kay relaxed a little.

"No, I didn't," she said truthfully.

"Do you like being in service—here to-day and gone to-morrow—Mrs. Green as a companion—no home, no friends, no money?"

This was easy too. She relaxed a little more.

"I don't like it very much," she said.

He was watching her. Those cold, pale eyes never left her face. But he was smiling quite pleasantly, and his voice was pleasant too.

"Of course you don't. No one with any intelligence would like it. You'd like a home—friends of your own—pretty clothes—dances—theatres—a car. Perhaps you'd like to travel. How does all that sound to you?"

Kay opened her lips to speak, and shut them again.

Mr. Harris slapped his knee.

"You think there's a catch about it—eh? Well there is and there isn't."

Kay thought to herself, "He's watching me. He's cold and—secret. He isn't really laughing. He's—cold—and cruel—" The last of this only just touched the edge of her mind and faded away. She didn't keep it, but it had been there, and it tinged her thought.

"Now, Kay," said Mr. Harris, leaning forward, "I'm going to tell you just how things are. I'm not going to keep anything back. You said Rhoda didn't tell you anything about yourself. Well, I'm going to tell you now. You're not Kay Moore, and you're not Rhoda's niece. Your name is Kay Macintyre, and if you can prove that, you'll come in for a fortune. But—and this is where the catch comes in—you can't prove it, and you never will be able to prove it, unless I help you. It may take time, and it's almost certain to cost a lot of money, and—well, I'm not a philanthropist, my dear, so I don't mind telling you plainly that I'm not prepared to take the matter up for somebody else's benefit. But if you were my wife, it would pay me—so there you are!"

Kay shook her head. She really couldn't speak. How could she be Kay Macintyre? Miles had found the real Miss Macintyre—he had told her so. She was a girl called Flossie Palmer.

She found her voice, or some of it, and said with breathless urgency, "I can't be—I can't!"

"Well, you are," said Mr. Harris. "And the sooner you get that into your head, the sooner we shall get on."

He got up and strolled across to the stack of old boxes piled in the corner of the room. He took a bunch of keys from his pocket, unlocked one of the trunks, and came back with a shabby old-fashioned desk in his hands. Kay knew it at once, and barely restrained herself from crying out. Aunt Rhoda's desk! Then it was Mr. Harris who had had it stolen—Aunt Rhoda's old shabby desk. She had a quick picture of Rhoda Moore propped up in bed, writing, writing, writing, and putting away what she had written in the secret drawer. She wondered if it was still there.

Mr. Harris came and sat down opposite her with the desk across his knees and opened it.

"Rhoda's desk," he said. "I see you recognize it. I had it fetched away after she died, because I thought she might have been fool enough to keep letters which she had been told to destroy." He gave a strange cold laugh. "She had too—and I don't mind telling you it was luck for her that she'd gone where I couldn't get at her. That's another thing I'd like you to get on to—when I give orders it's better to obey them—much better."

Just for a moment Kay met his eyes. There was something in them which she didn't know—power—cruel power. This thought faded too, but it left her shaken.

He had taken a packet of letters from the desk.

"These aren't my letters. I burnt mine. These are Rhoda's to me. Her whole *dossier* is in this desk. Now here's one I should like you to read."

He leaned across, and she took the letter from his hand. It gave her the strangest feeling to touch it and to see Rhoda Moore's writing again. What he had given her must be the second sheet of a letter. It began right at the top of the page without heading or address. She read:

"I have called her Kay. I have no other children with me now. I don't know why you expected me to keep her all these years without being paid. If I hadn't been fond of her, I wouldn't have done it. If there's a chance of getting this money for her, I shall expect my share, but you can't do anything until she's of age. Send me something on account. You know I've had nothing all along except for the first month—and that time Knox Macintyre was ill and you thought there was a chance he hadn't made a will."

"Here's another," said Mr. Harris. "The last few sentences—you needn't bother about the rest."

Kay read where his finger had pointed:

"What are you worrying about? The Macintyre child is perfectly strong and healthy. She passes as my niece, Kay Moore."

"That convince you?" said Mr. Harris. "Ah, I thought it would. But you see, you can't prove you're Kay Macintyre without those letters and the others I have here. They would be available for any claim my wife might make—naturally. Thanks, I'll have those two sheets back again."

He put them away in the packet, stood the desk in the seat of the chair, and got up.

"You can have a pretty good time with that money, my dear," he said. "You've never had one yet, but you might, you know. You're a pretty girl, and you ought to have pretty clothes. What do you think of these?" He went over to the pile of dress-boxes and began to open them. "What do you think of my taste? It's a pity you can't have a regular wedding-dress, but we don't want to make a splash. That will come later."

He rummaged among rustling paper and produced soft folds of Angora and a billowing mass of fur.

"What do you say to brown and beige, and a fur coat? You'd look nice in fur. I don't suppose you've ever had a proper evening dress in your life—have you? Well, what do you think of this?" He held up a glittering garment in which Kay felt she would look exactly like a mermaid.

She shook her head, and quite suddenly, right in the middle of everything being so dreadful, she wanted to laugh. And then, cold as ice, came the sense of utter danger. If she laughed, if she made him angry, something dreadful would happen. But she was going to laugh— she couldn't stop herself. There was only one thing she could fall back upon—the age-old device which covers laughter with tears. Without any conscious thought she bent over the arm of her chair, covering her face with her hands and shaking with sobs. The curious thing was that after the first moment she didn't have to pretend. Real tears came pouring down her cheeks and real sobs nearly choked her.

And then all of a sudden everything stopped—the tears, the sobs, the desire to laugh. There was a moment which was like the moment immediately after some deafening noise. There seemed to be a sort of terrified hush. In that hush she lifted her head and saw Mr. Harris coming towards her. He was still holding the fur coat, but Kay didn't see it. She met his eyes, and they froze her with terror. They were cold, and cruel, and pleased. But that wasn't all. The coldness and the cruel pleasure seemed, as it were, out of balance. There was something that Kay had no name for, except that it was danger—imminent, deadly danger. The fur coat dropped to the floor and lay there unregarded. Kay's lips parted to scream. But no one—no one would hear if she screamed.

Mr. Harris stood over her and laughed. He spoke her thought—her own despairing thought.

"No good screaming, because there's no one to hear you."

And just as he said "no one" and bent nearer, Kay saw over his shoulder the door handle turn and the door swing slowly in.

Chapter Thirty-Nine

MILES LEFT the house in Merriton Street without any clear idea of what he was going to do. He was going back to Varley Street, because he was now quite sure that Kay was in Varley Street, but what he was going to do when he got there he had no idea. Useless to ring the bell again and question Mrs. Green. He wondered what would happen if he were to pound on the front door till Nurse Long came down and then force his way in to look for Kay. He would probably get himself arrested, and then there would be no one to look for Kay. The phrase kept coming back—he'd got to look for Kay until he found her. But it was no use looking for her in No 16. If he were to go there with a search warrant and a dozen police, it wouldn't be any good, because Kay wouldn't be there. They would have taken her through the hole in the wall into No 18, and that was where he must look for her. At once. Before anything happened... Nothing was going to happen except that he was going to find Kay.

It was when he was actually walking up Varley Street that he remembered Barnabas Row. Barnabas Row ran parallel with Varley

Street. It was the lane that ran at the bottom of the Varley Street backyards. The garage was there. He had been round to it with the police, and as he thought about the garage and about Barnabas Row, a picture began to form in his mind of a narrow, ill-lighted lane, a place from which it might be possible to approach the back of those Varley Street houses. As soon as he had realized this picture he knew exactly what he was going to do. The phrase "breaking and entering" described it very appropriately. He was certainly going to enter, and if he couldn't enter without breaking, he was going to break. It was extraordinary how the weight which had been upon him lifted as he turned out of the Square into Barnabas Row.

The picture in his mind had been surprisingly accurate. If there was a darker and more deserted-looking lane anywhere in London, he had yet to come across it. Not a light showed in any one of the ill-assorted jumble of buildings between which it ran, and the distant glimmer of the street-lamp at the corner soon ceased in any way to mitigate the gloom.

He knew that the garage was at the back of No 18. Like everything else in the Row it was now dark and silent. Feeling along the wall, he found a narrow cut or passage which seemed to follow the side of the garage. It was very narrow indeed, and it ended in another wall. No, it didn't end; it turned at right angles and went on behind the garage. After a few steps it opened out. He had to pick his way over odd bricks, tin cans, rubble heaps, and broken bottles. Then, right across his path, a railing. As far as he could make out, the garage must run back into at least part of what had been the yard or garden of 18 Varley Street. A railing had been run across the lot—and a nasty brute of a railing it was going to be to climb. There was barbed wire on it and a *chevaux-de-frise* of iron spikes, but in the end he got over it by dint of making a pad of his overcoat, which suffered a good deal in the process. He had still to get into the house, but any house can be burgled by a desperate young man who has ceased to care whether he lands himself in prison or not.

He was presently inside a stuffy, pitch-dark room on the basement floor. He took it to be the scullery or kitchen. Yes, the scullery, for it had the feel of a small, enclosed place. It was icy cold. The stuffy smell was not the smell of food. It was the smell of a damp unused place which had forgotten the kindly heat of a fire.

He went forward, groping for a way into the house. Bumping against a doorpost, he came to the empty and deserted kitchen. The whole house had that same deserted feeling. It was curious that Miles' reaction should have been, "Kay in this horrible place!" and not, "Then Kay isn't here."

He got out of the kitchen and found his way up a steep flight of steps to the ground-floor level. A door at the top of the steps brought him to the hall. Like both the other doors he had encountered it was open, and open in rather a curious way, as if a careless push had left it in a half-way position. He crossed the hall, came to the foot of the stairs, and stood there listening, one hand on the newel-post, the other stretched out before him. Up to that moment he had heard no sound in the house or been aware of any presence except his own. His certainty that Kay was there sprang from a deep inward conviction, and not from any sound or sense. But now, as he lifted his foot to the bottom step, for the first time sound, actual sound, reached his ears. It came from somewhere above him in the house, and it was of two kinds—one formless and blurred, and the other quite faint but unmistakably nearer.

In straining to catch this second sound he lost the blur. He had to strain, because what he had heard puzzled him. He couldn't place it. He thought something moved, stopped, and moved again—draggingly. But what moved like that? An animal? A hurt animal? A dog? A dog would whine... A cold horror pricked him, and he took the stairs three at a time in the dark. They ran up straight, turned at the half landing, and went by six steps more to the drawing-room floor. As he came round the corner, he saw a line of light under the drawing-room door, and as he jumped for the landing, the line widened suddenly and the door swung in. There was a man before him, holding to the doorpost, swaying. He heard him groan, and beyond in the lighted room he heard Kay make a faint sound that would have been a scream if she had had enough breath to scream with.

The things that happened next were so mixed up that they all seemed to happen together. Kay saw the door swing in, and she saw Cal Morgan, ghastly, with a bandage round his head. She heard him groan, and she screamed, or tried to scream. And then Miles—*Miles* was in the room, and Mr. Harris whipped round with a pistol in his hand. This time Kay really screamed. But she did something more than that. She sprang with all her strength at Mr. Harris and hung upon his arm, and almost in the same moment Miles made a dive at his knees, the pistol went off, and they all came down together with a thud that shook the room.

"Attaboy!" gasped Mr. Cal Morgan weakly. And slipped to the ground. And fainted.

Chapter Forty

"FREDDY, I WANT to go home," said Lila Gilmore.

"Darling, aren't you well?"

"I don't know," said Lila. "I want to go home."

She looked so pale that Freddy was really alarmed. That Lila should wish to leave a party before eleven o'clock was unheard of.

In the taxi he put his arm round her and felt her shiver.

"Darling, what is it?"

"Freddy—"

"Yes, darling?"

"I've remembered something. I don't like it—it frightens me."

He held her tight.

"Silly darling!"

"No, I'm not. It's horrid to remember a little bit of something and have the feeling that there's a lot more. It's—it's like someone hiding behind a door all ready to pounce. Oh, Freddy, I *don't* like it! Oh, Freddy, you will keep me safe—won't you?"

"Of course I will! Now look here, darling, suppose you tell me what it is you've remembered, and then I can tell you just what a silly ass you are and you'll feel a whole lot better."

Lila put her head against his shoulder.

"It's that girl Kay Moore."

"Well?" Freddy looked completely puzzled.

"Freddy, when Miles said her name, I remembered it—I really did. I didn't *like* it, but it went away again. Now it's come back."

"What has come back?"

"Kay Moore. Freddy, I've remembered about her—and about Rhoda Moore—I used to call her Aunt Rhoda."

"Lila, what *are* you saying?"

"It's where Mummie left me when she went out to India. It was 1914, and she didn't come back till I was five years old because of the war and getting married again, and all that."

"Well, darling, I don't see why that should frighten you."

"It does," said Lila with a sob.

"But why, darling?"

"I don't know. It wouldn't frighten me so much if I did. Freddy, please don't let me go—*please!*"

Freddy soothed her as well as he could, but she continued to tremble and cling to him until they got home. He was very glad to get her there. But what he hadn't bargained for was another tearful girl in the hall. He had no sooner shut the front door than he was aware of Flossie, pale and incoherent.

"And I didn't mean to, but ooh—I can't hold out longer! Mr. Miles he begged and beseeched, and I wouldn't—not if it was ever so, I told him. But I got to—ooh, I *got* to! And if they put me in the river I got to go, and it can't be worse than what I've been through ever since I said I wouldn't!"

Lila opened her blue eyes and stared.

"*Miles?*" she said. "What did he want you to do, Flossie?"

"The police," said Flossie in a desperate voice. "He wanted me to go to the police and say what I seen in that house in Varley Street—and I dursn't. And if that other girl's been done in, it'll be my fault.

"What girl?" said Lila quickly.

"Kay Moore," said Flossie with a sob, and as she said it the telephone bell rang close by in the dining-room.

Freddy went to it with relief. He hadn't the slightest idea what Flossie was talking about. He wondered if she had gone suddenly off her head. He thought it would be quite good for Lila to have to cope with her. He shut the door and put the receiver to his ear, and heard Miles Clayton say insistently,

"Hullo—hullo—*hullo!*"

He said, "Hullo!"

"Is that you, Freddy?"

"I think so. What have you been doing to upset our staff? It's having a nervous breakdown in the hall."

"If you mean Flossie, she damn well ought to."

"Yes, but what's it all about? She says you wanted her to go to the police and she wouldn't. Now she will. At least I *think* that's what she's saying. We've only just got in."

"It doesn't matter now. Tell her I said so. Now look here, Freddy, I've got Kay, and I want to bring her along to you straight away. Is that all right?... Thanks awfully. And—I say, Freddy, if you know where Ian is, you might be ringing him up. I've just pushed a bloke off to hospital who wants to see him—American sleuth of the name of Cal Morgan. He's been shut up in a cellar and he's pretty bad. He says Ian knows all about him."

"I say, Miles, are you pulling my leg by any chance?"

He heard Miles laugh.

"No, I'm not. I've been mixing it up a bit to-night, I can tell you. The villain and villainess are in the hands of the police, the sleuth is on his way to hospital, and Kay and I are snatching some food while we're waiting for a taxi. By the way, we've found Mrs. Moore's statement about the Macintyre baby. It settles the whole thing once and for all. I'm bringing it along to read to you and Lila. I think Flossie ought to be there too... All right, there's the taxi. So long."

Freddy came out of the dining-room to find the two girls standing where he had left them. Lila was very pale. She had an odd withdrawn look, but he thought Flossie had been listening. She took an eager step forward.

"Ooh—what did he say?"

Freddy addressed himself to Lila.

"It's all right—he's bringing her here."

"Who?" said Lila faintly.

"Kay Moore."

Flossie gave a loud gasp of relief and the colour came back to her face with a rush. Neither of them took any notice of her. Lila said in a piteous voice,

"I don't want her to come."

"But darling, you told Miles he could bring her here."

She shook her head.

"No, *you* did."

She began to go slowly up the stairs, her fur coat falling back from the pale gold of her dress. She walked as if she was very tired, but even in fatigue every movement was graceful. About half way up she turned, looked down at Freddy with a faint smile, and said,

"It doesn't matter."

Then she went round the turn and out of sight.

Flossie straightened her collar and her cap.

"Well, I suppose I'd better make the spare room bed," she said.

Chapter Forty-One

MILES AND KAY came into the drawing-room about ten minutes later, Kay in the fur coat which Mr. Harris had offered her as a wedding garment. It was quite a nice coat but she hated wearing it, only as her own clothes, such as they were, had vanished into the blue and she had nothing but her thin uniform frock, she had given in to Miles' peremptory command and put it on.

Lila looked at her strangely as she came in. They looked at each other. Then Lila said,

"You're Kay—I'm Lila," and Kay said, "Yes." And then quite suddenly Lila kissed her and the strangeness was gone.

They sat round the fire—Freddy, Lila, Flossie, Miles, and Kay— and first Kay told her story and then Miles told his, and when he had finished telling it he took out of his pocket a thin tightly folded packet.

"Mrs. Moore's statement," he said. "Kay knew that she had written one when she was dying, and she knew where she had put it—in the secret drawer of an old desk. That desk was stolen the night after Rhoda Moore died. Harris had it stolen because he wasn't sure whether she had kept any of his letters. He didn't find the statement because he didn't know about the secret drawer. The desk was at 18 Varley Street, and we found the statement quite safe where Mrs. Moore had hidden it. Kay and I have read it. Now I want to read it to you. It's—it's rather surprising."

He unfolded the sheets and began to read:

"I am writing this for you, Kay, because when I'm gone he will try and get hold of you for the sake of the money. Now you'll begin to say 'What money?'—because we've never had any, have we? Well, I'm going to tell you about the money and about everything. I've never told you anything before, partly because I wanted to be everything to you, and partly because I didn't dare. I shouldn't dare now, only I'm going to die, so it doesn't matter any more.

"Now right back to the beginning. In July 1914 I was living at Ealing, and I'd just had my sister's baby thrown on my hands at a month old. Never mind about that—it's not your story. And never mind how I came to be at the beck and call of the man whom I'm going to call Harris, because that's a name he uses now and again. He has a dozen names, but he was calling himself Harris when I first knew him and when he sent me the Macintyre baby.

"Now I've got to explain about the Macintyres. There were two brothers—Americans—very rich. Knox Macintyre married and quarrelled with his wife, and she came over here and had a baby and died in July 1914, and Harris sent Addie Long to fetch away the baby and Mrs. Macintyre's jewels. Addie pretended to be her sister. She brought the baby to me. I think Harris' first idea was to try and get money out of Knox Macintyre for the return of the child, but the war began and everything was hung up. I was paid a good sum down and told to keep the baby. I was trained, so I could do it all right. I was told to keep my sister's baby too—I hadn't meant to. Then my next-door neighbour, who was a Mrs. Lestrange, asked me if I would look after her baby while she went out to India to her husband. She was frantic to get to him. I asked Harris about it, and he said the more the merrier. You see, if I made a regular business of it, there was much less risk for me and for everyone. The Macintyre baby would be lost in the crowd so to speak.

"Well, there I was with three babies on my hands, all about the same age. I had to get in a girl to help me, and I found out afterwards that she knew who the Macintyre baby was because she'd been in service in the house where it was born, with a Mrs. Smith who let rooms. Mrs. Smith had a sister called Florence Palmer who had taken a crazy fancy to the baby. She followed Addie Long when she fetched it away, and she got this girl Ada to come to me as a help on purpose to keep an eye on it.

"Well, there were the three children. Mrs. Lestrange's little girl was called Katherine. The other two hadn't any names when they came to me, and Ada called them Lily and Rose. They were both very fair, but she called the Macintyre baby Lily because she had such a white skin, and my sister's child was Rose because of her bright colour. Have you got that clear? Katherine Lestrange—Lily Macintyre—Rose Moore.

"When they were a year old, Florence Palmer turned up. It was the first I'd seen or heard of her, but Ada came to me and told me how she used to have this craze about the Macintyre baby. Only then she had a baby of her own and cooled off. Now it seemed she'd lost her husband and her child, and she wanted to adopt Lily Macintyre. Well, it was months since I'd had any money from Harris. If it hadn't been for Mrs. Lestrange's lawyer paying me regularly, I couldn't have kept going. As likely as not Harris had lost interest and I might never hear from him again. I didn't know where he was or how to get at him. The war was smashing everything up. I was very much tempted to take Mrs. Palmer's offer and get the child off my hands, but I just didn't dare. If you ever run up against Harris, you'll know why.

"And then I had a brain wave. I couldn't let her have Lily Macintyre, but she could have Rose Moore and welcome. They were both pretty, fair children. She hadn't seen Lily for months, and I thought I could bank on her not knowing that she hadn't got the one she'd asked for. I had to square Ada. Five pounds did it. Mrs. Palmer fetched the baby away and gave it her own name, so Rose Moore ceased to exist. I was left with Katherine Lestrange and Lily Macintyre, and a month or two later Ada left me to go and do munition work, and I moved away from Ealing. I moved several times in the next few years.

"Mrs. Lestrange was still in India. Her husband was killed in Mespot, and she couldn't get home because of the submarines. In the end she married again, and after the war was over she went round the world. The children were five years old before she came back. All that time I only heard once from Harris. He sent me a message saying that I was to keep the Macintyre child and he'd settle up with me later. That was in 1917. Mrs. Lestrange came home in 1919. She had married again, and she was now Lady Latimer. I was quite ready for her when she came, because I had made up my mind a long time before and I knew just what I was going to do. You see, I hadn't meant to get fond of any of the children. I'm not fond of children—I very nearly hated my sister's child—but right from the very beginning that little Katherine Lestrange got hold of me somehow. I struggled against it hard. I tried not seeing her, not doing things for her, but it wasn't any good. I didn't want to love her, because what's the good of loving another woman's child? Just heartbreak and misery. But there it was, I did love her—I've never loved anyone else in the world as much—and when I found how it was going to be, I made up my mind that no one should come between us and take her away. It was quite easy really. No one bothered about the child. The lawyer paid me. A cousin of Mrs. Lestrange's came down once or twice the first year, but after I moved away from Ealing no one came. You've got to remember the war was going on. Everyone was taken up with their own affairs.

"The day that Lady Latimer came down to fetch her child, I sent Katherine Lestrange—I sent *you*, Kay—out for the day. When Lady Latimer arrived, there was Lily Macintyre waiting for her as pretty as a picture. Only we didn't call her Lily. She'd made it into Lila as soon as she could speak, and we slipped into calling her Lila too. Lila Lestrange was what I'd been calling her for two years or more. My servant only knew her as Lila Lestrange, just as she knew you as my niece Kay Moore. Lady Latimer was simply delighted. I told her we'd slipped into calling the child Lila because that was what she'd made of Katherine when she began to try and say the name herself. She was delighted with that too. She said it was the prettiest name, and that the child was the prettiest child she had ever seen. So she was—and I never cared a snap of my fingers for her. I only wanted *you*, and I saw to it that I got you. Lady Latimer went away as pleased as Punch with Lily Macintyre, and I had you.

"Now have you got that perfectly clear? You are Katherine Lestrange, and I took you when you were five years old, and sent your mother away with Lily Macintyre. Lady Latimer was pleased, and I was pleased, so where was the harm? You weren't nearly as pretty as Lila, so she probably wouldn't have liked you half so well. That closes that chapter.

"About six months later I heard from Harris again. Better not ask where he'd been or what he'd been doing. He sent me some money. Knox Macintyre was ill. There was a chance that he hadn't made a will. I told Harris that I had still got the Macintyre child, that I had called her Kay Moore, and that she passed as my niece. Well, Knox Macintyre recovered. Harris lost interest again. And then all of a sudden he was more interested than ever, because he found there was a lot of money that was bound to come to the child from an aunt of Mrs. Macintyre's.

"I never knew the ins and outs of what had been going on between Harris and Knox Macintyre. I think he had tried to blackmail him, and I think he had found Knox Macintyre too hard a nut to crack. He was always very bitter about him. But this other money was a certainty. It was to come from an old Miss Basing who was out of her mind and shut up. She'd made a will years before, leaving her money to Mrs. Macintyre and any children she might have. So there it was—she couldn't alter the will, and as soon as she died Lily Macintyre would inherit the Basing millions. Well, at first I meant you to have them. If I'd been going to live, I'd have let you have them and fought Harris to keep you safe, but I shan't be here to look after you, and you can't fight him yourself. You're safe as long as Miss Basing is alive, but the minute she's dead and the will is proved, he'll try and get hold of you. That's why I'm writing this statement. You are not Mrs. Macintyre's child—you are Lady Latimer's daughter, Katherine Lestrange. I've thought it all out, and you will be quite safe if you do what I tell you.

"You won't read this until I am dead. I'm going to get the doctor to witness my signature. Take the statement to him and get him to read it. Then ask him to put it in the bank in his own name. After that you had better go and see Lady Latimer. I don't want you to, but I don't see any other way of keeping you safe. Her lawyer is Mr. James Ellerslie, 75 Broad Street, Exeter. He will give you her address.

"Well, that's all. Harris won't want to meddle with you if you're not Lila Macintyre. You'll be safe, and Lady Latimer will be bound to provide for you. But she'll never love you as I have. No one will.

RHODA MOORE."

Miles read the signature and looked up for the first time. How were they all taking it? If it had come as a smashing surprise to him and to Kay, what was it going to be to Freddy and Lila? Flossie knew her part of it already, but it wasn't all jam for her hearing that Rhoda Moore, her own aunt, had come near to hating her. *Why?* There was some dark story there, and perhaps just as well that Rhoda had held her tongue about it.

He looked at Flossie first. She was flushed, and her eyes were unbelievably bright. She said in a voice which trembled with anger,

"If I've ever said things about Aunt I'm sorry for it—yes, that I am! That Moore woman—what call had she got to hate me? A shame, I call it! And the wickednessnd left as if they were so many puppies and kittens! I never heard anything like it, and don't want to! And—and—" She choked and ran out of the room.

Her outburst had relieved the tension. Miles felt now that he could look at Lila. Freddy had his arm round her. She was sitting as if she hadn't moved at all since he had begun to read. There was no colour in her face. Her eyes had a fixed, bewildered look. At the sound of the closing door she shivered a little and said,

"I don't understand."

Freddy said, "It doesn't matter, darling. It won't make any difference."

Lila turned her head a little.

"You don't mind?"

"Not a bit, darling. You're still Lila."

She nodded.

"I called myself Lila—Mummy always said I did—Aunt Rhoda said so too—I called her Aunt Rhoda. I remember—her—and Kay—I remember Kay."

Kay came and knelt beside her and took her hand.

"Please, Lila, don't mind—*please.*"

And all at once it came over Miles that they were all concerned with Lila—begging Lila not to mind having the Basing millions and goodness knows what else besides. It tickled him, and yet he could see that Lila was that sort of person. She would go through life with silken carpets under her feet and pearls to hang about her neck. Oh well, it was a lovely neck—

The door opened and Flossie came in with one hand held behind her back.

"Ooh, Mr. Miles," she said, and when he went to meet her she dropped her voice to a whisper. "I come over so angry, I can't be sure I've got it all right. It *is* Mrs. Gilmore that's the one you've been looking for—the Macintyre baby?"

Miles nodded.

Flossie gave a faint giggle.

"First it was me—and then it was your young lady—and now it's Mrs. Gilmore. Bit of a queer start, isn't it?"

Miles nodded again.

"Well, Mr. Miles, such being the case, those beads of mine what the old gentleman said was pearls—I suppose by rights they're Mrs. Gilmore's?"

"I suppose they are."

Flossie giggled again.

"Coo! It makes me laugh when I think how they've just kicked about in my drawer all these years—and me thinking nothing about them except for their having belonged to my mother! Well, seeing as they're Mrs. Gilmore's, I'd sooner she had them—so here they are!" She pushed them into his hand and ran away.

Miles came back to the group by the fire.

Kay and Freddy were still fussing over Lila. And it was Kay who had been chloroformed and locked up in a cellar for hours, besides being nearly frightened to death. But Kay would go through the world looking after other people, while Lila would always be waited upon. He thought it was time that someone looked after Kay. His little Kay—his own darling little Kay—

He came up to the sofa and dropped the black pearls in Lila's golden lap.

THE END

Printed in Great Britain
by Amazon